Fat Chance

A love story of food and fantasy

Deborah Blumenthal

**RED
DRESS**

First edition March 2004

FAT CHANCE

A Red Dress Ink novel

ISBN 0-373-25050-9

Visit Red Dress Ink at www.reddressink.com

Printed in U.S.A.

ACKNOWLEDGMENTS:

There are several people that I would like to thank for making this book possible: Claudia Cross, my agent at Sterling Lord, for her quick and spirited response to the book, and Sarah Walsh, her assistant, for handling business so quickly and efficiently, even when computer glitches threw themselves in our path. Renni Browne and Mary Costello are writing teachers extraordinaire, and I thank them both for their vision. My editor, Ann Leslie Tuttle, deserves special thanks for being such a hearty supporter of the book from the start. She was a joy to work with. She is gracious, elegant, supportive, sensitive and always available. I would also like to offer deep-felt gratitude to Margaret Marbury and her associates at Red Dress Ink for their unswerving enthusiasm.

My husband, Ralph, my best friend and mentor, is always having drafts of my work dropped on him, and, as ever, I am eternally grateful for all his guidance. Our daughter Annie was also a faithful reader and editor as well as an overall great kid, and much love and appreciation goes to her for her unflagging support. Our younger daughter, Sophie, also deserves thanks and love for putting up with seeing my back at the computer for as many years as she has been with us. Thanks to Connie Christopher for offering her wise counsel. To all my other friends and family who have had to listen to the whining all these years, thanks for staying on the line.

To Ralph

Prologue

Chewing the Fat

How could I forget the way it started? We chewed the fat—on our filet mignons that were charred to blackened perfection outside, bloodred inside, topped with a pebbly crust of crushed green peppercorns. We were having lunch at Gallagher's, Bill's favorite steak restaurant, and the more excited he got about the idea, the more he waved his fork through the air like a conductor's baton, never mind that the end of it held a wedge of baked potato enveloped in sour cream that I feared he might inadvertently fling down on my head.

"The entire planet is fat, Maggie," Bill said, shaking his head. "Between 1991 and 1998 alone, the incidence of obesity almost doubled, and you know better than I do that the only people who benefit from bestselling diet books are the people who publish them." I opened my mouth to answer, but he went on.

"So here's my thought," he said, pausing just long enough to reach for the salt sticks. "Why not cover it in a regular space? But not the pap weight loss stuff—"

"A counterculture perspective," I said, finishing Bill's sentence.

"That's right, that's right," he said, the fork alighting once again, this time precariously freighted with a dollop of creamed spinach. "Your audience is bigger than ever—one out of every four adults is fat—and they're crying out for compassion."

"Bill, it's time for someone in the media to stand up and offer America an alternative vision about their overweight: 'Live with it and love it.'" I could almost hear the first stirring strains of "America the Beautiful."

"Exactly! You'll be their counselor, Maggie, you're perfect for the job."

I put down my fork and pressed my hand to my fluttering heart, as if to recite the pledge. "I'm speechless, Bill, it's brilliant. I'm behind it a hundred percent."

"We'll move you into a new office," he said with mounting excitement, "and you'll have carte blanche to indulge yourself at the city's finest restaurants."

With a fine stroke of the knife, I teased off a sliver of beef. "I can't wait to get my teeth into it."

Within a week of my lunch with the managing editor, my column was announced in the paper, and from then on my wit and wisdom sparked nationwide attention, leading not only to an outpouring of calls and letters from desperate readers, but also radio and TV interviews, and speaking engagements. In January, just nine months later, yours truly's face adorned the cover of *People* with the headline: "The New Face of Fat: Is Maggie O'Leary America's Anti-Diet Sweetheart?"

"Fat Chance" was launched, and I was becoming a rising media star. And readers? Well, they were eating up my words.

one

Five minutes to deadline and adrenaline surges through my gut. Eyes on the screen, I pound the keys with my usual vigor, stopping only to sip my Rhumba Frapuccino Venti—Starbucks' malted-rich, soda-fountain-sized coffee drink that tamps down a leaning tower of reader mail. A perfect marriage with the cinnamon-dusted apple pie from the Little Pie Company down the street. Mmmm... Nobody could beat their pie crust. And they got the chunky consistency of the apples just right. Texture. That's what perfect apple pie is all about. I turn back to the computer, dropping a few flakes of crust between the keys. The phone rings.

"I'M FED UP, YOU HEAR ME?"

I jerk the phone arm's length from my ear, but the voice rockets. "I CAN'T LOOK AT MYSELF ANYMORE. I'M FAT AND—"

"Wait, please I—"

"I'M DESPERATE…NO ONE UNDERSTANDS…"

"*I* do, but—"

"I'm all alone and unpopular. None of the friggin' diets—"

"—LISTEN, I'll call you back," I insist, wagging my foot. "I'm just on—"

"So what do you suggest, huh? You say live with it and love it, but how am I supposed to love fat dimpled thighs that are like, *so repulsive,* you know?"

"DEADLINE. I'm on D-E-A-D-L-I-N-E! Eat some comfort food, and call me in the morning." I slam down the phone, and check the clock. Minutes before deadline I finish, hit the send key and feel the familiar rush of having dodged another bullet.

I lean back, exhale and reach around to close the button on the waistline of my skirt. Time for dinner. I reflexively tap out Tex Ramsey's extension—1-8-4-5—the year that Texas was admitted to the Union. I know he arranged that, but how? As it rings, my eyes sweep the corkboard wall speckled with bloodred pushpins piercing ads for dubious achievement products: Dr. Fox's Fat-Blocker System, Appetite Suppressant Brownies and Seaweed Thigh-Slimming Cream. A magazine article, "Ideal Weight is an Ordeal Weight," takes center field, with a quote from Phyllis Diller: "How do I lose unwanted pounds? I undress."

Framing the perimeter is eye candy: Brad Pitt on the cover of *Vanity Fair,* his tanned, sinewy torso sheathed in a sleeveless white undershirt; a Marlboro Man, weathered complexion, cowboy hat tilted provocatively shadowing soulful green eyes; James Dean, the prototype haunted bad boy in *Rebel Without a Cause.*

Dreamboats. That's what girls used to called alpha hunks

like that. Taut, archetypical physiques, suggestive gazes that held your eyes promising long steamy nights of…

"Metro."

"Tex," I say, coming up short. "Dinner *ce soir?*"

"Barbecue?"

"Mmmmm. Virgil's?" I ask, naming a popular joint in the Manhattan Theater District.

"Great, pick me up."

Dinner plans on short notice. No pretense. No frantic search for something to wear: *"Does this skirt make me look like the back of a bus?"* Why couldn't romance be as easy?

I ring Tamara, my assistant and trusted confidant. "What are you doing?"

"Answering your fan mail."

"Do I have to call the producer from *AM with Susie* back?"

"You dissed her when she called."

"I was on deadline—"

"—she's doing a show on the fat phenomenon."

"Get her on the horn, I'll grovel for forgiveness." I turn back to a talk I'm preparing on the traumas of extreme weight loss, prompted by the story of a surgeon who was not only overweight but also a smoker. Facing the upcoming wedding of his daughter, he went on a crash diet, quickly dropping fifty pounds. The morning of the wedding as he dressed to go to the church, he slumped to the ground suffering a massive heart attack. His death was caused by the drastic diet, doctors ruled, not his excess weight.

The intercom beeps. "Wanta play cover girl for the Lands' End plus-size catalog?"

"Fat chance."

Another beep. "Wanna talk to a South Carolina group about leading the next Million Pound March?"

"Not in a million years."

I search my mail for readers' stories on the perils of extreme weight loss. It's one thing to champion fat acceptance, but another to convince readers. Actually, a tiny microcosm of them sits right outside my office.

The cherubic Arts secretary is slightly—but only slightly—over her ideal weight. Still, every bite is contemplated, measured out and then double checked using both the imperial and metric systems.

"It's simply a matter of sheer willpower," she says.

I want to strangle her.

Then there's fashion reporter Justine Connors, a former model who works in a Fortuny-swathed cubicle down the hall. She isn't fat, just obsessed with it. Every nugget of food is eyed as a bullet destined to destroy her reed-like shape. The only other thing you have to know about her is that she swears thong panties and stilettos are comfortable, a physiological impossibility, as I see it. When the office was chipping in to buy her a thirtieth-birthday gift, my suggestion:

"Why not a gift certificate for a colonic?"

Tamara is yet another veteran waist-watcher whom someone at the coffee cart once described as a slightly overblown version of sultry model Naomi Campbell. She's category three: Lost. The New York Lotto slogan is her own. "Hey, you never know." Tamara's bookshelves are a Library of Congress for the overweight, holding every weight loss tome ever published. It starts with golden oldies, like the quacko *The Last Chance Diet,* by Robert Linn, advocating a liquid protein regimen that the U.S.

C.D.C. later pronounced could lead to sudden death; *Triumph Over Disease* by Jack Goldstein (stop eating altogether); *The Rice Diet* by Walter Kempner (nutritionally unsound, but lowers blood pressure); the *U.S. Senate Diet* (no promise of a Congressional seat); *The Prudent Man's Diet,* by Norman Jolliffe M.D. (became the basis for the Weight Watcher's diet); *Live Longer Now* by Nathan Pritikin (tough to follow); *The Amazing Diet Secret of a Desperate Housewife* (you don't want to know); *The Paul Michael Weight Loss Plan* ("If your intake of carbohydrates is low, some of the fat will pass right through your system without being broken down and stored in adipose tissue"— "Pure nonsense," said *Consumer Guide* magazine); and on and on, up to and including prestigious tomes of today such as *Eat, Cheat, and Melt the Fat Away,* and *The Zone.*

Tamara can leave any diet bigwig on the mat with her grasp of diet lore, but all for naught. None of the regimens work for long, and the proof hangs limply in her closet. Dresses starting at size 12, barreling out to 18. Yo-yo couture.

A copy editor pokes his head into the office, jarring me from my thoughts. "You sure the fat doctor you mentioned is affiliated with Yale?"

"Let me check."

I press play on the VCR and am about to fast-forward it, but I freeze. What's wrong with this picture? Instead of a medical conference, the screen explodes with an odd menagerie of Great Danes, goats and horses jumping, panting, pushing, heaving, whining and neighing in the midst of sexual delirium.

"WHAT IN THE WORLD?" I pop out the tape: *Mammals Mating.*

Barsky—*that* animal!

I peer into the newsroom to make sure Alan Barsky is there, then grab the *Yellow Pages* and phone a West Village sex boutique. For the next hour, I monitor the newsroom until I see a delivery man hauling a carton in his direction. The bold black typeface reads: CONDOMS FOR SMALL PECKERS: ONE GROSS. Over the hush of the newsroom, a single voice rings out.

"WHAT THE HELL IS THIS?"

I ring his extension and at the sound of his voice, I sing the Marvin Gaye song "Let's Get It On."

Time to get serious, and I turn back to my work. I make a note to do a column on the down side of exercise—in rats, anyway. *Science News* reported that rats who were forced to run on treadmills had lower antibody levels than the ones free to run at will. Of course. Can't trick the old immune system. If exercise makes you miserable, you might get thinner, but your killer cells pay the price.

Another column I'm sketching out looks at the pressures of dieting on women as a form of oppression. By starving, they put themselves at a distinct disadvantage to their energetic, burger-and-fry-packin' male counterparts in the workplace. In effect, dieting is political suicide. It not only reduces women's stamina, but also leaves them handicapped because they crave satisfaction.

That hits close to home. After living under the tyranny of a diet binge, I once walked into a chocolate shop and bought a giant replica of the Statue of Liberty. Bitter chocolate. First I bit off Ms. Liberty's head, then I devoured the rest of her. It felt…liberating.

Reggie, the mail carrier, empties a canvas sack of letters on my desk. "You really read all this crap?"

"It's my bread and butter."

From the day I started the column, the mail was my window on the world. Hard to imagine that it's been only four years since giving birth both to the column and the realization that in losing—again—the war against fat I've fought all my life, nature has the upper hand. The size-sixteen rack was my destiny, and the only real choice I had was whether or not to accept it. But instead of looking at fat in terms of defeat, my publisher and I used it as a springboard to offer America a fresh take on obesity. As I made that quantum leap to fat acceptance, I've been crusading to carry overweight America with me. What I never imagined was that I would become not only a columnist but also a "Dear Abby" to the weight challenged.

Dear Maggie:

   I'm twenty-five years old and fat. I've been trying to lose weight since I was six. I diet and diet, lose a few pounds, and then gain it all back. Everyone makes fun of me. My parents nag me all the time about controlling my eating, and it drives me insane. They say they'd stop if I just lost the weight, but I can't. What should I do?

Women of all sizes, shapes, ages and temperaments now seek me out as a sounding board, shrink and diet counselor. But so do some censorious health experts who insist that I'm in perpetual denial, advising me to get my "fat head" out of the sand. Either way, the calls and letters never stop. Yes, I'm popular—at least with readers.

Popularity, of course, is a rare commodity for the overweight, and sympathy is, well, slim. We're blamed for lacking willpower, and self-control. Few can fathom the intractability of the problem. Ironically, the overweight resent each other. One reader said:

> *Even though I'm heavy, I still feel that I can control myself and can lose weight if I want to. But other overweight people disgust me. I think that they're just indulging themselves, and not showing any self-control.*

There is no shortage of themes. Overweight infiltrates every part of one's life, from bedroom to boardroom to the altar. But who said life was fair? Remember what the jury did to Jean Harris? No, she wasn't fat, she was just mad. Okay, okay, so she killed a man, but you know, not so terrible—after all, he *was* a diet doctor. In some circles, women thought she deserved sainthood. Personally, I'm not against killing certain men. I doubt that there is any woman over thirty who hasn't *already* come across at least one guy who deserves a toxic martini.

My phone rings nonstop, and even though I'm no longer on deadline, I try to avoid answering it. But where is my so-called secretary?

"Tamara? T A M A R A?" It's futile.

"Maggie, my name is Robert Clancy. I'm an executive producer with Horizons Entertainment in Los Angeles."

Ugh. "What can I do you for?"

"We're starting production on a new blockbuster movie called *Dangerous Lies.* We're all very excited it about it. It's going to be a very, very big film about a diet doctor in a weight-loss clinic who has to care for women obsessed with becoming thin…"

"Sorry, I can't take the lead. I've already committed to playing Scarlett in the remake of *Gone With the Wind*…."

"Cute…but…the movie's cast, Maggie. What we'd love to do is hire you as a consultant."

"Pourquoi?"

"To coach our lead actor about the milieu of the over-weight world and bring him up to speed on the mind-set of weight-obsessed women…"

What? No overweight women in Los Angeles? He had to call me? But to be fair, maybe there were some before they were all forced out of the city limits under the cover of darkness by a death squad of diet police.

"Look, Bob, I'm pretty tied up here with the column and—"

"Of course, I understand, but this wouldn't take that much of your time, maybe just a couple of weeks."

"Weeks?" I start opening the mail.

"We pay pretty well…would you just consider it?"

"Mmmm…I doubt it, but leave me your number." I grab a Chinese menu and jot it down along the border next to the two-red-chili-peppers rating of the Orange Beef. "I'll get back at ya." Tamara walks in, as if on cue.

"HOLLYWOOD!"

"Run that past me again," she says.

"They want me to fly out to Hollywood. Do you love it?"

"I hope you told them that I'm free to go as well. How much moola?"

"Not enough to get me on a plane."

Celebrating the Gift of Ampleness

Like an overprotective parent who lends you the family car with spare tires in the trunk, nature is looking out on your behalf. Natural selection provides a surplus, and the reason is obvious. Just listen to former Yale surgeon Sherwin Nuland.

"An injured creature is more likely to survive and reproduce if it has a surplus to fall back on." The human body is made with an abundance of cells, tissues, even organs. "We really do not need two kidneys or such a huge liver, or more than twenty feet of small intestine."

While Voltaire might not have been thinking about the fleshy woman when he said, *"Le superflu, chose trés nécessaire"*—the superfluous, that most necessary stuff—his words make biological sense too. The generous female body is the fertile one. Anorexics don't menstruate, well-fed women do, a fact that tells us that we need sustenance to nourish our children and continue the species; reserves to carry us through periods of disease; and ample stores to sustain us in case of starvation. So bless your flesh. Look at your generous, sensuous, nubile body as a miracle of scientific engineering, a delicate, responsive, harmonious creation designed to perpetuate life and keep the human spirit burning.

At the very least, your lush human fat cells now come with a newer, higher price. Stem cells, harvested from fat, represent the new frontier for scientists in search of high-tech treatments for disease.

Why? Because they have the magical ability to turn into a variety of other types of cells. In other words, sometime in the near future, stem cells taken from your glorious globules may be used to replace injured or worn-out cells.

"It's not a static spare tire around our waist. It's really a dynamic tissue, and there are a lot of things in it that could help us fix people with diseases," said Dr. Marc H. Hedrick, a University of Pittsburgh researcher.

So next time you look down at the scale, smile, don't frown.

two

To know Tex Ramsey is to love him. I'm perched on the corner of the Metro desk—he's the big honcho, Metro editor—with my legs crossed coquettishly, chewing a wad of purple bubble gum to get myself noticed, reading *People* magazine and waiting. You always have to wait for Tex, especially when it's dinnertime. It's not that he doesn't have an appetite. Just the opposite. It's just that dinnertime is synonymous with deadline, and the phone next to him rings constantly. He glares at it momentarily and then looks back at the computer screen.

"Don't we have a secretary around here?"

"Out sick, Tex."

"Sick of what, this joint? Anyone think to call a temp?"

"Don't think."

Business as usual.

"T E X, you cut *half* the story," the police reporter's

whine fills the room. "I spent three hours with the commissioner and you give me four hundred words?"

"No space. We'll do a follow."

"Follow? He won't spit at me after this abortion."

"Bring me a hankie."

A general assignment reporter shows up next, a Columbia University Graduate School of Journalism graduate, with no obvious pathology, who in two short years at the paper has developed a tic. He's smacking a copy of the newspaper against his hand in fury and grousing about a typo in his story about a hero cop. He closes his eyes, dropping his head in despair.

"We said he's been with the department for ONE HUNDRED years."

"Only an extra zero," Tex says, waving it away with his hand. "Look at the bright side. Now the department thinks they owe him 90 years of back pay, the guy's rich, and he's eligible for immediate retirement."

He winks at me, then fogs his glasses, wiping them on the sleeve of his shirt, before turning back to the lead story on his screen about a supposed affair between the mayor and his press secretary. At the press briefing, they decided, uncharacteristically, to take the high road and play it down, hiding it deep inside. The mayor already hated the press. They had alienated him sufficiently with their in-depth probe right before the election. But now that every gossipmonger in the city had weighed in, it would be the cover.

Tex stretches his legs up over the desk, crossing his scuffed Tony Lamas. "Here's our head: CITY HALL HOTBED. What the hell—it would sell papers. If the megalomaniac mayor couldn't stand the…"

"I'm starving…." I sing out sweetly. "Ribs encrusted

with honey and teriyaki glaze." I dangle the thought before him. If that doesn't work, I'm going to start filing my nails. Bingo. He looks out at the copy desk.

"Okay, bro's, put it to bed. I'll be at Virgil's if you need me."

"You and Maggie eatin' Pritikin again, eh?"

Tex snorts. "Not likely. No spinach salads and Diet Sprites for her," he says, punching my arm. "She's the only girl I ever met who knows how to eat." That's a compliment, I think. He grabs his coat and we hail a cab. I can't wait to tell him about California.

I gnaw off all of the red caramelized beef on the baby back ribs and then soak up the remaining droplets of amber glaze on my plate with a slab of doughy bread. The oval platter between us that had been heaped with crisp golden brown shoestring fries is now bare except for a sprinkling of burned crumbs and flakes of coarse salt.

I lean back on the thick wine velvet banquette and sigh. "So then the phone rings, and guess who called yours truly?"

"The papal nuncio?"

"Negative."

"Temptation Island?"

"No, and I'll spare you your remaining eighteen questions. A hotshot from L.A. who wants me to fly out there and help with a movie they're making."

Tex closes his eyes and looks down. "You're such a pushover. It was Alan Barsky."

"It was *not* Alan Barsky."

"How can you be so sure?"

"Alan Barsky would have said he was Steven Spielberg."

"Hmmm...I see your point...so what did you say?"

"I said I'd drop everything and be there in a heartbeat."

Tex guffaws. "They sending a Lear?"

"No, a Peter Pan Bus ticket."

He shrugs. "Hell…you're on a roll, why not? You've got the media eating out of your hand, go for it. It could beef up your career even more. Celebrity fat columnist reaches to the stars. Definitely a sound career move."

I'm suspicious now. "Why are you so gung ho?" I can't help but think of Tex as, well, my protector. Maybe it's his build. Former star tackle—the kind of guy who'd smile as he was hauling your couch up a flight of stairs. He hoists his beer bottle and drains it. That's the sum total of his daily exercise, not counting the jaw work of the job.

"You'll be the next IT girl and I can say I knew you when."

"Naw, it's not me…. I'll just forget the whole thing," I say, flicking bread crumbs into a miniature replica of the pyramid at Giza. "I mean, even though it probably means mega bucks—you know how these movie companies pay consultant fees when they want help—I despise L.A. anyway. I mean who doesn't?"

"Remember that Woody Allen movie?" He works at keeping a straight face, but his own stories always set him off. He leans back into the seat to get more comfortable before he starts spinning the yarn.

"You know where he's in the car with Tony Roberts who's got on this space-age, silver Mylar jumpsuit? Roberts zips up the hood that just about engulfs his entire head, like he's going to be launched to Mars, and Woody turns to him, deadpan, and asks, 'Are we driving through plutonium?'" Tex almost doubles over with his loud, roaring laughter. I give him a small tolerant smile.

"Yeah, the clothes, the cars, you can't walk anywhere," I say, "except for the treadmill in your home gym. And then there's the Freeway. What an oxymoron. The Freeway, where you sit in traffic, looking at the guy in the next lane. How did *he* get *that* car? What does *he* have that *you* don't? The car and the phone, the phone and the car, that's their whole shtick. I think they all have phones jammed up their asses, I swear. What a disgusting way of life!"

"Maybe you'll get into it, who knows?"

I look at Tex and wonder. What if he got a call from, say, someone like Gwyneth Paltrow or Kim Basinger asking him, in a breathy voice, if he could tutor her for an upcoming role as a newspaper editor? Would he go? I can only imagine his reply. "Let 'em try."

"So," he says, slapping his hand on the table, "how about we go to that Italian bakery on Third Avenue for tiramisu?"

We walk across town and up Madison Avenue. The trees in front of the Giorgio Armani shop are laced with tiny sapphire Christmas lights, arboretum couture, while window-lit mannequins wear strapless gowns and tuxedos of tissue-thin silks and crepes, and high-heeled sling-backs encrusted with ruby crystals. We pass candlelit restaurants where dark-haired men with romantic eyes face blondes in white wool suits with minks draped over the backs of their chairs, while just outside on frosty street corners open to the sharp wind lie vagrants with unkempt hair under cardboard shelters offering bent paper cups for spare change. The fragmented New York mosaic.

For all its opulence, and all its shortcomings, the city tapestry seduces me. Why would I want to leave it for L.A.? Who wants to spend half a day flying out to a place where nobody thought about anything but competing for parts and coveting awards for pretending that you were someone you weren't? They were all bent out of shape, pretentious. The whole damn place was pretentious.

We walk to Third Avenue, passing the Tower East movie theater and a Victoria's Secret. The long expanse of windows is devoted to sherbet-colored Miracle Bras that can incrementally ratchet up your cleavage, a "have it your way" for bras instead of burgers. They're paired with matching thongs as sheer as snowflakes. I'm watching Tex.

"So what was the name of the movie anyway?" he says, raking a hand through his dark, curly hair as he finally turns from a blond mannequin in a sea-green thong.

"What movie?"

He shakes his head in disbelief. "The one they asked you to help on, darlin'."

"Oh…. I forgot…. Hmmm…dangerous, dangerous something…oh…I think *Dangerous Ways, Dangerous Lies.* That was it."

"Gossip's doing an item on it tomorrow," he says offhandedly, and snorts. "The sleazy jerk who's starring in it has this global fan club that issues daily reports on 'sightings,'" he says. "Get this. Never mind that he was busted once for drunk driving, and likes coke, Hollywood doesn't hold that against him. They paid him twenty mil for his last movie. And you know what he tells Cindy?"

I shake my head.

"'Money doesn't mean that much to me. It doesn't buy spiritual fulfillment. It's something that you barter with. It has no intrinsic worth.'" He laughs out loud. "I'm going to use that on my landlord when he asks for the rent," he says, deadpan. "'It has no intrinsic worth.'"

For some reason my skin is starting to prickle. "Exactly who are you talking about?"

"The guy from that TV show…that hustler astronaut from *The High Life*."

I slow my pace. "What?"

"Yeah," he says. "Gelled hair, what's his name?"

"Mike Taylor?"

"Yeah."

I've fallen out of step with him now, dragging my feet. "Would you mind if I took a rain check on dessert?"

"You okay? You're lookin' a little pale."

"I'm fine…it's just been a really long day, and suddenly it's all hitting me."

Later on, I sit back and go over my phone messages. Shortly after I started the column, my phone started ringing with offers to do TV. Initially, I ducked them. How would it feel to be in front of the TV camera? I had this frightening scenario in my head: I was in an electronics store and everywhere I looked I saw my full face on all the screens of the demo models. Twenty different Maggies, starting with a ten-inch screen, graduating up to one the size of the eight-story Sony Imax screen, all in different gradations of harsh, artificial color. A too-red me, a pink-and-fuchsia me, a yellow-green me, a harsh black-and-white version, all color leached out. A flat-screened Maggie, a fat-screened Maggie. A United Nations of Maggie O'Learys. A fun-house house of horror come to life. Halloween. The vision makes me cringe.

Then there's the business of speaking my mind without the safety net of print. Would I start to stutter and stammer? Could happen. There was no delete key on a live TV show, and I wasn't used to expressing myself in sound bites. It was safe to work behind a computer screen. But ultimately, what it came down to was that I was never one to retreat in the face of a challenge…so…

First stop on the *AM with Susie* show is makeup. They redden my cheeks, add more lipstick to return the color that the lights wash out, then dust me with a giant powder brush to cut the shine. I'm ushered into the studio, and seated in front of the audience. The camera rolls up, the eyes of America are on me, and I feel as though the spotlight will imbue my words with greater meaning. I envision viewers alone in their kitchens or bedrooms, sipping coffee and eating coffee cake. They stop in the middle of paying bills or maybe cleaning the sink, hoping to come away with some moral or inspiration that will elevate them from the state of feeling disembodied, alienated, in perpetual despair about their weight and their lot in life. The effect I can have on TV dwarfs anything I can offer in print.

Susie cross-examines me. In a nice way.

"As America's antidieting guru, Maggie, tell us a little about your own struggle. Was being overweight an issue for you all your life?"

"Well, I got my workouts in the family bakery in Prospect Park, instead of the playground, as a child," I say, evoking sympathetic smiles from the audience. "I blame my weight problems as a kid on after-school snacks of hot cross buns, crullers and scones instead of carrot sticks and celery. And then, rather than climbing monkey bars and getting real exercise, I rolled dough in my parents' bakery. Arts and crafts was decorating cookies with colored frosting and rainbow sprinkles, then gobbling up my jewels."

"Didn't your parents see what was happening?"

"In those days, feeding your kids was a way of showing you could love and provide."

"So they were blind to what food had become to you?"

I weigh that for a moment. "Let's say their gift was disproportionate. When you take a vitamin in the recommended dose, it keeps you healthy. Overdose, and it can be lethal."

The discussion opens up to the audience, with no time to describe how I continued to overeat as I grew up. In my teens, I got my just desserts—Saturday nights in my room staring at rock-star posters on the walls, and listening to a blaring boom box while entwined in marathon confessional conversations on my pink princess telephone with desperate girlfriends. The secondhand stationary bike that my parents bought me soon became invisible, slipcovered with rejected clothes. If only abandoned exercise equipment could speak.

I was incarcerated in my room under self-imposed house arrest. Everyone else was out on the weekends, at movies, parties or concerts, and I was a prisoner of both my body and the four walls. One night, after going to a dance with my best friend Rhoda, wearing too much makeup and high platform shoes, we ended up in a back booth of Tony's Pizza parlor at eleven o'clock. There sat Rhoda, black eyeliner melting, sipping Diet Coke and reaching for a third slice of pepperoni pizza. She smirked.

"At least it doesn't walk away from you."

It didn't. Food was the gift that kept on giving.

To make things worse, my parents lightly brushed aside my preoccupation with my weight like crumbs on the counter, seemingly unaware of the pain and disappointment of growing up invisible to boys.

"Just use a little willpower," my mother would say. "Learn to control yourself."

Not my sister Kelly's problem. Like our father, she could eat anything she wanted, and never gain. But I took after my mother. Our bodies followed some Manifest Destiny theory, expanding beyond appropriate borders and nothing could be done about it. Once the fat cells developed during early childhood, the number stayed constant for life. All that diet could do was shrink them down.

"Have you always been at war with your body?" Susie asks after a commercial.

"I can't remember a time when I wasn't wending my way through cycles of gorging, deprivation, self-punishment, anger, resentment and rebellion, all of it siphoning off feelings of self-worth."

Susie turns to the audience for reactions, and a teenage girl in tight jeans with short wavy hair stands.

"I was chubby, as my mom put it, in elementary school and my body made me feel like I was a living sin." She pauses, taking a breath, then stares into the camera.

"I'm four-nine and I weigh 142 pounds. I feel suffocated, trapped in a dark hole, hopeless." She looks out beyond the audience. "At first I isolated myself from everybody and all I did was eat, then at the age of thirteen, everything changed."

"What happened?" Susie asks.

"I became anorexic. I was so paranoid about my unhappiness, I went on for two years being like that. It got to the point where if I had more than thirty calories a day, I would literally hurt myself." She pushes up the sleeve of a baggy gray sweatshirt to reveal an arm disfigured by the rubbery red scars. "I am a cutter."

There is stunned silence in the audience. Susie says nothing, as though participating in a moment of respectful observance.

"I know that wasn't easy," she says finally. "Thank you." Thunderous applause rings out, then she turns back to me. "At what point did your thinking change?"

"Staring down at the scale one day. The numbers hadn't changed and I was ready to smash it to see if that would make it budge. Maybe it *was* broken. I wanted to pick it up and see, the way you check the phone to see if it's working when the boy you're in love with doesn't call. But then it struck me that there was another option. I could triumph over that meaningless rectangle of steel that I had inveighed with so much of my self-worth by ignoring it and taking back charge of my life. Instead of wallowing in embarrassment and self-hatred, I would take my liability and flaunt it. It was time to fight back against the western world's prejudice toward a condition that most people couldn't change. From then on, I refused to dress like a mourner in black to look thinner. I opted for hot pink, chartreuse. I didn't care if it had horizontal stripes and made my waistline as wide as the equator. I'd go over the top. 'Too much of a good thing can be wonderful,' as Mae West said. Diets were a sham, biology was destiny, so I ran with it."

"What did you do?"

"Aside from shopping sprees in plus-size stores where things actually fit, I turned my attention to my soul. It was time to get in touch with who I really was because everything inside of me that was real and vulnerable had been buried. I started going to Overeaters Anonymous where they began each session by holding hands and saying a prayer: 'God grant me the serenity to accept the things I cannot change, courage to change the things I can and wisdom to know the difference.'"

"The same prayer that AA uses," Susie says.

"Yes. And that environment made me realize how much I needed spirituality in my life because I had become so closed off to love and meaning outside of myself. I was turning to a higher power for the love, strength and generosity that I couldn't find in myself anymore. Until then, I was locked in a one-dimensional life that was consumed with what I weighed and ate, not who I was or could become."

There are murmurs of agreement from the audience.

"I had lost my place in the universe. *Everything* in my life was out of proportion." In the eye of the camera, it all comes back to me. The hot TV lights shine down on me like heavenly beacons there to illuminate the truth, and I'm sweating as if I'm arriving at some religious epiphany. The studio is silent.

"Night after night, I sat in a windowless basement of an East Side church where compulsive eaters shared their stories. One night a withdrawn teenager told of being afraid to fall asleep at night, staying up listening for the sound of her abusive father's footsteps approaching her room. Strawberry ice-cream sundaes in the kitchen after school were the only thing that made her feel good, and forget his touch, at least for a while.

"A bearded man, very overweight, spoke of atrocities in Vietnam. He had nightmares of seeing the bullet that ripped through his buddy's chest, and getting there too late to save him. Eating was his escape from the guilt he had over his own survival. Others described stultifying days filled with nursing aging, bedridden parents; facing job loss; empty existence after retirement; the death of a spouse, all tales offering pinholes of light into their intimate worlds of grief and despair. So many people felt orphaned, split off from a world where everyone else seemed to be living purposeful, fulfilling lives.

"Eating filled them all with comfort and satisfaction, but like a euphoric drug, once the high wore off, it left them more despondent than when they started. Watching these people reveal themselves helped me. So did the idea of living life one day at a time, and drawing strength from this community."

A Clairol commercial prevents me from talking about how science writing connected me to the outside world in a more concrete, expansive way, and how the column and my like-minded thinking with Wharton later propelled me, Maggie O'Leary from Brooklyn, New York, to cult celebrity. Back in the eye of the camera I end by telling viewers:

"Eat to appetite instead of eating to extreme. I'm not saying don't lose weight if you want to, but I think you should do it without making your life miserable and impossible and unfortunately that's what very restrictive regimens do. And if you choose to remain at a weight that America deems 'fat,' well, that's okay too if you're okay with it because in the long run it just might be better than cycling over and over.

"What I hate to see are people subsisting on diet foods that they hate. Food is a source of pleasure, and we should enjoy it. I'm not saying that many of us don't have terribly serious food issues—it would be disrespectful to be glib about it. There are suicide eaters out there, and they need therapy, not chocolate Kisses."

"And, Maggie, let's talk about your column," Susie says. "Isn't 'Fat Chance' really a rallying cry for women all over

America. Isn't it really about a lot more than the issue of fat?" As I nod, she goes on.

"Isn't it about accepting yourself no matter what it is in life that you're at war with? Isn't it about giving yourself a break and loving yourself no matter what kind of pressures you perceive that society is putting on you to change, even when those changes may be biologically impossible for you?"

"That's exactly it, Susie. Fat is something of a metaphor for pain and unhappiness in a world that appears to be filled with people who have it all. The truth is that women everywhere, no matter where they come from, no matter what they do for a living, no matter whether they're married, or single, rich or poor, famous or utterly anonymous, have issues to deal with and things about themselves that they'd like to change. Ultimately, though, they must come to terms with those issues, because if they can't or they won't, they're destined to be at war with their—"

"And, Maggie—"

But I'm fired up now, and I don't let her break in.

"And despite liposuction, dieting, exercise, plastic surgery, or what have you, we are a product of our genes and our environments, and the whole business of living the best life that we possibly can means making peace with who we are and overcoming our private saboteurs."

The audience busts into applause, and I feel the color in my face rising.

"Thank you, Maggie," Susie says. "Thank you for being with us today. You've brought a very sober perspective to the issues that plague all of us."

I walk out, surprised with all that I said. A biology

teacher of mine once told me that he never really understood his subject until he had to teach it. Now I know what
he meant.

Out of the Running

The widespread ill will toward the obese leads to
discrimination in schools and the workplace, and
reduces chances of women going the old-fashioned
route and climbing the social ladder through marriage.

When was the last time a society column pic-
tured a fat woman at a social event? Or sitting on
the board of a major corporation?

Undoubtedly, being overweight sabotages success. Ninety-seven million of us are overweight,
but when it comes to fame, celebrity, recognition
and status, we are invisible.

Over and over again, I hear about discrimination
at the office—how women are passed over for
promotions. Some are too embarrassed to sue, unable to handle the attention that would put them in
the spotlight. Instead, they endure lower-level jobs,
less pay and the anger that comes from being vic-
timized and unable or unwilling to fight back.

But should you have the courage to stand up and
fight back, the sad truth is that juries often show the
same lack of sympathy toward the overweight that
is mirrored in the real world. Out of the entire
United States, only Michigan, Washington, D.C., San
Francisco and Santa Cruz, California, make it illegal

to discriminate against the overweight. Every place else, society is largely off the hook. The rationale: If you're fat, it's your own fault.

And here's the saddest evidence yet of how much society despises overweight. In a national survey done by Dorothy C. Wertz, an ethicist and sociologist at the University of Massachusetts Medical School, 16 percent of the general adult population said they would abort a child if they found out that it would be untreatably obese. By comparison, the survey found that 17 percent would abort if the child would be mildly retarded.

three

I hear my phone ringing before I even turn the corner to my office.

"It's Our Lady of Prospect Park," Tamara calls out when she sees me.

How could my mother *not* have seen the show? The TV was background music in the bakery. Always the drone, the predictable barks of laughter, applause. It would be a miracle if I could just get some work done.

"It's *my* fault that you're fat?"

"I wasn't *blaming* you, Mother." Oh, here goes. "It was the lifestyle—"

"You never learned self-control, it's—"

"*Mother,* it's a little more complicated!"

"What did you ever want that we didn't give you?"

"That's just it," I say, pounding my fist silently on the desk. "I have to go, Ma, I'm on deadline. I'll call you."

★ ★ ★

Several hours later, I look up to see a messenger at my door, bearing a large golden shopping bag imprinted with one of the most welcome names on earth: Godiva. The bag is filled with the signature gilded boxes with samples as opulent as Fabergé eggs. But these ovoid wonders are edible: Godiva's new truffle collection. I lift the first. Outside is a domed shell of black-brown bittersweet chocolate, a confectionary canvas covered with Jackson Pollock–style café-au-lait drippings. I bite. My tongue is having a party for my mouth as it is washed with cappuccino cream. I take another, milk chocolate with a hint of hazelnut. The third is bittersweet mocha chocolate filled with cherry cream.

"I've found religion. Tamara, you have to try these." No answer. "Tamara?" The phone rings again. Is Godiva publicly held? I lick my fingers and lift the receiver. Does that count as exercise?

"Maggie O'Leary? I have Robert Redford on the line from Sundance…"

I bite into another—"Mmm mmm mmm"—then swallow. "I know Bob, and I'm on deadline, *mon cher,* bad timing." I slam down the phone. It rings again, but this time I lift it up and then drop it into the garbage pail.

"Do you know how low you are Barsky? You're in the bottom of the garbage pail, you swine." I hear his signature nasal laugh as I fish the receiver out of the garbage.

The morning a pail of bulls' balls was delivered from a Ninth Avenue bodega, just after I got the column, I filled Tamara in. "He's been at the paper forever, and pulling this stuff keeps him awake between stories."

"You could ignore him."

"But then he'd stop."

I consider returning fire using a foreign identity. German? Dietrich? No, I can do better. Later. Now I have to apply ass to seat and get to work.

"SHIT." The phone's ringing again. "Tamara! Tamara! Tell Barsky to cool it." I wait, but my phantom assistant is gone. I snatch up the phone.

"Enough, asshole. I have work to do. This *is* a newspaper, remember?"

There is silence on the line.

"Alan! Don't ignore me and don't start that sick breathing thing again. You don't sound sexy, you sound like you're having an asthma attack."

There's a silence, and just as I'm about to hang up I hear the voice.

"Maggie? I'm sorry, I hope this isn't a bad time…. I'm, this is Mike Taylor, I'm an actor in Los Angeles. I don't know if someone from the studio ever reached you or not, but I'm about to start working on a new movie here, and that's why I'm calling. I need your help."

My eyes open wide, then wider. An alarm goes off deep inside my head. *Not* Alan Barsky. *Not* Alan Barsky. He wasn't *that* good. It was… My skin starts to prickle. It did sound like him. Oh God, I am such a complete moron.

"Sorry…SO-ORRY…just fooling around here…." I clear my throat. "I…I know who you are…" I say, trying to conceal a certain shakiness that's starting to spread over me like a violent onset of the flu. *Who could ever forget his rippled abs on that Calvin Klein underwear billboard in Times Square!*

"Oh, okay, well, I thought I'd try you myself because…anyway…I'm going to be starring in a new movie about a diet doctor, and I'm so out of my element with this. I wondered if there was any way that you could help me out."

The Mother Teresa of journalism to the rescue… Oh…what-EVER you need. But I say nothing, half out of fear of saying the wrong thing, the other half because I'm afraid that if I hear my own voice, I'll wake up and the dream will be over.

"Maggie? You there?"

"Yes…I… Sorry, I'm in…I got distracted for a minute—"

"Oh, well, anyway, I wondered if there was any way you might be able to come out to L.A. for a couple of weeks?"

"Weeks? A couple of weeks?" What the hell is happening to me, echolalia?

"I know you're working, but we could get you a suite at the Beverly Hills Hotel. There are amazing restaurants here—you could take lots of time for yourself and—"

"I don't think I could just—"

"Well, we could make some other arrangement if you don't like it there… L'Hermitage or… I mean, you could even stay here if you'd be more comfortable. I have a pretty big place—you could have your own wing—there's an office…and I have a great kitchen. You could make my place home base, and just give me some coaching—you know, background stuff—on the way overweight women think, and how they'd react to me. I usually spend a couple of months preparing for a role, and it would be a tremendous favor if—"

"I…I don't know—"

"I realize that it's not easy to just get up and leave—"

"No, but—"

"Don't answer now, just think about it."

"Well—"

"We would pay all your expenses, and a consulting fee. The studio is usually pretty generous, I'm sure we could work something out so that at least financially it would be worth your while. Just consider it, okay?"

"Maybe, maybe, Mike," I say, coiling a strand of hair around my finger like a tourniquet. "Can I get back to you?"

"Sure, sure, Maggie. This is great. I'm thrilled that you'll even think of helping me." Then his rich voice turns softer, *intime*. Caressing. And by God, it's working wonders.

"Honestly, people out here really look up to you, you know? This is a crazy town, everybody's into some diet routine or other, nobody's happy with themselves the way they are. That's why it would be so helpful if I could hear your take on it all."

There are other experts—I can rattle off a dozen names off the top of my head. Bloated, academic types, but they knew the stuff, they could fill him in. Or he could read my clips. The column was easy to call up, why did he need the flesh-and-blood me? On the other hand, SHUT UP. Did it matter WHY he called me? He *called me*. ME. He wanted ME. Needed ME. Maggie O'Leary.

We say goodbye, but I'm still holding the phone. Finally I place it in the cradle, gently. Mike Taylor. Mike Taylor.

I lean back in my chair, pressing my fingers over my

eyes, seeing shapes and colors collide like shooting stars. How often does someone get offered her fantasy on a silver platter, there for the taking? Lotto Jackpot. *And the winner is…* I'm nervous now, uneasy. Is my breath getting short? My panic circuitry is supercharged, as though my insides are a pinball machine and Mike Taylor the little steel ball that has been spring-loaded into my body and is ricocheting around, slamming the buttons and bumpers, setting off ringers and bells and arcades of pulsating lights.

I tear open the suffocating top button of my blouse, grab for my fan and open the bottom desk drawer where I stash the omnipresent reserve sack of Rainbow Chips Ahoy. I reach in and pull out a handful of cookies, admiring the gems of green, red and yellow chocolate that stud their rough surface. I lift one toward my lips. I can already taste it. My mouth knows cookies the way the fingertips of the blind know braille. Each pillow of chocolate…its dense, creamy center oozing satisfaction out along my tongue…washed down with a tall glass of chilled milk…comfort, fulfillment. I bite down and chew it slowly, as if mesmerized. Then another. But as quickly as I raise the third cookie to my lips, I pull it away.

Suddenly it becomes a grenade and I'm considering suicide. I hold it, just hold it, and wait. A moment later I put it on the edge of the desk, and, like a kid shooting bottle caps, use my thumb and pointer finger to flick it into the garbage where it lands with a resounding ping on the empty metal base. I shoot another and another until I'm out of cookies and the bag is empty. Bingo. I smooth out the bag and pin it to the bulletin board. It's flat now, thin, and it weighs next to nothing.

Breaking the Mold

"Don't change your body, change the rules." Those aren't my words, they're Jennifer Portnick's. Jennifer who? A girl after our own hearts. Jennifer, who weighs 240 pounds, and is 5' 8", is an aerobics teacher who reached a settlement with Jazzercise Inc. after being rejected as a Jazzercise franchisee because of her weight—she then proceeded to file a complaint with the Human Rights Commission.

In a decision that every plus-size woman should rejoice over, Jazzercise said, "Recent studies document that it may be possible for people of varying weights to be fit. Jazzercise has determined that the value of 'fit appearance' as a standard is debatable." The announcement was made at the 10th International No Diet Day in San Francisco, which was dubbed a celebration of "diversity in shape."

Ms. Portnick's lawyer, Sandra Solovey, who is the author of *Tipping the Scale of Justice: Fighting Weight-Based Discrimination,* told the New York Times that Ms. Portnick was lucky to be a resident of San Francisco, one of only four jurisdictions in the country where it's against the law to discriminate on the basis of weight.

"On one side of a bridge you can be protected from weight-based discrimination," she said of the Bay Bridge between San Francisco and Oakland, "and on the other side you're vulnerable."

★ ★ ★

I'm about to press the send key on the column when Tamara struts in like a windup doll on a talking tirade that has a long way to go before it fizzles.

"So I'm in your office, on my way home, about to turn out your office light."

I wait.

"I'm about to flick the switch on the M&M's lamp, and what do I see?"

"I give up."

"Your pink phone-message pad with doodling all over it."

"Your point is?"

"Not just *any* doodles, Maggie…." Her voice begins to trail.

I won't go for the bait.

"*Mike Taylor* doodles in all kinds of cutesy-poo little writing."

Unmasked.

"Block letters, puffy pastel two-dimensional letters, calligraphy, flowery script, and then little red hearts."

I'm not in the mood now for the drama queen who is studying me. She switches gears and is trying another approach as she drops the armload of mail she's been holding onto my desk.

"You okay, Maggie? You been acting a little strange lately, you know what I'm sayin'?"

"Strange how?"

"Strange like…" She drums her iridescent green fingernails on top of a thick hardcover book called *Aberrant Eating Behaviors*. "Uh, aberrant…you're not here, your mind is elsewhere."

"My mind's right here, Tamara, you want to take a CAT scan?"

"I'm not your doctor, babe, I don't want to take no CAT scan. But I'll tell you that you are most definitely not your ever-lovin' self. You are adrift. Something bothering you?"

"My job, my column, a water pill, my next meal, the exchange rate of the yen, that's what's bothering me, okay? What else could be on my mind? WHAT? WHAT? There is nothing else whatsoever. End of discussion. You read me?"

Tamara holds up her hands in surrender. "Not another word from me, I swear. I'll just sit myself back down outside and let you have your estro/progestero hissy fit. I'm out of here." She cha-chas toward the door.

I should let it go, but I can't. "Come back." I point to a chair opposite my desk. My pencil turns into a drumstick. Tap tap tap tap. "You're right. You know me. I wear my heart on my sleeve. I can't hide anything from you…although Lord knows I try." We eye each other over a drumroll.

Tamara crosses her legs and leans forward, twirling a cornrow around her finger. She raises her eyebrows and checks her watch. Then she sits back, and uncrosses her legs.

"H-E-L-L-O—"

"WHO has a body like no other man?"

She screws up her face. "Fabio?"

I fling open the paper to the TV page. "Ever heard of a show called *The High Life?*"

"Starring that lowlife…er…what's his name?"

"That gorgeous lowlife, yes."

"So?"

"So? The SO is that *that* sexy lowlife, Mike Taylor, called me last week. He needs my help. He wants me to fly to L.A. and help him with a movie he's making."

This is apparently the funniest thing that Tamara has ever heard. "You've been had, girl. Barsky's at it again. That guy slaughters me, I swear—" She smacks her thigh and laughs harder.

"No, my child, no no no no—"

"That man should sell a CD. 'Get 'em going with Alan Barsky.' God, he EXCELS! Barsky RULES!"

"Fine then, ask for a transfer and work for him if you're so tickled with his bullshit. Of course, you won't get Godiva truffles, chanterelles, tins of Beluga caviar. On Metro you'll get Tic Tacs. You like Tic Tacs, Tamara? What color? Or more likely you'll get gift baskets of poison apples and hemlock." Vicious pencil tapping now.

Tamara waves her arms over her head as if to clear the air.

"Girl, you are a pushover. Barsky is head and shoulders above you in the pranks department. You are just not up there in his league. Boy, do we have to bring that boy to his knees, make him pay. Oh, I love this…it's gonna take some thinking, but we can do it, we—"

I stare at her unflinchingly. "Barsky was out on assignment."

One perfect eyebrow arches up, then her whole body slumps. "You mean…?"

"Yes…it really was—"

"Mike Taylor?"

"Mike Taylor." I take an Internet picture of him out of my desk drawer. We both stare at it for a moment. "How could anyone not want to help that?"

"Lord have mercy. What are you going to do, Maggie?"

"After I have my heart massaged? What do you think? I'm going to give him the name of a diet doctor I know out on the coast, and then go back to my column and forget the whole thing. Do you think I'd just take off because I get a call from a smart-ass in Hollywood? Yes he's gorgeous, but out there they're all gorgeous—"

"Well, they're not all THAT—"

"They're plaster casts created in operating rooms. The plastic surgeons out there can carve George Clooney's face out of Danny Devito's behind. Tight skin, nipped eyes, shaved noses, chins, cheekbones, six-pack abs. The only thing they don't do yet is head transplants. That is one sick universe. So that's your answer. That's what I'm going to do."

"Good for you, Maggie." She high-fives me. "You are your own person." She walks toward the door, and then does a 180-degree pivot.

"Want me to arrange transpo?"

"Done."

"Huh?"

"DreamWorks booked it. How's that for a perfect name?"

Tamara turns again, but I'm not done. "One more thing. Of course you have to swear on your life—"

"What life?"

"—not to tell another living soul."

She shuts the door, then stands there, the other eyebrow raised.

"When I got home last night, I stripped off all my clothes and took a long look in the mirror, and let me tell you there's a reason my bathroom mirror is the size of a postage stamp."

"Amen."

"I stared at a body that I wanted to divorce, uncontested. I saw someone who didn't look like the real me that was trapped inside. So I declared war. The Maggie O'Leary who's going to L.A. in eight weeks will be nothing like the one that this world knows and loves."

"You lost me."

"I'm going to do something utterly heretical, and I need you to be my partner in crime."

"Maybe you better just tell me."

"You have to swear, *swear,* not to tell a soul, otherwise I'm going to be burned at the stake, excommunicated from the National Association to Advance Fat Acceptance. They'll haul me before them, like Martin Luther at the Diet of Worms—"

"Never tried *that* diet, any good?"

I drop my head in prayer. "The Maggie who's going to L.A. is going to attempt something more far-reaching than ever before."

"Like?"

"With my motivation at an all-time high, I'm embarking on a stealth-bomber food plan and will emerge my thin twin." I hold up my fist triumphantly. "Chiseled, whittled down, tight, taut, tantalizing, terrific and T-H-I-N!"

"Say it," Tamara says. "Say it."

"THIN."

She smiles, then suddenly her eyes cloud over. "But how? You can't *diet,* you don't, you won't. Diets are a sham, a lie, a trap to undermine the empowerment of liberated twenty-first-century women, enslave them mentally and hold them politically hostage. Your whole theory of who you are, self-love and acceptance and all that bologna that you've made your name by, not to say a career out of, is going out the window because some movie maharaja calls you up and asks for a little advice? Keep it together,

Maggie—we're talking just another M A N—so maybe you want to think this one through a little more. Maybe you're bein' just a trifle rash, you know what I'm sayin'?"

"I'm doing it, Tamara—total body and fender work. This is just a short leave of absence from my public persona. And it will surely be my last attempt to shake my booty and get it together. I'm doing it because if there was ever a motivation for me to recreate myself, this is it. If the thought of coaching Mike Taylor can't fire me into a body makeover and be successful where legions of others have failed, then there's no hope for anyone—EVER! This is the acid test, Tamara. BIOLOGICAL WARFARE! I can't ever really and truly accept the concept of self-acceptance unless I know what my capabilities are. I need to do this. You with me?"

"Spreadsheets are starting to call my name again," she says, going out the door.

"Now, that's aberrant. C'mon, Tamara," I yell as she leaves. "This is going to be fun!"

four

Don't Worry. Be Happy. Weigh Less.

Stress. I'm an expert, aren't you? Isn't everyone?
Does it make you eat more? Duh.

Who doesn't walk, zombielike, into the kitchen
for comfort as soon as the world gets too much to
handle? Well, now the scientific community weighs
in (ha) with this news and I hope it helps rid you
of some of your guilt because, dear hearts, it's not
just a matter of willpower: Your body chemistry is
partly to blame.

Stress does make you eat more—especially
sweets—because it causes the body to produce
more of a hormone called cortisol. And not only
do you eat more, but the fat that you put on as a
result, is the "deep-belly" stuff that's associated
with a higher risk of health problems such as heart

disease, high blood pressure, diabetes, stroke and cancer.

And while some women experience elevated levels of stress and cortisol periodically, depending on what is happening in their lives, others suffer from "toxic stress," in the words of Elissa Epel, Ph.D., a health psychology researcher at the University of California at San Francisco. "Toxic" or long-term stress is associated with feeling helpless and defeated. It leads to perpetually high cortisol levels that invite deep abdominal fat to be deposited—and that can happen whether you're fat or thin. So bottom line: It's a lot more complicated than just blaming your paunchy gut on the fact that you can't resist that second or third Krispy Kreme.

What to do?

* If stress is long-term, ditch the lousy job, or the lousy husband, or at least think about therapy to change the dynamic.

* When you're tempted to pig out, try to steer clear of the refined, sugary stuff that causes insulin levels to soar and then drop, making your urge to eat even greater.

* Try to counteract the urge to eat by doing something physical—sweeping the floor works and so does scrubbing the bathroom—at the very least, get yourself out of the house, and particularly away from the refrigerator.

* Next time you do head to the refrigerator, stop and ask yourself: Why am I eating? Better yet, needlepoint those words onto a pillow that you can stare at every time you get up off the couch

heading for the kitchen. If the answer, honestly, isn't hunger—assuming you remember what that feels like—get yourself into another room.

"So you're heading home?" I look up from my column to see Tex carrying his briefcase. He looks like he could be a poster boy for my article on stress.

"Mitchum's on the late movie," he says, as if that explains it all.

Tex, the movie buff, worships Mitchum. I'd heard it all before. Mitchum, the sadistic ex-con in *Cape Fear;* the American destroyer skipper in *The Enemy Below;* the cool American up against Japanese gangsters in *The Yakuza.* The heavy-lidded, laconic Mitchum.

"No one came close," he said. He had seen every one of his movies three, maybe four times. "That swaggering stride," he says, "the great laid-back antihero. So completely his own man, no matter what the role. And so cool."

I bought Tex Mitchum's biography and we laughed over the part about the end of his life. When Mitchum's emphysema worsened, he had to be put on oxygen. His droll comment: "I only need it to breathe."

When Tex walked into the office the next morning, it was clear that his moviefest had included a six-pack, maybe two.

"You okay?"

"If you don't count the fact that the back of my head feels like it was slammed with a brick."

Before he opens the mail, he reaches into his bottom desk drawer and shakes out two extra-strength Excedrin. He grabs his University of Texas mug, and goes over to

Metro's Mr. Coffee and fills it too full. Coffee starts to flow over the rim.

"Shit," he says, trying to sip it down, failing miserably, not to mention scalding his tongue. "What a piece of shit this is," he says, slamming the coffeepot.

Tex puts on a good show. I sit down to enjoy it. I consider telling him he's cute when he's mad, but decide against it.

"With Brauns, Toshibas and Cuisinarts, what MORON spent the company's money on a Mr. Coffee?"

The secretary's back becomes his target.

"Not that nine-tenths of the idiots in this office know the first thing about good coffee anyway."

He picks up a coffee can bought at the supermarket and looks at it mockingly. "I should shove the poor excuse for a coffeepot—and the swill that's in it—off the shelf, but as sure as day follows night, it will be magically replaced the next day with another one, a clone, that makes the same weak, lousy, piss-poor excuse for coffee."

The moment he sits down at his desk, he reaches for his prop: the black cowboy hat that he wears when he wants to disappear. He pulls the brim down, nearly covering his puppy-dog eyes. It looks good, actually. What is it about the cowboy mystique? He glances at the slew of mail that always greets him.

"Releases, releases, more releases," he mumbles, tossing a pile of them in the garbage. They land with a thwack that makes the secretary turn and give him a stern look.

"What a job it is to sit in an office all day and write pumped-up garbage about your client and their great new innovative product. NEWS. EMBARGOED UNTIL…" He laughs weirdly. I should be going, but I stay.

Larry Arnold, the number two man on Metro, sits down at the desk next to him and peers under the brim of the hat. "So, who are you doing? What news from down under?"

Tex massages his temples. "Actually, I feel like complete shit."

"PMS?"

"Caught it from you, sucker. What's goin' on?"

"The mayor's holding his press conference at eleven to put the rumors to rest about his affair, so now we're more convinced than ever that he's getting it on the side…. There's a school board meeting tonight that we have to cover because it's rumored that the chancellor's going to be ousted. The police commissioner is holding a press conference this afternoon about the police brutality investigation in the Bronx. *The Lion King* is opening in yet another theater, a murder in Brooklyn and your mother called to tell you her 'dawg's' vomiting."

Tex closes his eyes and shakes his head. "Get somebody down to hammer the mayor. Payback time. And send someone to get a quote from his wife. See how she's reacting to the mess. Let's do a man in the street, too. We'll give it a full page."

"Boy, you really are in a pissy mood," Larry says, heading back to his desk. "Sharon dump you for a fatter guy?" Sharon was Tex's latest flame.

Tex pulls the hat down lower. That's my cue to get to work.

Instead of research, I do something that shows my true colors. I log on to Google, opening one after another of the Mike Taylor entries. I want to see the pictures, read interviews, hear his words. I can't help looking over my shoulder. Not a smart move to be caught by the publisher while gawking at movie-star pictures when all of America is waiting for my next column. I open up one of "Melanie's pages," a picture gallery of "gorgeous Mike." There's a shot of him in a black T-shirt and a black leather jacket at a movie premier; hair gelled back, dark eyes sparkling, dressed in a tux at the Emmy Awards; shirtless in a tight bathing suit playing basketball at the beach. I enlarge it.

In another, his arm is locked around the waist of his current flame, French model Jolie Bonjour. Clearly, she is having many *bon jours* these days, thanks in large part to the fact that she's probably the one broad who fits into those stupid size 0 clothes, or worse still, 00, that always piss me off because they're made to fit only anorexics or eleven-year-old adolescents, in which case they belong in the children's department. To boot, Miss Bonjour is barely drinking age, and has luminescent blue eyes, and poreless skin. Was there even a word in French for *zit?* And that platinum hair. No wonder hair color manufacturers offered five hundred shades of blond that were used by more than a third of the women in the world. Now, brown hair, on the other hand, came in something like three shades. Light brown, medium brown and dark. End of story. Dullsville, really.

The plastic-Barbie image of perfection never died. No matter that if Barbie's body were translated into human scale, her measurements would be 38-18-34. So what if no one on the planet had those proportions, women still wanted them.

At least, to their credit, Barbie's manufacturers were now giving the dolls wider waists, smaller busts and closed mouths, a far cry from "Lilli," the prototype for Barbie—

dating back forty years—who was a German doll based on a lusty actress who was in between gigs.

This *poupée* smiles widely in every shot. No wonder. Mike Taylor's arm was hooked around her waist.

I open up interview after interview with Taylor. Thank God for the Internet. Actually, his life was an open magazine—just this past month the six-page cover story in *Architectural Digest* with the headline: "Perfection in Pacific Palisades." It began with a double-page spread showing the cobalt blue of the Pacific as a backdrop to the bright Southern California sun glinting off the polished steel of the Nautilus machines in his sprawling home gym. Fifteen behemoths in all, each with a precise function, either to tone and strengthen a specific muscle group, or offer an aerobic challenge. A trainer visited as often as the postman, the story said, to take him through the routine.

Sotto voce, Taylor admitted that he loathed exercise, but his romantic roles made it mandatory that he stay in shape. Legions of fans just waited for the moment when they would glimpse his contoured physique as he pulled off a snug T-shirt and fell into an embrace with a lush-lipped nymphet.

"Part of the job," he said.

According to the cover story, Taylor had been in Los Angeles for twelve years, but had quickly gained fame and fortune after a TV pilot based on the lives of a group of elite NASA astronauts was picked up for a regular series on CBS.

In *The High Life,* he played womanizing Scott Bronson, a rocket scientist who joined the space program and rose to become one of its top advisors, a job which had come to define who he was. His exalted standing didn't hurt his appeal to the nubile NASA recruits—whom he had a reputation for quickly bedding—or the thirty-million fans who watched—captivated by Mike's work—his long-term relationship with a curvaceous fellow astronaut, his secretive one-night stands, and all the bizarre twists and turns that his life took on this earth and beyond. In addition to the show, he told the writer that he spent weekends and vacations making films.

"Exhausting? Sure, but my career's on a roll, and that's not something you take lightly in Hollywood. I started out doing some awful TV work, and now, finally, at age thirty-eight, I feel that I've hit my stride."

"Where would you like to see yourself in the next five years?"

He shrugged. "No clue, man. I just take it from day to day, and I've no idea where this frantic roller-coaster ride is headed. All I know is that I'm holding on tight, and enjoying the ride."

His day started at sunrise, and his bedroom, the story showed, was a marvel of simplicity—a gray granite floor and a king-size bed covered in gray linens. He worked out in the gym, showered in a glass-walled bathroom with a panoramic ocean vista and had coffee in a cavernous granite, concrete and stainless-steel kitchen. The story followed him through the gardens outside the house, where he chatted with the writer about his future projects. One of them, he said, was a movie called *Dangerous Lies*.

My stomach is growling. It's almost one o'clock. I bookmark the site.

"How about some lunch?" I call out to Tamara.

"What's your pleasure?"

"Greens," I whisper pathetically.

"Can't hear ya."

Would she hear beef goulash? Fettucini Alfredo? It reminds me of the painful day that I went to buy my first bra. The hearing-impaired saleswoman walked to the back of the store toward the stockroom and yelled out for every New Yorker to hear, "What size bra did you want again, honey?"

And my pained whisper. The trainer, 34 triple A. Was that how it felt for a guy who bought his first box of condoms?

"Hey, big guy, you want the ribbed for extra stimulation? And what size? Small, medium? Behemoth?"

I get up and go over to Tamara's desk.

"A double order of gale-force greens," I mouth, "with balsamic vinegar and a large mineral water." Then I can't stop myself and shout, "Ahh, screw it, put an order of potato salad on top."

Wilhelm's sandwich shop. I adore it. Never a wait. Never a tie-up. It's run with military precision by a highly trained staff of beefy Bavarians who stand elbow-to-elbow behind a thick wooden cutting board where they prepare football-sized sandwiches. German heroes, as it were. Despite the long line snaking around the glass-covered counter, there's never more than just a moment's wait, the piercing cry, "WHO'S NEXT?" serving as a cracking bullwhip that keeps patrons rhythmically goose-stepping up to the counter.

Wilhelm's has become an institution in the East 40s, and I am one of their cherished patrons. Who else but yours truly is intimately familiar with every one of their thirty-three sandwiches? Who else calls on them to cater parties? An autographed picture of me with my chunky arm around owner and sandwich meister Wilhelm Obermayer is mounted on the wall as if I'm a visiting dignitary. It says, "To Wilhelm, my hero."

There is a reason for my devotion. A sandwich from Wilhelm's isn't a sandwich, it's an indulgence. Who doesn't wake up at night hankering for the smoked chicken salad, a marriage of white chicken, chunks of tangy blue-veined Stilton, ruffles of bacon and slivered red pepper, all lovingly dressed with a dollop of mayonnaise mustard sauce?

Or the Zeitgeist tuna salad blending white tuna with sun-dried tomatoes, mayo, fragrant dill and bits of sautéed Vidalia onions. Some prefer the Mediterranean version with chopped calamata olives, pimentos and anchovies.

In the mood for egg? Maybe the egg salad with caviar? The curried egg salad cradled in arugula and packed into a crusty French roll? Or the jalapeño egg salad?

For beef lovers there's a Hero, combining thin slices of rare roast beef, red onion rings and watercress, dripping with honey mustard and enjoyed with a side order of Wilhelm's coleslaw made with thickly sliced green cabbage, chunks of carrots and a thick coating of mayonnaise.

Tamara's face is familiar to the staff at Wilhelm's, but when she orders the triple-size greens topped with potato salad, order turned to chaos. I double over, laughing in pain as she describes it.

"VAT?" Chief sandwich-maker Brunhilde Braun shakes her head in denial. "Nein, nein. Das is nicht für Maggie. Corned beef, eh? Das is guuuut."

"You know you're right. I got mixed up," I told her.

Brunhilde shoots me a wide gold-toothed "I told you so" smirk, and I say, "It's actually TWO orders of triple greens."

According to Tamara, she was the only one smiling as Brunhilde attacked the luncheon board, lifting a lump of greens and looking at them disparagingly while shaking her head. Tamara stares at Brunhilde as she leaves.

One sour kraut. It wouldn't surprise me if she tries to right things by sending me a quart of fat-glutted chicken soup with a note, "Get Well Soon."

So there we are, sitting on opposite sides of the desk, working our way to the bottom of the mountains of greenery.

"Damn this chomping. We sound like machetes cutting through jungle grass," Tamara says.

"At least it's high fiber. High-fiber foods are supposed to have high satiety value."

Tamara gives me a blank look. "Like the movie, *High Society?*"

"They fill you up, keep you satisfied."

She grimaces then smiles conspiratorially. "I have a bag of Doritos in my drawer. Want some?"

"Desperately, so would you please throw them out immediately." Suddenly, I have this wellspring of self-control. But how long can it last?

"An unopened bag of Doritos, are you nuts?"

"Closet eating is not part of the plan." Right.

"And what about this great potato salad?" Tamara asks.

From the corner of my eye I see the Gestapo. Justine, dressed head to toe in a bias-cut Donna Karan dress in navy blue velvet. Now I'm glad I ordered it. For camouflage.

"Cover the greens with it, quick."

"Not MORE German potato salad. GIRLS, I swear you're going to develop waistlines like the Hindenberg," Justine says in her high-pitched, painful whine. She shakes her Frederic Fekkai–coiffed head. "Well, since no one's going out, I guess I'll head over to the park for a power walk. See y'all later."

"Y'all? God, I hate her," Tamara says. "I'd like to put fat pellets in her food."

"She's insufferable thin, can you imagine her fat?"

"What's a power walk, anyway?" Tamara says.

"Something masochists do. Not bad enough they go on marathon walks, they shlep weights." I consider stealing the running shoes she hides in her closet, so she'll have to walk in stilettos, but decide against it.

"Never mind her, let's dump this potato salad. It's time to do the video."

"Video?"

"*Lose It with Lisa.* For forty-five minutes, we're going to work out in here."

"Ugh, I'm getting indigestion already. We're working out here?"

"Should I put on a thong leotard and breeze on over to New York Sports?"

"Maggie, how are you going to hide this whole thing anyway? It's bound to come out."

"I'll cook up something. As you know by now, I'm a whiz at putting my spin on reality."

She closes the door, and we turn on the video. The face that greets us looks like Britney Spears—three decades down the road. What should I expect when I pick up a fitness tape from the giveaway table at the used bookstore? I'm surprised I don't have to crank up an RCA Victrola to hear it.

"Hi, I'm Lisa and I feel sooo good about exercising, sooo good about mySELF. That's why I made this video. I used to be forty pounds heavier, imagine? I ate everything in sight. UGH! I felt down, depressed, all I wanted to do was sleep. Then someone told me about a system of doing aerobics with light weights. I tried it,

adapted it to my own special needs and, girls, it forever changed my LIFE. I'm a CONVERT. Now I'm going to share my success with you, because YOU deserve it. Are you ready to work with me? Ready to develop the beautiful body that beautiful you deserve? You can do it, you know. All you have to do is stay with me. Give me a little itty bitty bit of time each day. Just forty-five minutes. Okay? LET'S EXERCISE!" The sound of Madonna's "Like a Virgin" pulsates throughout the room.

"I do *not* like her," Tamara says, shuddering. "Something about her hits me wrong. Bitch," she mouths at the TV screen.

"She's thin, she did it," I say, suddenly jumping to the defense of this baby-boomer Barbie. "*That's* what's so obnoxious. We have to show some tolerance, Tamara. We can't victimize *thin* women. In their own way, they suffer as much as we do, maybe more. At least I hope so."

"Right on," Tamara says. "We'll be PC. Equal opportunity haters."

"Amen." I wrap a pair of weighted cuffs around my ankles and wrists, then toss some to Tamara. We both start moving to the beat, ignoring the fact that outside the office door, someone is calling my name. There's a lock on the door but I, of course, didn't take the time to turn the brass knob, and already I'm regretting my carelessness.

five

I had this horrible nightmare last night. All about Jolie Bonjour. She was lying on a coffin-shaped tanning bed, her body slick with Chanel bronzing oil.

"*Seulement cinq minutes,*" she was mumbling. "*Le* tanning bed" wasn't a good idea, "*mais non,*" she was telling Mike Taylor over and over, but she couldn't resist "*un peu*" so that her skin looked, not bronze, *mais non,* but just "ze beige" to set off her white teeth, golden hair and sparkling blue eyes. She was the type, of course, that didn't get freckles or mottling. She got tan. Just tan. A moment later, she jumped out of the tanning bed and headed for a quick swim, her leopard-patterned beach towel knotted smartly, sarong-style, around her hips.

There was Mike stretched out in the sun alongside his Olympic-size pool, scripts everywhere. He was contemplating a lead role as a marine biologist working out of a laboratory in Bora Bora. The biologist finds the embryo of a unique sea monster that has a mutant strain of DNA, giving it the potential to grow larger than any marine creature that had ever lived. The dilemma: Destroy it and safeguard the world, or keep the fascinating specimen in the lab, running the risk that if it escaped it could wreak world destruction.

His concentration was broken by the sight of Jolie strolling out of the house. She untied the sarong to reveal a scarlet thong bikini and red patent-leather high-heeled mules. She stopped behind Mike's chair and draped her arms around his neck, her nipples tickling his back, her perfume pricking his senses.

"Swim *avec moi*," she whispered, caressing his ear.

He told her to wait, he had to read more scripts. Moments later, he was on the phone with his shrink, confessing, "She says she loves me…I told her I love her. She's good in bed, we're compatible…"

"But?"

"…something's missing."

Then I walked in, my head on her body, wearing the same bikini. He was mesmerized…. Okay, so I'll never look like Julie, but after two weeks, I've already lost ten pounds.

But then I wake up in a sweat, sheets tangled around me. I am sick. So sick. Along with the weight, I'm losing my grounding.

If it isn't bad enough that I'm involved in an underground makeover, the phone rings and it's a call from a local gourmet store that asked me many months ago if I would help them taste-test a new line of pasta sauces from a famed Italian importer. Who was I to say no, especially since the freelance change would help pay for the maintenance surcharge that my East-side co-op had just tacked on to cover waterproofing the aging bricks.

But now, who needs this? As if it weren't hard enough to resist temptation, I now have to deal with a team of white-clad Italian chefs who walk in promptly at eleven o'clock on the dot, bearing steaming pans of penne, rigatoni, linguini and farfalle, each covered with a mound of rich sauce. Instantly, the air is perfumed with the scents of garlic, onion, sun-dried tomatoes and olives, and my "friends" from the news department, who have noses as keen as bomb-sniffing dogs, come flocking to my door, ready to pounce.

Tex, who is usually glued to the computer screen, leads the parade, working hard to pretend that he's surprised to find food.

"Hey, what's this?" he says, acting like it's the first time he's come upon Italian food.

"Pasta," I answer dryly. "You know the starchy stuff they serve in Italian restaurants?"

"You wouldn't happen to have an extra bowl for a man who's had nothing the entire day except bacon and eggs for breakfast and a meager muffin and coffee, over an hour ago, would you?" he says, ignoring my sarcasm, and trying to get on my good side by coming up behind me and massaging my shoulders. I'm tempted to close my eyes and promise him anything if he continues since it's been so long since I had a pair of hands working on me, but I snap to.

"It's barely eleven-thirty, Tex."

"Exactly my point," he says, sliding the bowl out of my hand. "My blood-sugar level's starting to go south." He lifts a giant forkful to his mouth and tastes.

"Definitely respectable, if you don't count the fact that

it really needs a little more garlic and maybe some dill," he says, continuing to eat.

"But that's not stopping you."

He shakes his head and continues. "Not terrible. About equal to Ragu. Not close to Rao's."

How would I know? I haven't had a forkful yet. "If you're going to eat my portion, you might as well fill out the questionnaire," I say.

"I'd love to, sugar, but I've got a mountain of work waiting for me," he says. "I just came by looking for a stapler." He waves a piece of paper in the air as if that explains it. Tex starts to leave and then comes back and hands me the bowl. He pivots only to face a stack of garlic bread. In a nanosecond, his hand clamps down over a piece.

Tamara stares at him, saying nothing.

"Now *this* is good," Tex says, reaching for a second. As he turns, Larry makes his entrance and they nearly collide.

"I knew I wasn't crazy. I knew that I smelled garlic." He laughs hysterically. "How 'bout sharing the wealth?"

Tamara looks at me and shakes her head. "Are we running a soup kitchen here?"

"What?" Larry says, holding his hands out helplessly. "We're helping Maggie."

"Do you think you could find room in your heart to leave just a little behind so that I can get just a forkful and fill out the survey that they're paying me thousands of dollars to complete?" I ask.

"Nobody can judge food after just one tasting," Tex says. "Tell them to bring a new round of plates over the course of the next few days," he says, trying to wipe a red spaghetti stain from the front of his shirt that resembles blood oozing from a chest wound.

"I think you'd better get back to Metro," I say softly. "I just heard that the stock market took a nosedive and the Dow slid to a record-low level."

Tex and Larry look at each other, drop their plates and go running out of my office.

"Is that true?" Tamara says after they're gone.

"So, I heard wrong," I say, helping myself to just a strand of spaghetti with each of the different sauces.

I fill out the survey, and then, don't ask me how, put the leftovers out into the newsroom, then write my column as the sharks attack.

Diet Foods: High in Calories, Low in Taste

America's obsession with losing weight is to blame for the food industry's outpouring of "low-fat" and "no-fat" versions of virtually all the foods we love: low and no-fat ice cream, yogurt, cookies, pudding, whipped cream, mayo, cream cheese, cottage cheese, milk, cake, chips, and my—ugh—favorite, fat-free salad dressings that are gluey-tasting syrups made up basically of sugar.

The truth is: Not only doesn't the low-fat stuff taste good, it's finally being unmasked for the fraud that it is. The idea behind low-fat foods is that they're supposed to save you fat and calories, make you healthier and help you lose weight.

The truth is: America is getting fatter because of low-fat products. Guilt-free goodies, people think, give them license to eat more, and eat with impunity.

The truth is: Not only don't low-fat and no-fat NOT mean low in calories, these poor imitations are often HIGHER in calories than the original, because they have added amounts of sugar in an attempt to mask flavor that is lost when fat is reduced.

When I go to the grocery story, I look for food-food. What does that mean? The real McCoy. Plain butter. Not air pumped. Plain milk. Not the kind where the fat is removed. Nothing added. Nothing taken away. Nothing genetically engineered. Do I have to buy a farm? Raise my own animals? Grow my own crops? It may come to that. Stay tuned.

It's almost become a routine now. Every month or so, Bill Wharton takes me to lunch. Very simply, I'm his cash cow, and his goal in life is to keep the paper a success, something he's done for over twenty years by vigilantly watching the bottom line. The *Daily Record is* having a banner fourth quarter, and Bill is particularly proud of "Fat Chance." But also, he likes me. Somewhere in that enlarged, underexercised heart of his, he has a soft spot for my loud mouth and pleasing plumpness, I think, not to mention my irreverent wit and occasionally off-color jokes. He's got five boys, and, well, you get the picture.

Of course, not all of Wharton's innovations at the paper are as successful as the column. The style section's recent cover stories make him wonder if he's getting too old for all this stuff.

"Cross-dressing birthday parties; Upper East Siders who color-scheme their homes to coordinate with their dog's fur; and hair stylists who are buzz-cutting customers' astrological signs onto the backs of their heads. The editor is a moron," he hisses. "But I'll keep mum and give her more rope to hang herself before I pounce and obliterate her authority." He gulps down some Maalox and scratches his head.

"I used to have a handle on the news, a gut feeling about what was fresh," he said, one day over an osso bucco lunch at Carmine's. "Now that part of the job is in the hands of a bunch of kids who think that Charlotte Russe was a star of film noir."

So why, on this day, a full week after he called me, did I still not return his phone call?

"The fourth-quarter numbers look great," his message said. "Your column continues to be a smash, why don't we break out some champagne over lunch, restaurant of your choice."

In hindsight, I now realize what a mistake it was to ignore him. Just as Tamara and I were—for the tenth time—cranking up the volume of our nauseating fitness tape, we saw the door of my office open and who should stand before us, a horrified look on his face, but old Wharton. Shit. Double shit. And what did I do? Wave. He closed the door as quietly as he opened it.

Next thing I know, a messenger is delivering a Bailey's Irish cream cheesecake, to me, from, guess who? That was followed by a voice-mail message—"When your dancing fever subsides, call your publisher about lunch."

"Tex might be on to you," Tamara tells me after lunch one day.

This is not a particularly welcome development. "What did he say?"

I get the whole conversation verbatim.

"Something's up with Maggie," Tamara says he told her

one day while she was sitting with him and Larry. *"But I don't know what."*

"I looked at him straight-faced," Tamara says. "I asked him what he meant."

"She hasn't been herself lately."

"Probably something you said."

"Can't think of anything," Tex says, "but yeah, it doesn't take a lot to get women pissed. Once at a party, I got a drink for myself, but forgot to get my date one." He nods his head, as if remembering. *"I walk back to her and she says, 'Didn't it ever occur to you that I might want something to drink?' I said, 'I didn't think you wanted one,' then she pushes right past me and says, 'Right, you didn't think.'"*

Then Larry chimes in. *"Great material, we should write a screenplay. Once, I bought a gift for a woman. This black lace nightgown, great, sexy, I couldn't wait to see her in it."* He shakes his head. *"How was I supposed to know she wasn't an extra-large?"*

"Observant, aren't you, Larry?" I say. Tex laughs.

"So she takes it back for a small and finds out that it was the last one and came off the clearance rack." Larry looks down at his drink and mixes it with his finger and then licks his finger. *"So she says, 'The one thing I hate is men who are cheap and stupid!' So I said, 'That's two things.'"*

Tex nods his head. *"Yeah, the old one-two punch."* His voice trails off. *"I think there's some basic resentment of the opposite sex. It bobs along the surface until one day, propelled by some deep seismic forces, it explodes in your face."*

"PMS," Larry says.

"No, that's not it with Maggie. She's just distant…less eager to eat out. She's even starting to look different."

"Different?" I say. *"What do you mean by different?"*

"I'm enjoying baiting him, Maggie. He is so unbeliev-ably dense sometimes."

"I'm not sure," Tex says, as though he's afraid to divulge what he's thinking.

So Larry pipes up.

"Better," he said. "Maybe she's on a diet."

"Nah, impossible," Tex says. "Not old trencher woman Mag-gie. She never diets or takes off for spas like some of the women I know." He shakes his head. "She doesn't think about things like that. That's the great thing about her."

"Absolutely right," I say. "You guys read her stuff. Maggie doesn't diet."

"Take her out for ribs," Larry says. "See what's up."

"I looked at them both, trying hard to keep from laugh-ing," Tamara says. "If these two geniuses were directing the investigative reporting at the paper, then the *Times*, the *Daily News* and the *Post* could rest assured that they had nothing to fear."

six

FedEx parks the wardrobe-sized box in my building lobby with the doorman. No more nights spent cuddled up by the TV. No more evenings sprawled on the bed facing a snack tray with BBQ Pringles, Snyder's of Hanover home-style pretzels, Entenmann's chocolate doughnuts and Diet Coke. From now on I'd be quaffing Fiji Water and snacking on orange wedges. NordicTrack time. The Dominican handyman rolls it up to my apartment door on a dolly and hauls it into the bedroom.

He looks at the box and laughs. "Everybody buy these things, these equipments, but nobody use them."

"Well, it's good to stay in shape." *How would I know?* He looks at me, shaking his head, laughing, as if I told him a good joke.

After a lightning-quick smile, I double-lock the door behind him. It would probably be fun. I'd make it fun. Sliding, gliding. I'm not the most coordinated person in the world, but I'd get the knack of it. I am a quick study.

I change into my sole pair of cycling shorts, which were secreted in the back of my drawer years ago. I start to tug them on, but when I stretch the waistline apart, it stays that way. I fling them into the garbage. At least my dresser drawers are getting roomier. I pull on a dress-length STOP HUNGER T-shirt, sweat socks and sneakers.

I tuck my feet into the toeholds, reflexively stiffening up as I slide forward, then back. Thighs make up one-quarter of women's weight. Indeed. The effort brings me back to my first riding lesson and the resistance before it flowed. I was stiff, uncoordinated. Maybe if I try to relax and move a little faster, smoother. The phrase *fluid movement* comes to mind, whatever that means.

I step up the pace but the machine begins working against me now, like a frisky horse that senses the unease of a new rider and starts to snort and buck. Like Mr. Ed— the first horse I was on at Camp Camelot, a weight-loss camp. When other kids were munching on bags of buttery popcorn at the movies, we walked in with Ziploc bags filled with sour pickles on sticks. Anyway, my Mr. Ed was named after the funny-talking horse on the '60s TV show. Okay, maybe I'm heavy, and unsteady, but this Scandinavian-style Mr. Ed is starting to list and then lean and then… Ohhhhhhhhh, shit, I inadvertently lose my balance and vrooooooom, never mind riding, I am s-k-i-i-n-g over to the side as if part of a giant slalom.

Mr. Ed crashes down on me with the weight of a workhorse, viciously slamming into my poor dimpled upper thigh.

"JESUS, OH JESUS." It feels as if I just took a bullet. I

can only imagine what my downstairs neighbor is imagining as she hears the deafening crash. She probably expects my couch to come barreling through her ceiling any minute.

I rub and rub the spot to prevent it from turning blue and magenta, and hobble to the refrigerator for ice. I deserve a Sara Lee cheesecake for this. Or half a carrot cake. It's not fair. I have the noblest intentions, and it backfires. But I'm not going to be a self-saboteur. I grab a giant bag of frozen corn kernels and wrap it around my thigh like a blood pressure cuff.

I glare at the NordicTrack. I am *not* having fun. This is not about fitness, it is about pain and suffering. I feel desperately sorry for myself. All around the city, other women are dining out at restaurants, sitting in box seats at the opera, attending Broadway shows, or having marvelous mindless sex, and I'm here sweating like a pig with a black-and-blue mark the size of Texas tattooing my upper thigh. I want candy, a Milky Way. But there's no way I can even think of going out for one like this. I call Duane Reade.

"Do you deliver?" YES, there is a God. "Good. I'd like a Milky Way.

"A Milky Way. A MILKY WAY, you know the CANDY bar. Haven't you ever heard of it?" I cannot believe this. Is that such a hard question?

"Sorry? What do you mean, by 'sorry'? Why can't you deliver it? I realize that it's not medicine…okay…okay… but you happen to be wrong, dear heart, it most definitely *does* serve a biological need.

"So how much do I have to spend before you'll deliver it? What?" I slam down the phone.

I lie back on the couch and stare up at the ceiling. Why

am I doing this? Is it worth it? Maybe I will never get anywhere with the damn makeover anyway. Why am I putting myself through this punitive fitness crap? Am I a masochist? I want candy. I want to be happy. I don't like fucking cut-up vegetables. I don't want hot broth *without* noodles, and I happen to like the crispy chicken skin. It *kills* me to peel it off and throw it away, especially if it's sprinkled with salt and garlic.

But then the other voice in my head stops me. Do you like tight clothes? Do you like looking at yourself in the mirror? So stay the way you are. Eat candy and greasy chicken. Don't change. Don't pay your dues.

I vow to stop the negativity, the old excuses. No caving in to the self-saboteur. Hard work pays off. I'm going to succeed. The power is in my hands.

If you fall off a horse… I step back on and glide forward and back, steadier now. How dare they smile in the infomercials. Like sports, it looks a lot easier than it is. Bette Midler had it right. "I never do anything I can't do in high heels."

Of course there are some women—heels or no—who don't even need a piece of exercise equipment. They can open up a magazine and follow an exercise plan. They can simply look at a photograph of an exercise and know what to do by reading the instructions. Now, I know I'm not stupid, but when it comes to coordinating body movements and understanding which foot, knee, arm, etc. gets lifted while the other sits on the floor and waits its turn, I'm out of my element. Maybe it's like map reading. Some people are good at it and others have to ask directions. Left-brain/right-brain kind of thing.

So instead I shell out hundreds on this new roommate.

I brace my midsection against the padded center once again and try to coordinate the back-and-forth arm movements, but after only a few tries, I'm gasping for air. My body becomes sheathed in a cocoon of oily sweat and my T-shirt clings like my epidermis. I slow my pace and breathe deeply.

A nun in a Catholic school once chided a girl who complained that she was hot and sweating: "Horses sweat, men perspire and women glow." So I *am* the horse. I sling a towel around my neck like a prizefighter in training. If water loss counts, by the end of the night my tightest jeans will billow.

The phone rings, and I hesitate. Should I ignore it and just continue exercising? Of course not, I'm a firm believer in breaks.

"Want to go out for some paella?" Tex says. "There's a new Spanish joint that we're reviewing tomorrow. Tonight will probably be the last time that we can get a table before the four-star review comes out."

Spanish food. Paella. I love the way the sausage is mixed with chicken and the saffron rice. And who doesn't love a pitcher of icy sangria, the hearty red wine—and white is wonderful, too—lovingly sweetened with oranges and apples?

"Actually, I had an early dinner," I lie. Can he tell?

"So have another one," Tex said.

Tex is a man after my own heart, but somehow I summon the energy to keep my resolve. "Can I take a rain check? I'm kind of bushed anyway."

"Big mistake. Listen to this review—'The bunyol de bacalla, a mashed salt-cod-and-potato cake is ambrosial, teamed with a cilantro-mint salsa. Another favorite is the tortilla bandera, a frittata of tomatoes, Gruyere cheese and spinach—a party for your mouth.' Damn," Tex says, "let me at it."

I'm tempted to put the phone down and walk away as he continues to read the review. Are the gods testing me?

"Rain check," I say again feebly, then hang up and put on my favorite golden oldie CD, Donna Summer's "Endless Summer." Who said I can't take the heat?

Tamara and I had agreed to meet at the track around the Central Park reservoir. It's something we've been doing for two solid weeks now. Still, sometimes she shows, sometimes she doesn't. Often, she feigns sickness. One frosty morning I'm on the track with my face hidden behind a black nylon ski mask—one way to avoid putting on makeup.

"You look like you're gonna hold up Citibank," Tamara says, making my day.

"The only thing I'm trying to hold up is my behind," I say, puffing.

"And now there's twenty pounds less of it," Tamara says, slowing to a crawl and stretching her arms over her head while she gulps oxygen. "I wish I could say the same thing. I need a Wonderbra to give my saggin' ass some lift. I ran my fastest speed into McDonald's to get an Egg McMuffin. Another time, I ordered pizza, and then a calzone—"

"Oh, that warm, soft ricotta cheese, God, how I—"

"More guilt," Tamara says, "but that's progress, right? It means you know you shouldn't be eating things like cheese—"

"Can we talk about something other than food?"

To distract herself from eating, Tamara spends time in Barnes & Noble buying books and CDs. She dreams of writing a book, making a name for herself, earning more money and independence. On the weekends she's home reading and cooking, but these days the recipes are healthy ones. Tonight, instead of the brisket with caramelized onions and roasted potatoes that she would have gone with, she's making grilled shrimp and peppers. Her sister Flossie is coming for dinner.

She calls me up and describes the process. "Put the shrimps in a bowl and pour a dark ginger marinade over them."

"What's in the marinade?" I'm getting hungry already.

"Rice wine, soy sauce, minced ginger, garlic and toasted sesame oil. Next you mix the dressing—more soy sauce, vinegar, sesame oil, sugar, sake and chopped cilantro."

"Then?"

"You sauté fresh baby spinach in oil with fresh garlic, then thread the shrimp onto skewers alternating with chunks of red, yellow and orange peppers. Broil them, then lay the skewers over the cooked spinach. Last thing you do is pour the cilantro dressing over the skewers." I'm now considering calling the local Chinese restaurant and having them make the recipe for me.

After Flossie tastes the shrimp, she calls me herself. "You're definitely on to something."

We hang up and I can imagine how they're dishing over my born-again makeover thanks to Michael Taylor.

"Who would have guessed that rock-solid Maggie would go gaga."

"Honey, you never really know about people," Flossie probably says. "The smart, tough-talkin' ones are the quickest to become unhinged. There's no connection between brains and success and how smart you love."

In fact, despite all her dishing, Tamara was doing a great job keeping the makeover a tight secret. To throw off people in the office, we agreed to keep a box of Oreos on the desk, and a bowl of M&M's near her phone. I considered rubber-cementing some to the bottom of the bowl but decided against it. Someone would find out. Still, because it's a newspaper, people get paid for following hunches, and they were suspicious about me.

A comment or two had been made.

"Where's Maggie hiding herself?" Wendy the Weight Watcher asked Tamara.

My loyal assistant nipped that one in the bud. "Over at *Sports Illustrated,* being photographed for the swimsuit issue."

And Tex. Ever since I started having California rolls for dinner, our friendship seemed to have gone as limp as seaweed and rumors that came my way indicated he was wining and dining not only Sharon but other stocky blondes around town.

Where would it all end? In my wildest dreams, could I imagine a Hollywood hunk falling for me, especially if I wasn't fat anymore? I wondered how my own drama would play out.

The Skinny on Weight Loss Plateaus

So maybe you refuse to give up dieting. Fine. But before you start your next diet, and then abandon it because it "stops working," read this. Every diet works for a while, and then you diet and you diet and you diet some more, but the scale seems to stop getting the message. H-E-L-L-O—you're ready to start kicking it viciously. In fact, the problem isn't a dustball stuck in the mechanism. Something is going on with your body and that's why you're not losing those hard-fought pounds anymore, no matter what you do. But what?

Every dieter knows the frustrations of arriving at a weight-loss plateau, and the solution isn't to say screw it and down ten Hostess cupcakes. What might help is to look at what your body does with the calories that you're taking in.

About two-thirds of them go toward running your machine. In other words, fueling your heart, liver, lungs, etc., and regulating body temperature. Another ten percent or so are used to digest your food and utilize it. The rest go toward moving your ever-loving body around—or not moving it, as the case may be.

And, of course, we all vary tremendously in the amount of calories that we need. Two women may be the same height and weight, and age, but differ significantly, studies show, in the number of calories that they need just to keep basic body functions humming. After that, it's often a case of playing policeman with yourself. Buy a food scale and monitor the size of the portions that you eat. Every bite of food counts—even the free samples that you pick up in the supermarket, or the bites of leftover food that your kids leave. Have you been exercising? You may have built up more muscle, and even though the scale doesn't show less weight yet, you may have lost fat. Exercise more and then sit back (mentally) because the weight will continue to come off. In fact, at this point, shift your energies more toward exercise. Remember, weight loss slows down the more that you lose. It's the way the body protects itself against starvation.

seven

Yes, I felt guilty about ignoring Wharton. But how could I handle lunch with him in a four-star restaurant and order salad? If I didn't eat whole-hog, he'd be suspicious. After the second call, there was no place to hide. I decided I'd resort to the clichéd illness fable. Some sort of mysterious and lingering GI bug, just had to wait it out…these things didn't just go away overnight. I'd go without makeup so I looked washed-out, and order consommé, broiled fish, fruit. Ugh.

In the meantime, I'd hide the lost weight with camouflage gear.

"I need something to make me look fatter," I tell Tamara.

"That's a switch. Who you tryin' to impress, a sumo wrestler?"

"Close, lunch with Wharton. You think the Zoo has an online boutique?"

"Zebra stripe couture?"

"Oh, maybe elephant pants. Anyway," I yawn, "they couldn't look worse than this." From a mammoth shopping bag, I pull out a flouncy pink dress with puffy sleeves and crinolines under it. I pull it on over my dress.

Tamara's eyes widen in horror. "You trying out for Shakespeare in the Park? Give it up."

"I plan to. At the end of this charade it goes priority to Stratford on Avon—at least I'll get a tax deduction. But you have to admit, I *don't* look thin."

Weird clothes, plates of greens, my digestive system is in an uproar, my head is turned around, it was time to see my shrink.

I sit on her overstuffed down couch in her apartment on Central Park West and stare out of the leaded-glass windows at the tall trees. It's a co-op, in the kind of building that celebrities live in with mahogany-paneled dining rooms that can seat sixteen comfortably for Thanksgiving. Don't know who painted her walls, but they're lacquered to glossy perfection, free of cracks and goose bumps. I understand completely how she affords it—at one hundred and fifty bucks an hour, she should put up a brass plaque outside the office with my name on it, since I pay so much of the maintenance each month.

I sit in the corner of the couch, near the Kleenex box and the small gold Tiffany clock that she sees without looking at. I mean she must. We always finish on time, ten to the hour.

There's a pen-and-ink sketch of an oak tree opposite the couch, and one branch holds a flock of sparrows. All of the sparrows have their heads turned in the same direction, except for one. Guess who identifies with the oddball?

"One phone call, and I was the high priestess of the overweight, but enter Mike Taylor, and I came unglued."

"We all have uncertainties about who we are depending on—"

"Uncertainties? I'm a knock-kneed teenager waiting for the latest issue of *True Romance* to hit the newsstands. You know the word *crush?*"

She sits back in her moss-green velvet wing chair and smiles benignly. "Aren't you being a little hard on yourself, Maggie?"

I smile tightly. "It gets to be a habit." I turn and stare out the window. It always feels so safe here. All feelings are allowed. Tolerated. In fact, if things are going better than average, I almost feel I'm disappointing her. As if we need to do crisis management, otherwise what's the point? She doesn't take notes, and I can't decide if I like that or not. Does she have an extraordinary memory? Or do I just repeat the same stories and themes so often that there's no need for her to write the same things down, over and over. Or is it simply that she feels as though taking notes would inhibit me, as if she were a detective recording every detail for the record? This way, at least, no one can subpoena her notes.

"Okay, let's put another spin on this. A celebrity's call for help prompts a savvy journalist to offer her body in the interest of science. Can maximum motivation edge out body chemistry?" I rather like that.

"Maggie, maybe you've made a habit of putting your own spin on things, instead of dealing with what you really feel…"

"What I really feel? It's been so long since I've given vent to— I mean, I'm perpetually thwarted, dammit…" I reach for the Kleenex. I wonder how many boxes she goes through in a year. Do other women get as weepy as I do? I doubt it. I'm the type who cries at funerals even if I didn't know the deceased. I feel for the family. I know how I'd feel if it were my mother. Everyone else, however, always seems so self-possessed. What is that?

She sits forward in her chair. I know by now what that means. "I'm afraid we're out of time," she says. "Let's start with that next time." I go to the bathroom, and then pass the next patient who's waiting in the living room as I go out. As usual, I'm tempted to look at her, and ask her what her issues are. But I avert my eyes, and head out to the elevator, then step back and turn toward the staircase.

Wharton booked a table at Le Cirque 2000, the venerated four-star celebrity haunt, now gaily redone in harlequin-like decor.

"Bill, I wasn't ignoring you. I would never do that. I...I was out with some viral bug or something for a few days. I'm trying to slowly get back to myself. I mean, you lose muscle mass when you just lie there and vegetate." I hold my arms along my sides as though I'm an eight-year-old doing show-and-tell in class. He's not an idiot, why am I showing him what a prone position looks like?

"Mmmm," he says, with a bewildered expression on his face.

"I mean, it's like being weightless, like you're in outer space." I blabber on, filling the void. "You need to walk, move, do weight-bearing exercises or you just turn to mush. So I bought a couple of videos, and I'm trying to get my strength back."

He seems to be considering that. Actually, it's hard to

know what is behind the pained expression etched into his soft, punching-bag-shaped face. Those horizontal ridges etched into his forehead, the hangdog look. The man appears as though he's never had a truly relaxing day in his life.

"Well, I'm starting with the escargots," he belches out, as if to release the discomfort he is bottling up listening to me. "And then I'll segue into the ris de veau with the sauteed wild mushrooms. How about you, Maggie? Betcha can't top that."

I smile weakly. My eyes seize on the succulent lobster with coral risotto, the seared duck breast with its curry braised leg and desserts like crème brûlée and chocolate fondant.

"I'm really on culinary R&R right now. Just some consommé and then monkfish and fiddlehead ferns." I'm at a four-star restaurant, and I'm ordering like I'm in the ICU.

Wharton stares at me in disbelief. "Maggie, is there something that you want to tell me? You're not going through some conversion, some born-again fitness philosophy or altered state of consciousness, are you?"

I consider ordering fresh-squeezed celery juice to really freak him out, but no, it might be too jarring.

"Bill," I coo, elbowing him. "You know me better than that."

Wharton looks back at me for a moment without saying anything. He's about to break apart a second roll when he stops and turns to me.

"You're not unhappy at the paper, are you? I've tried to give you all the perks that I could to make you happy. Is there something you need? More file drawers? New office furniture? Even more vacation time?"

Now that I've lost weight, I consider asking for a wardrobe allowance, but then think better of it. "I'm perfectly happy, Bill, I swear. Relax."

Some of the tension melts out of him.

"Good," he says, patting my hand like the parish priest. "Good. Well, here come the appetizers."

I sit and glumly sip from the shallow bowl of pale yellow broth flecked with scallions, mesmerized by the sight of Wharton energetically downing his escargots and then soaking up their fragrant garlic-infused broth with thick heels of crusty French bread.

He passes his plate under my nose. "At least have a taste."

I smile brightly and shake my head, then glance down and catch the reflection of my shining green eyes in the shimmering silver of the oversize soup spoon. I might be starving to death, but I was proving to myself that I had willpower worthy of a listing in the *Guinness Book of World Records.* And now, for a change, my head is in charge, not my gut. Suddenly, my mood brightens. Three weeks down, five more to go. It was a piece of cake!

You're Not To Blame

Do you blame yourself for the way you overeat? Well, now new research comes to the rescue, offering some solid science to show that how you eat has to do with more than just willpower.

For years, researchers have suspected that the business of understanding eating disorders was far from simple. They just didn't have all the facts—the whole scientific picture. Well, they still don't, but some newly published research now shows that one form of a gene that's part of controlling your appetite occurs more often among anorexics.

What does that tell us?

That maybe eating disorders can be blamed in part on some malfunction in the way the brain normally controls food intake. The study—done by researchers from Germany and the Netherlands—revealed that 11 percent of anorexics had a variant form of the gene for agouti-related protein, a chemical in the body that stimulates appetite. Among people without anorexia, only 4.5 percent had this form of the gene.

While the causes of anorexia as well as other eating disorders may involve more than just one gene, and have to do with one's environment as well, the study gives ammunition to our argument that "it's not our fault."

After three weeks into my new routine, I decide pampering is in order. I wriggle my toes. Time to book a pedicure at Arden and then head over to the shrine. I deserve a gift. I had to reward myself. No one else would. Who was it who said we're becoming the men we want to marry?

I lean against the edge of Tamara's desk. "You're finished for the day. We're outta here."

"What's our cover?"

"A reducing seminar."

"What are we reducing?"

"Our wallets."

We enter the famed Red Door of Elizabeth Arden, walking past displays of lipsticks in tempting colors like cherry soufflé, strawberry ice and orange float, and take the elevator up. We sit elbow to elbow while our feet are buffed and sloughed, and our toenails painted persimmon. To prevent the polish from getting stamped with the impression from our shoes, the pedicurist slips plastic baggies over our toes before our stockings go back on. I grab the check. "It's on me."

"Let me at least cover the big toes," Tamara says.

"I'm buying your silence." I grab her arm. "Next stop," I say, ushering her into a cab, "is the shrine." We pull up in front of a store on West 55th Street.

"Shrine? What in God's name—"

"Genuflect and then saunter in as if you're a regular. And don't reach for your inhaler when you see the prices— which are in dollars, not in lira."

I see them the moment I walk in. They are on a par with no other. A black snakeskin stiletto with a four-inch heel and a stiff cord that snakes up the calf. *Helmut Newton, where are you?* No contest, these were Manolo Blahnik's crowning achievement.

"THESE!" I screech to the salesman. "THESE!"

Tamara crosses herself and looks up. "Forgive her, Father." She grabs me by the upper arm. "You're losing more brain cells than pounds." The look on my face makes her drop her voice to a basso profundo. "Twelve hundred dollars?"

"Don't put a price on my happiness!" I slide out of my pumps, forgetting about the wrapping around my toes, and grin sweetly at the salesman. "Condoms to protect the pedicure."

"And what size for madam?"

"Who cares, they'll kill no matter what size they are," I cry, as if suddenly high on laughing gas.

"Nine," Tamara says snootily.

He nods, failing to share the joke, then heads into the back. I stroll around the store, narrowing my eyes and examining shoe after shoe, lifting each one, turning it, holding it up to the light, studying the craftsmanship from every angle, as a diamond dealer might study each facet of a prized specimen. Finally, the salesman reappears, carrying a box that he places before me.

I separate the tissue gingerly, lifting out a shoe as if I am unearthing the Holy Grail. I slip one on, and then the other, and slowly stand. I've been reborn. I'm a contender. I'm feeling as beautiful as that cover girl, Giselle whatever her name is.

"Tall at last," I utter, walking my new seductive walk. "I'm breathless."

Tamara's not buying it and glares at the salesman's icy face. "Attitude sickness."

I teeter totter over to the mirror and study my feet. This is better than therapy. "I'll take them," I whisper, breathlessly.

"In what color, madam?"

I extend my platinum card between two fingers. "E-V-E-R-Y color."

eight

It was the memory of the chunks of ripe avocado ignited by zesty bits of onion, lemon juice and cilantro that was the lure at Rosa Mexicano. It was a tough reservation, unless you were, well, me. Tex and I always start with frozen margaritas, the widemouth glasses encrusted with a ring of coarse salt that bites gently into your lips. We go through one round, then another. They slide down easy with chips and guacamole served just right in a thick pebbly stone mortar. We follow with beef enchiladas, sizzling steak or shrimp fajitas, or maybe grilled pork chops with black beans and rice. South of the border soul food. Tex and I hadn't had dinner together in almost two weeks— a record—and now he was sitting opposite me and looking at me funny.

He scratches his head. "Something wrong, Maggie?"

"Why?"

"You lost weight. You okay?"

"Not 'You look good, you look thinner.' Duh, 'You lost weight.' Am I okay?"

Tex raises his eyebrows. He's on unsteady ground now, I know his every facial twitch.

"Yes, in fact, I've never been better." I toss my head back. "I am just *terrific*." I can't help snapping at him.

He holds his hands up in surrender. "You look great, you do, it's just that you never lost weight *deliberately* before…" He shrugs. "So I figured…"

"Well, stop figuring, and thanks for the left-handed compliment." It made me wonder about the kind of compliments he gave Sharon. Did he tell her he liked her dark roots? That he didn't mind the chipped red nail polish? That he found her hard edge appealing? I flash him a venomous look, then turn away.

"I never thought you needed to lose weight," he adds, almost muttering to himself. "I mean, I thought you looked good the way you were… I mean, who likes boyish, skinny women. They look sickly, underfed."

I'm dining with the village idiot. And it was getting worse. I stare at him incredulously. "I looked good the way I *was?* The way I *was* was *fat*." I shake my head and then reach for a corn chip, but think better of it and bury it in the salsa as though I'm stubbing out a cigarette.

"So what's happening on Metro?" I spit out the last word like a curse. Why was it that even the smartest men seemed to have these deep gullies of ignorance? I never could understand how a man could be so brilliant in one area—tort law, for example, or quantum physics—while showing himself to be totally ignorant in understanding the basic human needs for love and compassion.

In women, on the other hand, ignorance was spread

more evenly, like frosting on a cake. Tex could be so sharp when it came to the intricacies of a story. Every detail, every nuance, registered viscerally. But when it came to the fine points of anything to do with women, he was hopelessly dense. Was that why he went from date to date until he met Sharon, who, I was willing to swear, wore contacts to make her eyes look green? Sometimes I suspected that he even read the personals, and it wasn't to look for dangling participles. What was he looking for anyway?

Thirty-nine-year-old newspaper editor, former football star, warmhearted, well-intentioned, but brain dead on issues relating to women, in need of smart, sexy broad with thick skin and infinite tolerance.

"How does Sharon stand you?" I say, trying to hold back a laugh. "You're hopeless."

He looks back at me like a wounded puppy, then slowly, a glint appears in his eye and his frown turns into a grin.

"I grow on women. It just takes a while."

It's impossible to stay mad at Tex. While narrowing his eyes and holding my gaze, his fork surreptitiously slides underneath the leftovers on my plate. Without looking down, I trap his fork with mine, then push my plate over to him.

"Here, have my fat."

We talk about changes on the desk, and laugh over plans for the newsroom renovation. The only subject that never comes up is California.

Toes in position, my nocturnal track attack begins. Donna is wailing, "She works hard for the money, but he never treats her right." Left, right, left. I stop, lost in thought, arms clinging to the padded chest support as if it's a life raft.

It wasn't just battling to lose weight that fueled my unease, it was feeling in my heart of hearts that I had betrayed a trust. As a journalist, I'd be the first one to point a finger at hypocrisy, yet outwardly I was championing fat acceptance while inwardly eschewing meat and potatoes for fish, fowl and field greens.

I could blame it on Mike Taylor, but if it wasn't him something or someone else would have spurred me on to give it one last shot. The urge to get thin lingers in your system like nicotine. Years after giving it up, you're never completely released from temptation. It's an addiction, and you never recover, you are perpetually recovering.

It was consoling to think of this last all-out try as an outward-bound adventure. Living on the edge. It wouldn't work out, but it was exhilarating to think that it might....

Of course I was Irish Catholic with the genes for dark introspection and misery. I could envision myself as a desperate character in a play, fifty years from now, with long trailing tendrils of gray hair as coarse as a Brillo pad. I'd be sweeping, trapped in a stone cottage by the ocean, the waves pounding on the shore outside, and the NordicTrack—along with a carton of corroded weights—a memorial to the past, standing by the fireplace like the bones of a long-dead mate.

Well, maybe it wasn't guilt, just fear. I was in a panic at the thought of reaching out, stepping over the mundane borders of my life to make up for all those Saturday nights in my bedroom.

I head into the kitchen and start preparing dinner—a low-cal green pepper filled with rice and a smattering of beans. While I wait for the rice to boil, I watch the traffic outside going down Second Avenue. If I had any regrets in this life, I wanted them to be over what I *had* done, not avoided doing. I had already spent enough time on the sidelines.

Remember photographer Bert Stern writing that lame account of how he resisted the opportunity to sleep with Marilyn Monroe? He was glad, it would have ruined the fantasy, the myth of Marilyn, or some such nonsense. OH PUH-LEEZE.

Yet I have to admit I'm scared, panicked at the thought of doing something wildly out of the ordinary. Of course offers like this were as rare as fruitcakes in August, so why in hell shouldn't I follow my passion? No, I wouldn't think this thing to death. I'd just go—lightly—my luggage, the laptop, snug dresses, long-lasting makeup, a bottle of Contradictions, and...the SHOES.

Maybe what was slipping away was more than just pounds. I'd never felt better, and the truth was that thin was looking pretty good.

The Cure Can Be Worse Than the Disease

There's always a better regimen, just a diet book away. You feel as though somewhere out there is the magic plan that will erase a lifetime of fat and abuse.

Everyone who has ever been caught up in the dieting trap—that means all of us—is like a quick-change artist who reinvents herself on one regimen or another, any or all of them bound to help in the short run, but ultimately destined to rebound, leaving us not only heavier, but also deeper in despair. It defies logic. The diet mind-set has an insidious life of its own. It's about pipe dreams and prayers, not IQ.

If diets worked, no one would be fat.

But now experts tell us that while obesity might increase the risk of premature death to some degree, the risk is far less than they believed. By age 65 the risk was slight, and by age 74 it no longer existed.

According to the two top editors of the *New England Journal of Medicine,* "The cure for obesity may be worse than the condition."

Others go so far as to say that dieting itself is a risk factor for developing an eating disorder.

How much science do we need to prove that deprivation diets aren't the path to happiness and fulfillment? When does measured thinking take the place of drastic measures? Instead of zoning out on common sense, and opting for the life of pathetic greens and hard-boiled eggs and fly-by-night regimens that no one can stick with, it's time to eat well and instead make some long-lasting lifestyle changes if your aim is to shed pounds.

And if you need some math to convince you that dieting alone is doomed to fail, here goes:

Every time you diet without exercising, you lose one-quarter pound of muscle for every three-quarters of a pound of fat.

And while a pound of muscle burns fourteen calories a day, a pound of fat burns just two calories.

In other words, if you lose twenty pounds, you'll lose five pounds of muscle, reducing the number of calories you burn each day from muscle by seventy.

So say you go off your diet and gain all the weight back, what happens? The weight you put back—assuming you're still not lifting weights—will be all fat, not muscle.

Bottom line: Overall, your metabolism will have slowed down and you won't even stay at your previous weight. If you keep eating just the way you did before dieting, you'll eventually weigh more.

Five weeks into my routine, I am down thirty pounds, so what is wrong with the face that is staring back at me in the mirror? Not face. Faces, that's it. The glaring pool of one-hundred-fifty-watt, soft-white bathroom light was indisputably illuminating not a single, but a double chin. Contouring with makeup, no matter how awe-inspiring the artistry, couldn't make it disappear. Two palettes of Bobbi Brown's toasty blusher later, the futility of a brownout hit me hard. So instead of groping for the bible of self-acceptance, I reach for the phone book and the number of a plastic surgeon who has gained a reputation for facial microsuctioning. I put in for a week off—enough time for the bruising to disappear, and buy myself a jar of vitamin K cream and another of arnica that I'll use to ward off bruising.

"Here's the game plan," I tell Tamara, like a sergeant in the marine corps. "I'm out for a week of vacation. I'm tired, overworked, resting at home, doing a little apartment work. I'll be in and out a lot, hard to reach…and a week later, I'll be back, looking like the time off served me well."

"Maggie, this has gone way beyond that small-potatoes diet—"

"We don't use the *d*-word around here, remember?"

"You're entering the major leagues now—you're talking the knife, anesthesia—maybe you should think about—"

"No, I don't want to think, it doesn't burn fat. It's time to act, and I'm depending on you to run interference for me, keep the newshounds at bay and share in my passion play."

"You sure about that?"

"Yes, I'm definitely doing it."

"No, I mean about thinking burning fat."

"God, who knows?"

Tamara gives me that look.

"You think I'm nuts, okay, say it."

"Noooo, you're just being sucked off into a midlife twister—but go ahead, do the crazy shit, get it out of your system. At least you're single. Maybe it'll work out in the end like it did for Flossie."

"What did she do?"

"She got married and five years later ran off with the window cleaner."

"And what happened then?"

"He kept her windows so spotless—"

"What happened to *her?*"

"Well, the love affair didn't last but two months, and her marriage went bust, but Flossie's no dope. She rounded up all of that stud's friends, and started a house-cleaning service. Now she's making half a million a year, and has her pick of the stable."

Tamara sits in the softly lit waiting room with the husbands of other patients, waiting for me to emerge. When I come up, she's deep into an article called "Facial Sculpting," pinching the sides of her face and the slack under her chin. It's contagious, I think. It occurs to me that maybe the good doctor gives a bulk discount. Tamara tries not to look startled, but fails miserably. That's why I love her.

I know I look like the Pillsbury dough girl. The thickly

wound compression bandage snugly puffs out my face. She runs over and hugs me.

"You poor pathetic creature," she says, and her voice gives away the fact that tears are forming in her eyes.

"Don't get soft on me, Tamara. It's just like analysis, except the knife makes you feel better faster."

I drape a knockoff Hermès scarf flecked with horse bits and saddles around my head, '50s Italian-film-star-style and strut out of the office behind wraparound sunglasses. But nobody is fooled. Not one person comes running up to me yelling "Sophia Loren, *cara*."

We cab it to my apartment, past the silent stares of the doorman. I make Tamara leave. I can't stand to see her pathetically sad puss, and I go to bed with a Tylenol with codeine and the cold comfort offered by a body-bag-sized sack of ice. The old me is disappearing, a little more every day.

"So Larry comes by and says, 'Where's Maggie hiding out these days? Haven't seen much of her lately,'" Tamara says, in her daily phone report. "He pointedly left it unclear whether he was referring to your presence or your weight."

"What did you tell him?"

"Lectures, guest appearances, Maggie is everywhere. Want her cell number?

"'Cell?' he says. 'Where is she, in solitary at Rikers Island?'

"I yawn and tell him to go get someone indicted and then strut away in my Manolos. And you know what he says?"

"I give up."

"'*Mama mia*. What have you got on your feet?'

"'Just shoes,' I say. 'Shoes that show toe cleavage.'

"'What? Show what?'

"'Toe cleavage.'

"'And I thought I heard of everything,' he says.

"They work! THEY'RE BAD!" Tamara says.

I hang up. I can't laugh anymore, my face is too sore.

Minus a chin, and plus a new palette of earth-toned makeup applied with techniques I've culled from a *Vogue* beauty book, I make my grand entrance into the office.

"Maggie," the receptionist shrieks. "You are sumpt'n else."

I blow her a kiss. After intentionally threading my way through the newsroom and generating a buzz of whispering, I sidle into my office. *"Buon giorno."*

Tamara looks. Her look alone is worth it all. "Lord have mercy. Bless that surgeon."

I pat the underside of my chin, and smile. "What surgeon?"

Justine eyes me strutting through the newsroom and freezes. She comes running.

"How did you do it? How? How?" she says before she's crossed the threshold. She crosses herself. "What diet did you go on, tell me."

The health-food gestapo asking moi about *my* diet. This is great.

"I guess we all just have our natural set points," I say, tossing a green and then a yellow M&M up into the air and catching them in my mouth. "The weight at which our bodies feel most comfy. So I just let nature take its course. I grazed—had a little of this, a little of that, some German potato salad, teeny slivers of brat, a pinch or two of terra chips, and it just happened. Just like that." I hold out my hands, as if in wonder. "You know me. I don't believe in dieting."

Connors isn't buying it. "You had your stomach stapled, didn't you? Who did it? Was it that guy from Baden Baden who's at Mount Sinai?"

"WHAT?"

"Did you take Leptin? Or was it Fen-phen? I know it kills your valves, but it works, for God's sake. We've got more than we need anyway, haven't we? I mean, planes run on one engine, why can't a heart get by— So what did you use? You didn't go to Switzerland for the sleep cure, did you?"

My hand goes up around my throat. "Justine, you are truly making me nauseous. Other than my new DK contouring body stocking…there's nothing terribly different that I'm doing."

She shoots me a dirty look. "Fine, Maggie," she says, pivoting. She starts to walk off and then pivots once again. Is this a routine she learned from Martha Graham? "Just don't come running to me when you want the inside track on sample sales. I'll give you a map pointing you to Bergdorf's." I scrunch up my nose and rock back on my heels.

"The last sample sale she told me about was for Kalso Earth Shoes. I was literally off my rocker." I grab a handful of M&M's and throw them at her as she leaves.

Wharton is the next drop-in. News travels fast in the newsroom. He stares in disbelief.

"How was your vacation?"

"Great, fine."

"Go anyplace special?"

"Nah, just hung out at home. Did some sprucing up…"

Wharton sits silently for a moment like a husband knowing full well he has been cuckolded, but fearful of the consequences of acknowledging it. "Maggie…is there anything you want to tell me?"

"Yeah, I caught *Monster in a Box* on HBO last night. Did you see it? That Spalding Gray is a scream, I swear." Silence.

"Maggie," he says, resigned. "I guess I'll just come right out and say it. You don't look like our fat columnist anymore. I mean, you're just not fat anymore. I…I don't know what to say. I'm concerned. I'm worried—"

"Bill, I—"

"Your column is the most popular one in the history of this newspaper. We want to continue with it, build on your success. But what's going on with you? I mean, can you keep writing a column like *that* if you look like *this?*"

"So I lost a few pounds. I'm into exercise these days that's all. I still have the same beliefs, the same goodwill message to everyone else who's overweight. I—"

"Okay, if you say so. I hope you're not changing. You'll keep doing what you've been doing all along, right?"

"Of course, of course, Bill."

"Okay, okay," he says, getting up and leaving. "Okay." He keeps parroting it like a mantra. The next thing I know, a messenger is delivering two dozen Italian pastries to me from Ferraras in Little Italy. I take the box and put it out on the Metro desk for the staff. Half an hour later, the piranhas have devoured every crumb.

I lean back in my chair. For the first time there is more wiggle room in it now. Six weeks have gone by since I started dieting and working out. I've dropped thirty pounds and am down almost three sizes. Two more weeks to countdown. Still ahead: Body wraps to smooth the skin, capillary zapping to banish the pesky red threadlike streaks that cropped up on my cheeks, sclerotherapy to get rid of leg veins, a manicure, leg waxing, eyebrow shaping, bleaching to whiten my teeth, a hair trim, highlights to add mock sunshine to hair that barely sees the sun, and about one hundred more miles to run. Natural beauty? An oxymoron. This makeover was draining me physically and financially. I even considered taking out a second mortgage on my apartment. Well, priorities. In Brazil, where women make a career of looking gorgeous, there are more Avon ladies than soldiers.

I scan the medical journals to catch up on the latest findings about weight control. By now, someone should have given me an honorary degree, an M.D. No one would know that it really stood for a Master's in deceit.

nine

I've spoken to Mike Taylor several times since his initial call.

"We're still on, right?" he asks, and I want to laugh out loud.

Instead I answer, demurely, "I'll be there."

"Need anything special? A private phone line, a DVD player?"

"I'm easy," I say. *Am I ever.* "Just my laptop." *God, even that sounds... What is happening to me?*

"Any special foods?" he asks. Is he nervous? I'm loving this more by the minute. Just a few pounds of Beluga, I'm thinking, but I bite my tongue. "Nothing special at all."

Before heading to my apartment to pack up, I clean out my desk. Mike Taylor should only know the effect that his calls have had on my life. I'm lightening up everywhere.

There are two piles: save and toss. It reminds me of the fashion columns that offer a column of what's *passé* and *au courant*.

An unexpected advantage of losing weight, I've discovered, is that a smaller wardrobe takes up less room in a suitcase. And for once, I'm not embarrassed to wear clothes made of stretchy fabrics that don't wrinkle. A master of packing, I roll each garment tightly and find that I've room to spare. I'm now humming—"Pack up your troubles in your old kit bag and smile, smile, smile…" Songs fall into your head that way. The mind acts like a giant Kazaa that stores this huge inventory and then pulls out the appropriate song that gives quick feedback on what you're thinking before you even know it.

I zip the bag and sit on the edge of the bed like a kid contemplating running away from home. I want to go, I do, but I'm afraid to cross the street.

Everything's ready and I watch the red digital numbers change, second by second, on the clock radio like a little electronic guillotine, killing time before I fly from one zone and one kind of life to another. An hour until the cab comes.

I haven't seen Tex in weeks. Ever since the dinner at Rosa Mexicano, things have been strained. I never told him about the makeover, or the trip, but he knows. Even though he's just a friend, I don't need him holding up a magnifying glass and examining my motives. And certainly no guy needs to hear about how infatuated you are with another guy and the lengths you'd go to snare him. That was inside baseball—something best shared with another neurotic girlfriend, or better still, kept to yourself. The results would speak for themselves. Anyway, I know how I feel

when a guy starts raving about some fabulous broad.
SHUT UP.

I dial Texas's number and am surprised when he picks
it up himself, on the first ring.

"Hey."

"Hey back, where are you?"

"Home, I'm flying to L.A. later today."

"Panning for gold," Tex says. "Don't turn into one
of them."

"One of them?"

"Stay Maggie."

"Whoever she is."

"Quit the shrink talk."

"Not easy. It's been a lifetime," I remind Tex.

"Your life ain't over, sugar. Anyway, I'll buy you a steak
when you're back."

"Well, maybe some sole."

"Why, did you sell yours?"

"No, I didn't go that far.... Well, I'll miss you, Texan."

"Damn right you will. Take care, kid."

"Yeah." I cradle the phone in my lap before hanging up.

As the plane takes off from JFK, I listen to my scolding
conscience lash out like a genie that escaped from the bottle. *What the hell have you done?* How could I have been deaf
to it? Why am I all dolled up in shoes I can hardly walk in,
wearing a dress that barely fits my butt, and underwear that
has its own way and needs a good slap? Two weeks later
I'll be back, hit with bills for a second wardrobe that I'll
outgrow before I have time to save up and pay for it.

What do I hope will happen anyway? Is Mr. Movie Star
going to fall deeply in love with me? Is the divine Miss

Maggie O'Leary going to open his eyes to the fact that chubby broads can be as sexy as skinny ones? More likely I'm going to bat my Lancôme-sheathed lashes at the hunk and appear a pathetically sorry sight. A sinking fear begins to spread through my gut.

I have a respectable job back home, a column to write, readers who need me, believe in me, and here I am in LaLa land, deluded by fantasies from a grade B movie. What a stupendously stupid move.

Why didn't it occur to me to just e-mail him a contact in L.A. and be done with it? Was my life so bereft that I had to embark on this makeover charade? I've never really felt my age, didn't think I looked it, but playing the role of a groupie? The stage door matron, more likely, waving a playbill in the face of a departing actor. It's clear that I'm spiritually bankrupt, clueless about fulfillment and psychic rewards. *What in the world am I searching for?*

What I should have done was book a room at a spiritual retreat, or gone trekking in Nepal. Make a spiritual connection to the *universe,* not DreamWorks.

He called and I flipped, slimming down to a weight that in a million years I'll never maintain. One hour of abandonment—a plate of ribs or fried chicken (with garlic mashed potatoes, please)—and I'll unravel, pig out and slap it back on. Was there a parachute?

To calm myself, I breathe in, count to ten, and then blow it out. It's too late for regrets. *For the next two weeks, chin up, shoulders back, tummy tucked in. I am CONFIDENT, SELF-ASSURED, EASY, BREEZY, THIN AND GORGEOUS.* I repeat the words as if I'm parroting a self-improvement tape. If you assume a role for long enough, you eventually become that person. Someone said that, anyway, inane as it sounds. If that were the case, I would now be Kate Moss.

I pull a magnifying mirror out of my makeup bag and stare hard into it. I put on a light layer of lipstick, blot it, then dust my face with powder. I examine my teeth, and regret neglecting to bond my two front teeth. The hint of uneven color…. I begin combing my hair, then stop and pull the mirror closer, noticing for the first time what I think is a gray hair in the line of my part. Already? And not there at the beginning of the flight. Where was I going, back into the future? I search through my bag frantically and extract the tweezers. Narrowing my eyes, I trap the wiry rogue between the sharp tips and pull.

Then to distract myself, I open my laptop and begin writing:

When Food Becomes Ammo and You're Pointing the Gun At Your Own Head

Savor your food, inhale the aroma, feast on the flavor, enjoy and nourish. But leave the table content and thankful for the offering. Don't use food to punish yourself. Easier said than done? Undoubtedly, but to help, I offer just a few tips that I've stolen from others:

- Brush your teeth after every meal. That means you're finished. Don't go back. Want something to do with your hands? Knit. Sew. Black out winning numbers on your lottery tickets. Want to keep your mouth busy? Keep a thermos of hot tea within reach.
- Remember white space. On the printed page

that means a rest for the weary eye. On your dinner plate it means smaller portions or islands of food. Think St. Kitts and Nevis, not Australia.

- Where do you put leftovers? Not near the TV. Not on your night table. Not on your kitchen table. In the freezer—where it's too cold and hard to enjoy any more today....

I close the laptop when the attendant comes around to serve lunch. "Hamburger or fishwich," she asks.

"Fishwich?" my seatmate says. "Who's catering the food these days, McDonald's?"

"It would be an improvement."

The flight attendant turns to the woman, a cherubic blonde in her early thirties who fills out her pleated skirt.

"I'll have both," she says, laughing.

My kind of girl.

"No, just kidding. I'll have the fish too." She turns to me. "Perpetually dieting."

"It's the American way. You traveling on business?"

"I'm going home to see my parents." She stares off for a moment, her eyes vacant. "I left my husband."

I barely nod. *Should I say I'm sorry? Maybe he was a bastard and she was doing the right thing. Unfair to assume it was him, but wasn't it usually?*

"It must be hard."

"Not as hard as staying." She brushes a lock of hair off her face and shrugs. "The cheerleader grew up and let herself go." She pats her hips. "So I was replaced with a better-looking clone." She stares at the fingers of her left hand, studying the one that now has no wedding band encircling it.

"Maybe eating was your escape route out of the marriage," I suggest.

"Yeah, sometimes I think I should thank Ben & Jerry's." She starts to laugh, but the laugh gets stifled in her throat and escapes as a pained cry. She turns her head and looks out the window. The plane dips, as though the gods are admonishing her, and her salad tilts into her lap.

"Damn, now I'm a mess," she says, brushing furiously at her skirt.

I wet a napkin with club soda and help blot up the stain. "No, you're not," I say, touching her arm. "It'll be just fine. You'll see."

As we approach L.A. I stop writing to prepare for landing, and turn off the laptop so that the pilot doesn't lose contact with the control tower and mistakenly land in Libya. My seatmate is asleep now, and I can't help looking over at her now and wondering how her life will turn out. Maybe something or someone will come along, and like me, she'll do everything in her power to become the best of herself. Or maybe she won't. Maybe she'll give up, or just do nothing and go on for the rest of her life reexamining the past and being ruled by it, convinced that somehow she's failed and that she's now powerless to change that.

Out of the window, I see the unwelcome cloud of smog that hangs over the city like the exhalation of a wrathful automotive deity. I've never noticed the same dirty schmatte of smog over New York.

As the plane circles lower, I search for the legendary homes, and notice the tiny squares of turquoise swimming pools that dot the landscape like shimmering mosaic tiles. What would Taylor's house look like, the Getty Center?

Finally, the plane bumps down, and I feel like applauding. I can't help it. Sure plane travel is the safest way to go and all that—assuming no one from over *there* takes over the cockpit, but what a relief to hit terra firma. After all the work I've done, I'm sure as hell not about to be vaporized in a goddamn 747.

I pull down my ballistic nylon bag from the overhead storage bin and edge my way toward the front of the plane. Not a particularly challenging walk ordinarily, but in this case the forty-pound bag doesn't help me balance in four-inch high heels no thicker than #2 pencils, particularly when they have been off my feet for the entire flight, and my little piggies have expanded, inexplicably, and wee wee wee, I want to run all the way home and come back with my fat, wide, thick-as-a-mattress, unsightly Nike cross-trainers.

The L.A. sunshine embraces me like a lover's arms, hot, encompassing. Gray New York is now worlds behind. Nonexistent. Irrelevant really. My dour New York demeanor that I've long blamed on sun deprivation is a thing of the past. I can almost feel my vitamin D level rebound. INSANE, but HERE I AM. I feel like singing in a loud Ethel Merman voice.

I walk toward the exit, unconsciously going slower and slower, about to step off the gangplank. A few more feet… He's out there, somewhere. I walk closer and closer, remembering the child's game of hide-and-seek. You're getting warm, warmer, hot, HOTTER, HOTTEST, ROASTING!

A bloodred Ferrari Testarosa heads the line of waiting cars. I put my bag down, searching. I want to see him before he sees me. Sneak preview. I want to study him. I search the parking lot, and then, there he is, and I just stare.

The arms first. Tanned, strong, folded over the black vinyl roof of the Porsche. Then I stare at his body, which is muscular beneath a snug black T-shirt. Dark sunglasses, and a pulled-down red baseball cap that shadows the face. An insignia on the cap, but too far away to make it out. He stands out as if in bold relief, three-dimensional among a flat, blurred backdrop of moving cars, towering palm trees and passengers coming and going, like a movie clip that is played and replayed to make some existential point about rootlessness.

Involuntarily, I smooth my hair, pushing it back away from my face. I reach behind me and tug slightly at the black spandex dress to reverse its upward crawl. I step toward him and smile. At that moment, I feel blessed. Hundreds of thousands of women around the world would trade places with me right now. That's a situation that I've never ever been in before and that I'll probably never be in again, so I hold that thought. Bask in it.

He seems to look in my direction, but he doesn't move. No sign of recognition. I wave, but he hesitates. Then he quickly moves toward me, realizing that no, it's probably not a fan after all.

"Maggie?" he calls, a questioning look on his face. "O'Leary? Maggie O'Leary?"

"C'est moi."

"Oh, hey, I'm sorry, I didn't know for sure… I…" He doesn't finish the sentence for a minute. He's tongue-tied. Irresistible. He pushes his sunglasses down and looks over them. Who taught him that? *The eyes.* I feel a rush, as though I'm watching him strip.

"I thought you looked different," he tries, holding himself in check so he doesn't stumble over his explanation. He's self-conscious, almost embarrassed. I smile, looking down to stifle a laugh. I'm not helping him out of this one.

"Well, hey, it's great to have you here. Let me toss your bag in the trunk, and we'll take off pronto." I open the door and slide back into the soft black bucket seat, canvassing the car like a detective to find out whatever I can about him. An open wallet tossed into the leather compartment between the two seats, loose change, matches, folded slips of pink paper, the scent of cowhide, a faint whiff of smoke. No breath spray, thank God, or Tic Tacs. He slides in on his side, and slams the door. I'm now a part of his intimate world, and for the length of the ride, it will be just the two of us, just inches apart. He looks over, smiling awkwardly.

"Welcome," he says, pecking my cheek. "Welcome to L.A." I reach over and tug lightly on the visor of his cap.

"Thanks, Taylor," I say, suddenly overcome with an unnerving calmness. "It's super to be here."

ten

The speedometer needle quivers at around 90, and the world seems to be fast-forwarding past my window. Taylor leans back, at ease, his right hand loosely guiding the wheel. I steal a glance at his profile as he chats, hoping to find some angle, some wrinkle, a fat pad maybe, an ice pick scar, an incipient boil, something that I can seize upon to make me feel that "AHA! See! Even *he* really isn't that perfect in person after all." But, of course, there's nothing, not even an ingrown hair. Smooth tanned skin, a powerful neck, the perfectly sculpted jawline. A furtive glance at the way his faded jeans outline his muscular legs, the length of them, the worn black leather belt with the steel buckle, the swell of his zipper. Looking at Mike Taylor, it occurs to me that God has really put himself out. Gone that extra mile.

I study his features. The eyes dominate his face. Honeybrown, fringed with thick lashes. If he were female, he would have secured a lifetime contract with Maybelline.

Okay, his nose is just a mite too small—but all to the benefit of the eyes. Lips that are born to smile, that curl easily into a 1000-megawatt glow showing white teeth with just the barest hint of crookedness. Comfortable with himself, easy.

If he senses that I'm studying him, he doesn't let on. Used to that. He probably feels naked without eyes on him. We chat about the flight, how many years I've been doing the column, school—"NYU? Really? One of my directors taught at the film school"—and occasionally, he glances over at me offering that small, confident grin that my body registers in every molecule like a mini-Richter scale. He tells me how much he likes New York, and how sorry he is that he doesn't get there more often. I admire the car, and am about to change the conversation when he swerves off the road abruptly.

"Here, take over."

"I…I don't know how to drive a stick—" I'm stuttering now. That's cool.

"Come on, I'll teach you, it's easy."

"Now?"

"Now." He jumps out and walks around the front of the car to my side.

"Slide over, go ahead, it'll be fun."

Oh no. Well, at least I can now maneuver myself over the stick shift without becoming impaled on it and land—thump—in the driver's seat. Eight weeks ago, all of me would definitely not have made it. That accomplishment alone justified two months in the gulag of self-denial. The leather feels warm from his body. Can I learn to drive, feeling like this?

"Look," Taylor says, jumping into the passenger seat and

putting my hand over the smooth rounded head of the vibrating gearshift and covering it with his. It feels like…like… Oh God! My face is flushed. *Is he thinking what I'm thinking?* Our hands slide together—left then right. Up and down. *In… YES, YES.*

"Neutral, okay? Now think of the shape of an *H*." He moves it left and then up. "This is first, down to second, up, across and up here to third and then down to fourth. To go in reverse, you push it down across and back. Just remember to press down on the clutch when you shift, and ease your foot off the gas at the same time." He looks deep into my eyes.

"You got it?"

No, I don't think so, let's do it again. Damn, the telltale blush.

"You sure you trust me with this baby?"

He sees it and smiles seductively. "It's only a car."

"Tighten your seat belt," I say, doing my most polished imitation of Bette Davis. "It's going to be a bumpy ride." The car stalls at several points, and then lurches painfully at other junctures as I shift gears. We come to a fork in the road. As Yogi Bera said, "If you come to a fork in the road, take it."

"Right," Taylor says tolerantly. "Up that hill."

I turn to him and pat his hand. "You okay?"

He buries his head down under his shirt. "Who, me?" But he's smiling. I reach a set of gates and he grabs the remote and punches in a code. The gate opens. Then I drive up a long winding driveway to a second set of gates. I nearly stop short when I reach the front door of a contemporary glass mansion.

"Not bad for a starter house," I say, trying to sound blasé.

He smiles. "Three years ago, I couldn't have afforded the

pool house. But that's what happens around here. Make-believe city."

I pull up to a garage filled with L.A. status symbols—motorcycles, a Jaguar XKE, a vintage Thunderbird, a Range Rover, even a formula-something-or-other racing car. He smiles and gestures around. "My toys."

"You better pull it in. I don't have enough collision insurance."

"You can leave it right there. I'll show you around after you're settled in." He springs out of the car and grabs my bag heading toward the front door. A moment after he opens it, I catch my own reflection flung back at me in the cold blue orbs of the skimpily clad Jolie Bonjour. She's dolled up in a black lace tank top and white cutoffs that are so cut off that they reveal the rounded bottom of her doll-sized rear end.

"Jolie—Maggie," Mike says.

"Alo," she says with about as much enthusiasm as she would show to a tax auditor.

"She, ah, lives with me," Taylor says.

"Great to meet you," I say, graciously extending my hand, although I really felt like exhaling hard to see if I can blow her away, maybe all the way back to France. Introductions out of the way, he seems to forget Jolie.

"I'm sure you'll be really comfortable here," he says, his voice trailing off as he climbs the staircase, two steps at a time. I start to follow him.

With Taylor out of earshot, Jolie turns to me. "I thought you were a *fat* columnist."

That stops me. I turn around. Some Gaul. "I guess it's a matter of interpretation."

Jolie remains at the bottom of the staircase, glaring up.

★ ★ ★

Architectural Digest failed to do justice to the place. Aside from ten sun-flooded bedrooms—if I counted right—and an expansive living room, there is a library, a screening room, Taylor's office, his secretary's office, a gym bigger than the newsroom at the paper, and a kitchen with an island just smaller than Manhattan. The cabinets hold a kitchen computer stocked with international recipes, a TV, DVD player and sound system. I have lost count of the phones. There is a pool, two tennis courts and a handball court. Why no polo field or Alpine ski run? Why would anyone ever leave this Xanadu?

Wherever I walk, I see tiny red flashing lights. Security is Pentagon tight. "A royal pain," as Taylor puts it, but a necessary evil. I watch him sprawled out on the bed in what will be my room, marveling at his…at my good fortune, as he elaborates.

"I came home one night and found a dizzy blonde who had climbed through a window. I tried to talk her out the door with an autographed picture, but she pulled a knife and said she'd kill both of us if I didn't marry her." He shakes his head in disbelief. "I thought it was just a fluke until about a week later. Another nutcase showed up, this time sitting out by the pool naked. She was waiting for me to make it with her. Said it was the right time of the month, that she had taken her temperature."

"So you played along."

Taylor snorts. "Yeah, I told her I was going to the bathroom first and locked myself in the john until the cops came. Now you know why I host the annual fund-raiser for the Police Benevolent Association."

In addition to the sensors inside and out (*and I thought*

Tex's police lock on his apartment door was excessive), he tells me about the twenty-foot high fences. "Those went up the day that I saw a picture of myself inhaling an illegal drug."

"Men in glass houses shouldn't get stoned."

He smiles. "I see you're gonna be trouble."

"So, does tight security mean that bells go off if I touch your arm?"

"Not quite. Anyway, you get used to it, and since I couldn't get arrested in this town for years, I'm not complaining about the way things are…anyway, you hungry? I have a fridge packed with food."

"I ate on the plane, but maybe just some iced tea and fruit?"

He seems taken aback, then shrugs it off. "Done. Let's go down."

I can't help staring at the luminescent flecks that dance along the runway of black granite that is a kitchen counter, as if I am looking at a highway paved with diamonds.

"Do you *know* what a New Yorker would do for a kitchen this size? We cook in cubicles. If you're lucky, you can stretch your arms out to the side and make a 360 degree circle without banging into something." He watches me, amused. I open the refrigerator and stare.

"Party here tonight?"

He shakes his head.

"Why so much food?"

He shrugs. "You're supposed to like to eat, no?"

"I don't eat THIS much. But I'll tell you what. I'll cook you dinner. What do you like?"

His eyes widen. "Everything. Whatever."

"Why do you look so shocked?"

"The truth is that no one has made me a home-cooked

meal since the last time I ate shepherd's pie at my mom's house in Des Moines, maybe six months back—and to tell you the truth, she's not such a hot cook."

This surprises me. No women fawning over him, inviting him over for dinner? Maybe that wasn't an L.A. thing.

"Until I left home at eighteen, I thought mashed potatoes came out of boxes, and that gravy came in cans."

"Doesn't Jolie cook?"

"Cook? All *she* eats are fruits and vegetables and a sprinkling of granola." I see he's house-cleaned. There's nothing resembling granola or soy milk here, at least not that I can see. He smiles. "On Thanksgiving—hey, that was a feast—she diced up a salad."

Should I laugh or cry? "Well then, Super Sleuth," I say, now comfortable enough to call him by the title of one of his movies, "tonight you're going to eat big-time, some delectable treats from the mother cuisine." I look at his face. He has no clue. "Italian food. How does that sound?"

"I can't wait."

"Good, now get out of the kitchen and go learn some lines or something. I'll find you when dinner's ready."

"Whatever you say." He salutes, and walks out of the kitchen, but then he turns back and leans up against the door and watches me.

"What?"

"I don't know," he says, rubbing the back of his neck. "The house feels different now."

"It's probably the first time you've seen someone other than the maid in your kitchen."

He shakes his head. "It's not that. It's your energy... your...aura."

"My aura? Now I'm sure I'm in California."

He misses the cynicism. "Great," he says, striding off. "Great."

The overstocked refrigerator is like a giant orgasmatron. I inhale, get a grip on myself and then begin poking through shelf after shelf to come upon gastronomic glory in all shapes, scents, colors and tastes. It's like a VIP ticket to Fauchon, or the Food Halls of Harrods with the unlimited freedom to indulge. Obscene, excessive, overabundant—and alluring. And no one knows better than me what to do with all these delectables. The French Froz fruit had put Taylor's body into culinary deep freeze. I would shock him back to life.

After inventorying the contents, I decide on the menu: Semolina cakes with butter and cheese, baked oysters Florentine, veal marsala, meatballs, manicotti, escarole with garlic, mesclun greens, and zabaglione with raspberries and blackberries. (Maybe this should be a column: See, I'm not dieting!!!)

I press the power button on the CD player and the kitchen comes alive with golden oldies by the Supremes—*Baby love, oh baby love, I need you, oh how I miss you.* What I really want to do is jump up on the kitchen counter and dance, swinging a wine bottle over my head, but afraid of being caught and appearing bipolar, I channel my euphoria by chopping and sautéing to the beat, infusing the air with the redolent bouquet of garlic, onions and wine sauce.

"What are you making? It should be illegal." I jump. Taylor has crept into the kitchen behind me.

"Nuking Lean Cuisine."

He lifts the lid on a pot, but I smack his hand.

"Don't you dare!"

"Sorry," he says, lowering it. "Sorry. How about a little wine?"

"Let me guess, you have cases of the Richebourg '71, and as a backup, the Grand-Echezeaux '71 from the Domaine de la Romanee-Conti."

"Huh?"

"Don't tell me you don't have a world-class *cave* packed with priceless selections."

He shakes his head. "No *cave*. Don't know a damn about wine. I usually go with local California stuff—at least I can pronounce it. The only things goin' vintage in my cellar are the bones of producers who put me into pilots that went nowhere." He pours two glasses of chardonnay ordinaire and lifts his. "To you and to our collaboration. And boy am I glad you can cook."

I clink his glass a trifle too hard in return. "Here's to *Dangerous Lies,* the movie and all the ones I had to tell to get me here. Now if you want to eat tonight, I suggest you find something to do. I've got work ahead of me. See you at eight."

"I'm off to the gym," Taylor says. "If I'm going to feast tonight, I better get into shape."

Fat AND Fit

Remember all the research telling you that fat people die younger than thin ones? That less is more when it comes to how much you weigh? Well, now there's another piece to the puzzle. Stephen Blair, director of research at the Cooper Institute for Aerobics Research in Dallas, told colleagues attending a meeting of the Association for the Study of Obesity in London that if obese people are fit they have half the death rate of skinnies who don't work out. According to Blair, we're too busy obsessing about weight, and not busy enough thinking about fitness.

Does the dinner tonight include Jolie? I wonder as Taylor saunters off. The scent of sautéing beef probably sends her into spasm. *Merde!* Fatty food! Is she in the gym too? I can't get the vision of her in the gym out of my head. I see her riding on a bike next to him, purring seductively. Or lying down on a weight bench, trying to tease him into getting on top of her. Or worse still, following him into the shower while dear old me is in the kitchen fixing them both dinner. I turn up the CD.

In the middle of rolling out the pasta for the manicotti, I stop. Tim McGraw is singing "Please Remember Me." It makes me think about the paper, and I check my watch. What's going on now? The office seems a world away.

The scent of sautéing garlic and onions and browning beef makes me think of Tex and how he would have delighted in the feast I was preparing—especially in a kitchen this size. He would have rolled up his sleeves and joined me. He never cooked with a recipe. The proportions just seemed to come to him. Then he taste-tested.

When we met I assumed that his culinary repertoire began and ended with his kickin'-ass chili. And it wasn't the kind of chili that I knew, with red kidney beans and tomatoes.

"Cut up the beef, you *never* use ground beef," he informed me. I sat there, like an attentive student, watching him add water, chilies and garlic, and then cumin and oregano. Nothing else. He told me about the international chili cook-off that he entered in the West Texas ghost town of Terlingua—total population 25—fewer than the number of tenants who lived in my apartment building. That gave me just an inkling of his interest in food. It turned out that Tex had read more cookbooks than Tamara had tried diets.

He was the one who introduced me to Ligurian cooking—"La Cucina Profumata." One cold Sunday last winter, I called him after a brunch to whine about a disastrous blind date. He swore that his fish Ligurian-style would improve my mood. We met on the West side to shop for Gaeta olives and red snapper. When we got back, he presented me with a little gift sack of an appetizer: Basil leaves stuffed with minced prosciutto and Parmesan cheese then breaded and fried in olive oil. Then he taught me about Sicilian bottarga, the cured tuna roe that was salty and pungent and divine when mixed with olive oil, garlic and parsley, and served over spaghetti dusted with bread crumbs.

And technique. Tex knew every method, even how to use a pressure cooker. He walked me through the basics, one afternoon, demystifying the process.

"I know it's going to spew out of the pot and explode in my face," I said, holding an oven mitt over my face like a catcher's mask.

"Darlin', you have nothing whatsoever to worry about."

"Where in the world did this contraption come from anyway," I asked, lowering the mitt.

"Introduced at the 1939 New York World's Fair by National Presto Industries." What were the chances of any other guy in the world knowing that?

"And for the one-million-dollar jackpot, Mr. Van Doren, the category is food history. Who was the fierce conqueror who introduced the lowly potato to Elizabeth I? Tick tock, tick tock—"

"Sir Walter Raleigh."

"Jesus, Tex! How did you *know* that?"

"Trivial Pursuit, I think," he said, grinning. "Keep going."

I did. "If you're so smart, tell me about the origins of ketchup. And I'm talking about pre-Heinz."

I remember the way he stared back at me. "Ketchup, huh?"

I was so sure then that he was stumped. "Ketchup, you heard me."

Slowly, a smile spread over his face. "Ohh." He feigned confusion. "I think what you mean is ke-tsiap. It was a seventeenth-century Chinese brine of pickled fish and spices."

"Oh, stop it, Tex."

"I swear to you."

But he wasn't all business. I was over at his apartment baking chocolate cookies one day, got distracted and forgot about them until the smoke alarm went off. I raced to the kitchen, too late. Tex had to hold back a laugh.

"Guess Maida Heatter's job is secure." He lifted one, tossed it up and then caught it in his hand, weighing it. "Feels like buckshot," he said, eyeing me with a wicked grin.

"You want to *feel* buckshot?" I took a cookie and flipped it at his head.

"Naw, that wasn't buckshot," he said, taking aim, "THIS is buckshot." He flung it at me like a Frisbee and then ran out, ducking behind the couch. Men love this sort of thing. I think it's almost instinctual for them to go wild and act piggish, like out-of-control adolescents. Food fights, panty raids, activities of that high level of sophistication. No matter how old they are, or what they do, start the rumpus and you'll see how easily they'll join in.

Our food fight escalated to the point where both of us were running in and out of rooms, screaming threats and barricading ourselves behind furniture and doors. Cookies flew through the air. What did I care? It wasn't my place.

Eventually, we cleaned the mess up together and then, bereft of dessert, we went out for it. Then we just walked and explored some new neighborhood, and saw a movie. Sometimes our nights together ended up in a bookstore or a foreign magazine stand where we would share barbs about which books made the bestseller list, who was profiled in the news magazines and who should have been, or the ludicrous subject for a fashion magazine cover story: "Legs are Back."

"Didn't know they left," Tex said.

Nothing special, we just hung out. Together, just not on Saturdays or Wednesdays. Those were his date nights with Sharon. This was fine with me. We went to better restaurants than they did. She was a born-again vegetarian. At least this week.

Though it's late in New York, I dial and then punch out his extension. If he answered, it was never by name, in case he wanted to duck who it was.

"Metro."

"So how's the big cheese?"

"Turnin' blue without you," he says.

"Yeah, it's dead there without me, huh?"

"What's it to you? Was there a lull between sour apple martinis poolside and you remembered your roots?"

"Actually, they're drinking cosmopolitans out here, but more importantly, I needed help with a recipe. I'm making veal marsala and I forget how much wine to use."

"Whatever's left in the case after you drink yourself sick."

"That's helpful. Thank you."

"Why don't you teach the actor how to cook? You spent a summer at the Culinary Arts Institute, didn't you?"

I don't answer.

"Maybe you could give him some tips on roasting the high-heat method; reducing gravies—"

"You don't sound like yourself. What's doing?" The Texas drawl was back. Why was he pissed?

"Ah'm getting married."

"Tell me another one."

"Ah am serious."

I knew at that moment he was leaning back in his chair, stroking the side of his face. I start to answer, but nothing comes out of my mouth, then a rush like bullets. "Are you fucking kidding me?"

"Now, what kind of thing is that to say?"

"You're one of my best friends, and you didn't even *tell* me?"

"Ah'm telling you now."

I wedge the phone between my ear and shoulder and start mincing the onion, making very small, precise cuts with the knife. I don't know what to say. That doesn't happen often.

"Well…congratulations." I'm using the knife to push all the pieces into a neat pile. "I'm just surprised. Well, that's wonderful for you and Sharon. When's the big day?"

"If I had five minutes away from this damn place I could figure that out."

"So why don't you sound deliriously happy?"

"I'm in the middle of a mess here. Police reporter just quit, so it looks like there's going to be white space where his column belongs."

"I'll let you go. I was just cooking up a big Italian dinner here and I thought of you—"

"I thought you don't eat that way anymore."

"I'm keeping the franchise."

"Good, when you get back you can teach Sharon how to cook."

"She can't *cook*?"

"She does other things," he drawls.

I try to keep the laugh in the back of my throat, but like a wave in motion, there's no stopping it. Tex hangs up, and that makes it funnier. Maybe it was the wine, but I'm doubled over, holding my stomach envisioning the headline in a supermarket tabloid: Cuisine from Hell! The poor guy would subsist on boilable bag cuisine. His mantra would be "microwave ready." Served him right for getting involved with an investment banker. Well, at least I now know what to buy them for a wedding present: A Texas-size toaster oven, and *Cooking for Dummies*. If it didn't exist, I'd write it.

eleven

"Maggie, *que pasa, mama?*" Tamara says when I call her a few minutes later at the office.

"According to plan."

"And how is the hunkasauras? What is that bad little white boy really like?"

"Trash," I say. "No, sweet, really. I'd even venture humble. Unlike his pet frog here, I don't think he has a mean bone in his body."

"Are you lovesick? I mean how can you work with a guy who looks—"

"It's under control. What am I missing?"

"Page six in the *Post*. The headline, and I quote: 'Mega Morph for Mesomorph for Mega Mike—'"

"Yeeech."

"They said that you whittled down, glammed up and headed out to play houseguest of, quote, 'L.A.'s sexiest bachelor.'"

"Oh God. How the hell did they find out? This is going to poison my career. I can see the résumés pouring in to Wharton now for my replacement. He probably bought himself a cat-o'-nine-tails and is whipping himself for giving me the okay to come out here."

"Never mind the real world, you've got exactly eleven more days left in paradise. Knock yourself out."

"Thanks, Tamara."

"Maggie?"

"Yeah?"

"Is he hung?"

"Oh, Jesus, I am going to hang up in your—"

"One mo' thing."

"What?"

"Pro-tec-shun."

I'm about to hang up and then hesitate. "Did you hear about Tex?"

"Yeah, Sharon's really crazy about the guy."

"How do you know?"

"He told me," Tamara says before hanging up.

It was good to check in with the office. Dear, crazy Tamara…and the whole crew. But after today, no more "in the kitchen with Maggie." I'm out here working, even though in the sunshine it doesn't look like anybody does that.

I fish out a meatball. Mmmmm, perfection, and the recipe will die with me. Forty minutes to dinner. I sip the wine and look out at the gardens. Fruit trees—oranges, lemons, grapefruits, mangos. Eden. What would it be like to live in a house like this? Vistas of paradise, cascading vines of fuchsia bougainvillea, scarlet frangipani, spiky red-

and-yellow bromeliads… I'd be a fine gardener. I could barely remember to water my cactus.

This *was* a world away. The view over my kitchen sink in Manhattan was the traffic-choked entrance to the Mid-town Tunnel, and beyond it a sliver of the East River with a cylindrical concrete Con Ed tower, like a monument to steam, rising above it. And that was an improvement over my last apartment where my head abutted the kitchen cabinets when I did the dishes. Enter trompe l'oeil. But here, no ersatz panoramas needed to be painstakingly drawn.

Wasn't that what my makeover was all about? Repaint-ing reality? Toying with nature? Priming the surface with diet and denial, and then drawing a new figure. Making up a prettier face, a brighter hair color. Buying clothes to flatter the new figure. But would the paint stick over the old surface? Or would the true grain show through, and the new design warp and wear?

But I'm striving to stay in the moment. Some of my old self was surely shed with the weight, at least some of the negativism. And, for the most part, it seemed as though I had broken through old barriers and was now liberated from the burden that excess weight put not only on my body, but also my mind.

I set the table. Two plates, napkins, forks and knives. Oh…I've forgotten Jolie. Not too Freudian or anything. I quickly fling down another dinner plate. It crosses my mind to replace it with a teacup, but I restrain myself. I grab a carrot. There really is something to be said for the nib-bling (no, gorging) on vegetables while cooking idea.

Just before eight, Taylor's torso is silhouetted in the door frame. He's wearing a band-collared white linen shirt over jeans. Does he realize how it sets off his eyes? I try not to stare.

"I'm fashionably early, and starvin' to death."

"Where's Jolie?"

He shrugs. "Maybe undressing for dinner?" I smile at him. *Are we both making fun of her? Bitch that I am, I warm to that idea.*

"Well, while we're waiting, I'll give you a quick taste of my specialty to get your juices flowing." *Oh no, did I really say that? Doesn't look like he's reading anything into it, fortunately.*

"C'mere." I spear a meatball, blow on it, and hold it out to him. "Tell me what you think."

He closes his eyes and moans as his mouth moves. "I'm yours," he says, lunging at me.

"You pathetic creature. Is one miserable meatball all it takes to win you over?"

He's reduced to silence.

"Tell me something, Taylor. With all the women swarming over you, hasn't anyone ever cooked you a meal, for God's sake?"

"Can I count the chef at David K's?"

I shake my head in disbelief. "In a crunch you ever rustle up your own dinner?"

"I poured milk over corn—no—amaranth flakes once."

"What?"

"It's some grain they found in an Egyptian crypt, I think," Taylor says. "Tastes that way, anyhow. Otherwise, let's see. Sometimes I scramble eggs. Other than that, I don't think this kitchen has ever been used this much before. You christened it." He reaches for another meatball, but I push his hand away.

"Wait for your girlfriend."

He starts to turn away when Jolie walks in wearing a halter dress that I think is really a long blouse.

"I see that the party started *sans moi.*"

"No, we were waiting," I insist. I bring the dishes to the table and start serving.

"Taste Maggie's meatballs, you won't believe them," Taylor says, looking upward. "They're out of this world."

Jolie gives me the *mal occhio,* or whatever the *evil eye* is in French. *"Un peu,"* she says, holding up her hand. She cuts off a pebble-sized piece and tastes it, allowing me a small smile.

"You are a good cook. I have never seen Michael so excited—about food."

I'm about to give her a helping of oysters and manicotti, but the hand shoots up again. Two miserable meatballs and a glass of wine. Not Taylor. He's piling his plate high like a college boy home for the holidays, and popping the cork on another bottle of vin ordinaire. The more he and I eat and drink, the more explosively our stories erupt into laughter. By nine o'clock, Jolie has a splitting "mal à la tête."

"Please excuse me. I don't feel very well."

"C'mon, we haven't even had dessert yet," Taylor says. "Maggie made zabaglione."

She shrugs and walks off, turning back only once to glare at him over her shoulder. He's oblivious.

"So I'm up on stage in front of a group of Hollywood honchos," he says, trying hard to stifle a laugh. "It's my first audition." He puts his head down contemplatively to control the urge to laugh, then continues. "I walk up, working hard at looking laid-back, confident, and I clear my throat and get down to business." He slaps his hand on the table for emphasis. "I start reading and I don't stop, I can't, I'm off and running, flying high on my performance, my incredible virtuosity, oblivious to the words…the meaning…except five minutes down the line it hits me that unless this show is for transsexuals, I blew it big-time, because instead of reading Stanley Kowalski, I was a brilliant Blanche DuBois…."

By eleven o'clock one candle has burned out, and the other is just a flicker in a pool of melted wax. We sit opposite each other like old friends. Bizarre, but it feels like trading stories with him is the most natural thing in the world. Two empty wine bottles stand between us. He reaches for a third.

"I don't want to become a candidate for a liver transplant," I say, putting a hand out to stop him. "I don't know about you, but I need some air."

We walk down to the pool and stretch out on lounge chairs. My head is spinning, buzzing. I'm mesmerized by the luminescent turquoise water, and in the stillness, every sound filters through me. A helicopter sputters overhead and then turns silent, absorbed by the vast acres of darkness. The wooden chaise creaks, as if in pain, as I shift my position and lie back, tranquilized by the meal, the whir of cicadas, the comforting sound of my own breathing. Taylor lifts the wine bottle to his mouth then lets it slide to the ground. It hits the concrete with a ping. Why do I feel like a stoned, twenty-year-old stowaway who inexplicably ended up in a strange place with a celebrity rock star? I break the silence.

"Do you have some kind of herbal cure out here—some capsules from the health food store or Tibet or somewhere—to prevent hangovers, because I think I'm going to wake up with a raging one tomorrow, and I have a column to write."

Taylor rubs his chin. "Yeah, okay, here's what we do," he says, his voice booming. He starts to laugh, the slow, sexy laugh of someone who has happily been relieved of the burden of sobriety. "We wrap our heads real tight in towels filled with ice cubes, down some Vat 69, and then take off our clothes and go swimming in the buff." He laughs harder, and harder. It's contagious, we're both so ripped.

"I would sink. I would sink like a stone, like a medicine ball. They'd have to use a rope to haul me up." That sets me off and I can't stop. "Oh, God, it's not so funny." Inexplicably, tears fill my eyes. The line is blurring between comedy and tragedy. "Why am I laughing so hard, or whatever this is?"

"You're away from home," Taylor says, looking at me levelly. "And you're having an adventure."

I avoid his eyes. Heat is spreading over me. If I allow my head to turn one inch in his direction, we'll be on top of one another and this is moving far too fast for me. I'm so afraid of crashing, of having it all look so different in the morning light, that I put on the brakes. "Yup, that's it. A long-overdue R&R."

He's still staring and I'm pretending not to notice, but the power of his look seems to immobilize me. I'm about to tell him to stop, but stop what? Instead, I chide myself. *Do not move your mouth again. Stop before you blurt out something that you're going to die of embarrassment from for the next eleven days.* Abruptly, I get up on my feet. "I've got to go up," I say, crossing my hands over my chest for emphasis. "Do you mind if I leave you the dishes? I am so wrecked."

"Actually, I think I would mind if I had to do all of them

right now," he says in a goofy voice, "but the maid is coming bright and early. Come on," he says, managing to stand. "I'll go up with you."

I follow him as he weaves up the stairs. We're standing outside my bedroom door.

"'Night, Taylor."

He leans forward and runs the back of his knuckles along the side of my cheek. "G'night, Maggie. Thanks. Thank you. It was a great night." He doesn't move, and I don't dare draw breath. Finally, I ease back and look at him questioningly.

"What?" My legs are going weak. But he just smiles woozily, touches his finger to my lips and then walks off down the corridor.

Not all migraines are created equal. This one mimicks the pummeling given to a slab of veal being reduced to wafer thinness. The pulsations come in waves, the cerebral equivalent of what the poor uterus probably goes through as it contracts explosively in the last centimeters of childbirth. But nothing productive would come out of this torture session, other than the lesson to lay off wine and drink more mineral water.

But while my paddled brain might have been getting thinner, my waistline wasn't. The fat fairy has reappeared and waved her magic wand, causing my middle to swell. Then there was jet lag, topped off by exhaustion from going to bed at three, New York time, and the pressure to write a column when outside it was sunny and 80 degrees.

Are You Eating Your Heart Out?

You're home alone, the phone doesn't ring, your heart aches and you reflexively reach for a quart of

Rocky Road. Does it take away your loneliness, your grief, the pain?

You're in a rage. You head to McDonald's for a bucket-size family meal, only, you don't have a family to share it with and you're all alone. Does the feeding-frenzy stuff down the anger and get rid of your problems?

More likely your self-styled eating cure dooms you to suffer postmeal syndrome: Self-hatred, frustration, misery and helplessness. You'll never do that again, you vow—not until tomorrow, when you do. I know, I've been there. We all love to eat, but when eating isn't about love and nourishment, and instead becomes a weapon that you're using against yourself, it's time to put down your forked weapon and start exploring your inner landscape.

Roughly thirty years ago, an overweight California woman took a friend of hers with a gambling problem to a meeting of Gamblers Anonymous. She recognized that the men in the group suffered from an addiction that was the same one that she as an overweight woman had battled with all her life: Compulsive behavior. In her words: "As long as I live I will never forget that night. We were in a meeting hall with about twenty-five men and just a few women...I heard men talk about lives of lying and cheating, stealing and hiding...I'm just like that, I said to myself. The only difference is that I overeat instead of gamble."

Food was my drug of choice too. But it's not just eating the food, it's thinking about the food, not eating the food, and fantasizing about how your life is going to change when you lose the weight. The funny thing is your life does change, but what happens is frequently it changes for the worse. Suddenly you've got to face the real problems that were sitting there all along.

My thoughts are racing and I stop typing. The column is autobiography masked as journalism. Maybe that was why it had affected readers. But the end was a question mark. Would I triumph over my obsession with food, weight and body image and honestly accept myself for who I am? A month ago, it looked that way. But now, having lost weight at great expense, would I be going back in time, fighting the old battles—perpetually weight cycling—and again joining the ranks of the one third of all women, fat or thin, who despised some part of their bodies?

To make matters worse, with my first breath of California air, I become a hypocrite, hiding my crush. Diet guru? Hard-nosed journalist? Wise counselor? No, schizo.

A knock on the door interrupts my reverie.

"Maggie, you okay?"

Taylor is standing there, unshaven, barefoot, in bleached jeans and a torn black T-shirt. Was it worn to death or expressly made that way by an Italian designer? He looks even sexier all disheveled, of course, so good he might have been photographed that way—leaning up against a rusty pickup truck, say, among tall grass in the backwoods of Tennessee. There would be the tinkle of banjo music somewhere in the background. A heart-stopping *Vanity Fair* cover that someone like me would tear off and stick up on my bulletin board, or squirrel away in a marbleized paper accordion folder among a thick pile of treasured pictures and articles about a life more perfect than my own. I had lots of those photos tucked away. Fabulous men, triplex pent-house apartments, perfectly set dinner tables like the Thanksgiving table that featured a cranberry-draped turkey and take-your-breath-away hotel rooms perfect for honeymoons, including one I particularly liked in Marrakesh, and another, a Mediterranean gem on Italy's Amalfi Coast with an enormous window over the bathtub that opened out to the sea.

He's holding out a cup of coffee. "Thought maybe you could use some."

I reach for it and groan. "First aid, thanks. I'm just working frantically to finish. I need about another hour. You going to be around?"

"I have to be at the studio, and I'll be back late. If you want we can grab dinner later on this week and, if you're interested, one of the writers on the show is having a party in Santa Monica. We could go after I get back." He raises his eyebrows in question.

"Look, I'll be here for a while, so it's really fine if you want to go out, I understand. You have a life, a girlfriend, you don't have to baby-sit me. I'll be just—"

"Stop. I'd like to take you out. It can be fun here. We're not all cardboard cutouts, I swear." He makes a dopey self-mocking expression.

"Okay, I guess I can tough it out for dinner and then the party if you don't mind a third leg."

"Third leg?"

"You, Jolie, me?"

He shakes his head. "She's not coming."

"Oh," I say, nodding. I don't want to know. I look at the time, and gently close the door.

My makeover regimen also seems to be altering the

course of Tamara's life as well. She told me in a phone call just as I was finishing the column that she was sitting in the cafeteria in a new dress when a hot guy she had spotted in the elevator approached the empty seat at her table with his double cheeseburger and fries.

"We have to stop meeting like this," he said. She smiled back at him, and by the end of lunch, she had a date with the hot sports reporter to go to the next Knicks game.

"I developed a passion for basketball, right then and there," Tamara tells me.

It's been a long time since Tamara's dated, and I'm thrilled she has a new prospect. Smart move for her to eat in the cafeteria, instead of getting takeout. It certainly beat seeing Brunhilda's disapproving scowl ever since we started ordering salads.

I can't even remember the last guy she dated.

"I had a string of club dates with a rock star," she says, refreshing my memory. "GUI-TAR man. Not half-bad-looking, fun to be with, but his gigs started after midnight. I saw the pink slip on the wall if I kept stumbling into work after just three hours of sleep. Then there was the two-timer from advertising."

I groan. "That was when I was two sizes larger." We both remember the navy tent dresses. We each had one. They looked like they came from the camping department of L.L.Bean. What rags they were, but then again so were some of the guys we went out with when we wore them.

Actually, I could track my entire life—where I went and with whom—by the outfit I had on. I had an eclectic mix of sizes and styles, all revolving around the numbers on the scale. I never forgot the size-twelve events—so precious and rare.

Fortunately, Ty had a life that meshed with Tamara's and there he was, under the same roof. Not only does she check with the Garden to get the Knicks' schedule so she'd have enough time to find a new outfit, and get her hair done, she tells me that she's working more and more on her novel and the lead character is a photographer.

I end the call by promising to buy Tamara a camera and a how-to book. I make her promise not to take pictures of me, however. I can't forget what I heard in grade school. Models are much thinner than they look. The camera adds ten pounds.

She's thrilled with the gift. She's now buttering up the photo editor and plans to spend lunch hours with him. Since photographers always walk around with their cameras, and she's going to a game with Ty, she's getting ready to take basketball shots and doesn't want to come off like the novice that she is.

"We went out to dinner first," Tamara said, in one of our marathon conversations, and, "I found myself telling him all about my home life. For the first time in as long as I can remember, I was talking to a man who I could open up to. He's like the new acquaintance that you wouldn't have second thoughts about giving your house keys."

For some reason, Tamara and I have better conversations on the phone than in person. Maybe it's easier to talk when you're not looking someone in the eye, but we've got a country between us now and, for the first time, I learn about her family.

"I grew up in Harlem," she says. "Four kids, my mom—

my father died in a car accident when I was six —I don't really remember much about him. We lived in a cramped apartment, and went to an overcrowded school. There were classes in the cafeteria, even the halls. Sometimes not enough books to go around, and the ones they had were old." Instead of salads and seafood, she ate macaroni and cheese and fried chicken legs that they paid for with food stamps. She didn't know there was any other way to eat.

"It was humiliating going food shopping," she says, because their pockets held food stamps instead of money. "You could see what people were thinking," Tamara says, "even when their faces were blank." She lived on welfare, she adds. I'm quiet, saying nothing, not wanting to stop her.

"Do you know what it's like to go with your mother to sign the checks? There were these short little yellow pencils with no erasers in a size made for a child's hand so you feel like you don't even deserve a bigger pencil. I told him all that," Tamara says, "and you know what, Maggie?"

"What?"

"The man looked like he was going to cry."

A definite prospect. "How did he find his way to the paper?"

"Basketball scholarship to UCLA, and three years down the line he smashed his knee in a motorcycle accident. After that, he started writing about the games for the school paper and then moved to New York and started freelancing. He met Wharton through a friend in sports."

So it was Tamara's first live basketball game. The Knicks were playing the Pacers. It has been a dismal season for the Knicks. A string of losses with no expectations for things to turn around. But New York sports fans refused to lose their spirit and Tamara could feel electricity in the air. Ty had a chance to corner Lattrell Sprewell before the game and they were talking about what the future looked like. While Ty talked, Tamara stood back and took a few shots of Sprewell with the camera I'd given her. She also shot Allan Houston and Howard Eisley. When they got back to their seats, Ty turned to her.

"I think I'm getting some great shots," she said to him excitedly.

"I don't know an awful lot about photography," he said, lowering his voice and leaning close to her. "But I think it would be a good idea to take the lens cap off before you take any more pictures."

"I prayed for death," she says. But then she rebounded and turned to him. "Fast eye," she said, punching his arm. "I knew that you'd pass the test."

Ty looked away, stifling a laugh.

With the lens cap wedged in her hip pocket, she took aim. She shot Sprewell and then the oft-injured Marcus Camby, deciding to concentrate on him.

She was just about to lean down and get a second roll of film ready when her heart recorded what she saw before her eye. Camby fell hard on his side just moments after he attempted a driving layup shot along the baseline, after ramming into Jermaine O'Neal. Tamara got it all, including his crash to the floor. A crowd started to form around him, and the team doctor hurried over and kneeled beside him. It was hard to tell what was going on.

"I ran out of the Gardens and jumped into a cab," Tamara says. "I had to go back to the paper to find out what I had...."

twelve

Could there be a sexier place to take a bath than Mike Taylor's white marble bathroom? I don't think so. I tuck the shell-shaped bath pillow behind my head and lean back in the calm, white marble oasis, enjoying the geysers of scented water pulsating against me. If only water pressure could pelt away fat. Now, there was an idea. I reach for the seaweed soap, lather up, and then get out to write a column.

Will We Stop At Nothing?

How do we try to lose weight? Diet, exercise, fasts, massage, machinery. Why hasn't anyone come up with a fat-reducing bath?

Over the years, the overweight have made themselves victims to all sorts of harebrained schemes. Remember when your grandma went to the gym and wrapped a vibrating belt gizmo around her waist or hips hoping it would jiggle off fat? Or how about the rotating wooden rollers she pressed her thighs against to pummel off fat? (Today's version is the mechanical massage called endermologie.) Then there were herbal capsules to dissolve cellulite (a prescription pill now takes its place) and rubberized suits decades back that connected to the hose of your vacuum so that they filled up with hot air and you schvitzed away pounds through water loss. The market seems to be perpetually reinventing the same useless products and techniques.

When will women get it? Do we want to? Maybe saying no—even if the idea borders on the absurd—means abandoning hope, and giving up the dream.

Work aside, I think of dinner with Taylor and tomorrow's party. I'm not used to mingling with the beautiful people, and I have to psych myself up. Oh, I go out a lot, but mostly to give speeches, talk to women's groups, conventions and just revisit comfortable restaurants with friends. Even when I do television, it's the bridge-and-tunnel crowd in the audience. Not too many celebs in my circle. Where did all those physically perfect creatures hide themselves, anyway? Not at the paper, or my apartment building. They weren't riding the subway, pushing carts at the Food Emporium, or even shopping at Bloomingdale's. So who told the bookings editor of *Men's Health* where to look for their cover boys? Or Calvin Klein? How in the world did you get access to that glorified kingdom of male pulchritude—www.hunkdatabase.com?

I shimmy into a long sleeveless black jersey dress. Understated, unpretentious. My reddish hair just covers my shoulders and is slightly layered so that the waves frame the angles of my face. Hair—one of the few parts of the female anatomy where thickness is welcomed. For that at least, I'm grateful to my double helixes. I fasten a gold chain around my neck with a green tourmaline that matches my eyes.

It's the body that always haunts me, perpetually eroding my self-esteem. Even after losing weight, the mind's eye doesn't see it. Sort of like the phantom limb—gone, yet the sensation remains. You feel it, it itches. You live with that fixation of fat, the dark lurking shadow, despite what the scale reads or the mirror shows. You become blind to what you have become. The distorted image lodges itself behind your eyes like a bad dream, a nightmarish visitation that could never be forgotten.

Would I ever feel secure? Comfortable with my body? Have the confidence of Jolie? Wear a bikini brief or short shorts and put myself on display? I can't imagine ever casually flicking off a bikini top so that I wouldn't get tan lines. But being overweight and being secure don't go together. Maybe it has to do with the fact that you have failed repeatedly, every time you dieted, and eventually it demoralized you, robbing you of self-esteem. You hated your inability to succeed, and you hated your body.

What does someone like Jolie agonize about? There has to be something. Big ears? A high forehead? Bony shoulders? Nail ridges? That other models are more beautiful than she is? I open the *Vogue* that's on my night table—this man has thought of everything—and thumb through it. Even though the models on the magazine's glossy pages looked perfect to my eyes, well-known models had con-fided to me in their letters that they felt they were fat or that they hated their looks. One said she was haunted by an offhand remark tossed her way in jest years before. *You're an ugly duckling.* Someone else remembered being called pimple-face, just because she had the normal sprinkling of adolescent zits. The pimples went away, but the scars remained. Every mirror in the world reflected back the depression.

Every woman seems plagued by body dysmorphic disorder—a fixation on some body part that they view as unsightly. Some obsess about puffy midriffs, shopping endlessly for heftier control-top panty hose and camouflage clothes. Others target their wrath on billowy thighs or loose underarms, a fleshy face, a recessed chin, a protruding one, or worse still, a collage of imperfections, a smorgasbord of ills, that are magnified to ghastly proportions.

The only two parts of the body that women rate more positively about themselves compared to the way men rate themselves are the lips and the ears. Ears? I don't recall ever looking at mine closely—they are usually just buried under my hair. And lips? Finally, a place where plumpness was welcomed.

It has occurred to me that maybe I've just been born in the wrong continent. If I was born in West Africa where the ideal figure is fat, I'd be a different person. There's a contest called Hangandi, where women of the Djerma ethnic group gorge themselves and compete to weigh the most. And in southeastern Nigeria, brides are sent to fat farms for a few weeks before their weddings, and then are paraded in the streets where their fleshy figures are admired.

Men are a different story. They're rarely consumed with their weight, or tyrannized by the scales, from what

I can see. They coast along untroubled by their defects, if they see them at all. So many of them secretly consider themselves to be borderline Brad Pitt or Tom Cruise. Even Tex.

While I try to hide my stomach, he pats his and laughs. Of course, he doesn't spend bathroom time peering in the mirror and pulling back the corners of his eyes to erase the crow's feet, or stay up at night ruing the fat pads that time and good food have put over his football player's physique, like a thick extra layer of clothing.

So now I'm close to my weight-loss goal. I can't make myself taller, but oh, well, five-eight in spikes isn't bad. My hair is well cut, a perfect color. I know how to put on makeup. I've got a great job. But am I happy? Well…

Researchers found out that people have a set point for happiness, just the way their bodies have a set point for weight. And even though they shift up and down from that point, nature has mandated that they gravitate back to it like water seeking its own level. In other words, if you were the "sort of happy" type, not counting the day you won the lottery, or the time your dog died, then that was how you'd end up feeling much of the time.

Was I happy with my looks? Ha! I felt like a lacquered Russian doll that contained smaller and smaller ones nestled inside. While the outside shows a slim, confident red-cheeked Maggie, beneath the outer lacquered babe lay the inner unhappy clones. The ones who pop up in dressing rooms with garish fluorescent lighting and wavy mirrors, or emerge outdoors in the reflections of store windows, as if magnified by a fun-house mirror. Worse still, the one who appears on the beach to watch an endless parade of women, all with better figures, who don't have to hide under beach wraps. The dreaded creature, the unhappy clone of myself lurks beneath the surface, unseen, like a malignant cell.

Who do I really want to look like? Jolie, with Mike, her perfect knight, sweeping her up for a spirited romp beyond a mundane reality. If only… Why do I obsessively engage in sidewalk beauty contests, evaluating other women's figures, haircuts, makeup, skin? Inevitably, it leaves me feeling compromised.

For tonight at least, I feel good about myself. I'm looking forward to having dinner with Taylor. What a kick to go out on his arm. Maybe it's some newfound, if temporary, self-confidence and good cheer that came with weight loss. Or, more likely, just an upswing in the hormonal continuum that leaves me feeling that I can tackle anything that life tosses my way because I am basically smart and accomplished.

I put makeup on that face, and slip into my snakeskin Manolos. By now, I can walk in them as though they're Hush Puppies. I check the mirror once more, pull back my shoulders, lift my rib cage, and my chin—all to make me look slimmer and more confident—and head for the door. I pause for a moment, and then go back and grab my sunglasses. Hey, it is California.

We aren't arriving at the Academy Awards, just a restaurant; still, a gaggle of fans along with the ever-present paparazzi are clustered outside Spago. As soon as Taylor pulls up, cameras appear and frenzied girls seem to emerge from the shadows, slipping scraps of paper through the car window for him to autograph. He stops short.

"Mike, I'm so in love with you, I swear. Would you sign this for me, PUHLEEZE!"

He scrawls his name and mumbles, "Thanks."

"Thank YOU!" she shrieks. "I'll keep this for the rest of my life, I swear."

Another tries to wedges her mouth through the window and kiss him. "I'll go home with you," she whispers.

He eases back. "I'm driving the car, hon, I..." A blonde shoves her away and tries to lean into him, cleavage and all, as he's edging the car forward. I don't believe what I'm witnessing.

"Do you always have this effect on teenagers?" I say, half laughing.

"It depends. Sometimes after I make a movie, they throw food." He leaves the car with the valet, and we duck into the restaurant. We're ushered to a small table in the back. Taylor waves to Tom Hanks, and then leads me to a table. So maybe it isn't *just* a restaurant.

"Say hello to the dream team," Taylor says, introducing Steven Spielberg and his entourage.

Before we sit down, a patron with a menu in her hand comes over. "Would you sign this for my daughter. She's madly in love with you." Taylor obliges.

"Don't let me leave without an autograph," I say. "I'm so forgetful about those things."

"Now you're sticking it to me," he says, narrowing his eyes. "What do I have to do to impress tough Maggie O'Leary from New York?"

"Impress *me?* What for?"

"So that you'll stick around and cook for me. I'll never forget the meatballs."

"You're better off on Jolie's waif-loss diet, it's the only

way to stay thin. If I did the cooking, your career would crash in a month. Who would love a fat heartthrob?"

"At least I'd be fat and content."

"The two don't go together much in this world," I say, meeting his eyes. "That's why I write a successful column, and you have the role. Being overweight is to blame for a lot of misery, and unless you've been there, you have no idea—"

"I didn't recognize you when you came off the plane," Taylor says, finally owning up to it. "You don't look the way you used to. What made you change? How did *you* do it?"

No way am I going to admit that he was the prime motivator. I try to come up with something fast, but am saved when the waiter intervenes to take our drink order. I open the oversize menu, and put it between us like a bundling board, but he puts his hand over mine.

"So how did you do it?"

"It had a lot to do with someone I was seeing." Not much of a stretch, I was *seeing him,* on TV, in the movies, on the net. "It's a long story. Why don't we order, and then we can talk about what I'm here to talk about." So I was blowing him off, but what else could I do?

"Business, sure."

I study the menu, or rather, am transfixed by it. White asparagus soup with Parmesan croutons and chive oil. Crisp potato galette with smoked sturgeon and freshly grated horseradish. Maine lobster spring roll with Chinese apricot mustard and pickled vegetables. Seared foie gras with arugula and cherry chutney. Stir-fried Chinois lamb salad with ginger, scallions and sweet soy sauce. And those were just appetizers. *No wonder Jolie didn't come. One appe-*

tizer would exceed her calorie allotment for the month. She'd have to go to Lourdes for a cure. Then, of course, there were the famous pizzas, nothing like the soggy imitations from the frozen food cases. My eye scans some of the choices: pizza with peppered Louisiana shrimp; plum tomatoes, leeks and sweet basil; pizza with artichoke, seared eggplant, caramelized garlic and shaved Parmesan.

And the entrées—grilled white Copper River salmon with caramelized asparagus and lobster nage, crispy Mandarin quail with tangerine, pineapple glaze and Asian greens, roasted Sonoma lamb with fennel potato gratin, black olives and thyme, and on and on.

"What's your pleasure?" Taylor says.

E V E R Y T H I N G. "The lobster spring roll and then the black bass." I'll eat slowly, savor every bite. This was above and beyond sustenance. Art. Just recognizing this is progress. I congratulate myself as if I'm a nutritionist watching over a high-maintenance patient. Here I am, about to eat food prepared by an interior designer. I appeal to a higher power—*at least get spiritually filled*—to help me feel that I've had enough.

Taylor orders asparagus soup and the dry aged prime New York steak with arugula, grilled onion salad and crisp potato galette. Men always order the beef. Never a qualm. I look at him.

"Foods of love. That's what I'm writing about for Valentine's Day."

"Aphrodisiacs?" His eyes widen.

"Sort of. There are some great books about foods as aphrodisiacs. My readers love that sort of thing. Hard data may be scant, but everyone loves finding out that they're not the only ones seduced by great food. Two psychologists in Chicago did a study years back that found that heavy women liked to have sex more often than thin ones."

"Now you tell me." He looks into my eyes. "To think that all these years I've been hangin' out with the wrong women. So tell me all about the foods of love." He feigns a naughty grin. "What do you eat to fan the flames?"

"Fowl for foul play. No…ah, let's see, there are lots. Seafood, because of the high phosphorus content, shark-fin soup, don't ask me why, but the Chinese swear by it. Then there's the Japanese fugu fish. You do know about it?"

He shakes his head.

"Aka the puffer fish. It's been a gourmet food of love in Japan for centuries. But there's a catch—not to pun— if it's not prepared properly, it's deadly. It's supposed to be so lethal that just about an ounce can kill more than fifty thousand diners. And, by the way, there are no antidotes to the poison. By law in Japan, it can only be made by chefs who have taken a course and received a license, and only about thirty percent of the chefs pass the exam. But that hasn't stopped unlicensed chefs from preparing it, so you're playing Russian roulette if you order it. But I guess the game and the danger turns people on."

Taylor takes out his cell: "Hello, Japan Airlines?"

"There's more," I say. "The most potent aphrodisiac they say is made by mixing a teaspoonful of its testes with hot sake. Sounds yummy, right?"

"You think Wolfgang knows how to make fugu?" He slaps his hand on the table. "I'm in. Fugu sake this minute." He holds his hand up with a dramatic flourish as if he were summoning a waiter. I'm enjoying this.

"What else, what other foods?"

"I'll give you the column as soon as I write it. I can't give away all my secrets."

"Promise me you'll make me a Valentine's dinner using all that stuff. A steaming pot of it, okay?"

"Why do you need me? You mean to tell me that you don't have your own fugu chef? I can't believe that. I thought everyone in Hollywood did. Make sure that's written into your next contract." Neither of us says anything as the food is served. Then Taylor looks up.

"You love to make fun of us out here, don't you?" He shakes his head. "Betcha can't wait to get home to your snowy city, and tell all your friends how you goofed on us." I look back at him. Nobody is ever completely kidding.

"No…I'm sorry, Taylor. I'm acting like a jerk. I'm tough on people sometimes, I don't know why."

"You're funny," he says, levelly, "I like you, I mean it. I never met anyone like you."

"Too bad your luck has run out."

"I'm startin' to figure you," he says, nodding. I watch him slice off a triangle of rare beef and chew it slowly. The pregnant pause. Why do I feel as though his performance was rehearsed? As though he has the timing of a professional. I watch him chew. Even that's sexy. The rhythmical way that jaw worked. The man should pose for the National Livestock and Meat Board. Never mind mad cow, hoof and mouth, or animal rights, turn the camera on that face, and a diehard vegan would beg for beef.

He looks back at me. "It's warm out here," he says, as if in passing. "Maybe you should think about staying for a while. The house is big enough…you need a chance to chill."

thirteen

We drive to the beach after dinner. The mist-covered moon casts an opalescent glow on the black water. As I walk, the damp sand massages my feet, and I'm aware of the light touch of Taylor's hand draping my shoulder. My senses are elevated to a higher frequency whenever I'm around him as if I'm visiting some distant, more vibrant reality. When his voice breaks the silence, it almost startles me.

"Tell me about the mind-set of the perpetual dieter. Give me a day in the life."

I tighten my jacket around me. "She—because it's usually a she—is consumed with the idea of losing weight, but since her mind's always on *not* eating, she's obsessed—like a junkie—with her next fix. She has to eat, yet that's the very stuff that's killing her, so she has to develop a whole new framework for thinking about what food is, and what it does. Relearn behaviors that she's known from childhood."

"Brain surgery," he says, turning up the collar of his jacket.

"Mmm, hmm, but on yourself. And aside from the brain, the body is working against you. You know what the set point theory is?"

"No, but I think you're going to tell me."

"There seems to be a certain weight that your body stays at when you're eating normally and not trying to lose weight—the set point. The theory holds that there is an internal control mechanism tucked into the brain that seems to want your body to maintain a certain level of fat."

"Passport to survival," Taylor says, picking up a stone and skipping it across the water.

"Exactly. So when you diet and lose fat, the body adapts to protect you from starvation, and boom, your resting basal metabolic rate goes down—you require less fuel to keep the furnace going. Bottom line—especially if you've dieted a lot—is that you find that the same pathetic number of calories you're eating on your diet isn't meager enough to allow you to lose the kind of weight that you did before on that regimen. You're confused now. Why aren't you losing anymore? You plateau, get frustrated. Why diet anymore when it doesn't work? Screw it, you're angry and you start eating like mad to get back at yourself—"

"Half of L.A."

"You hate your stubborn, uncooperative body and want to punish it, so you eat and eat out of anger and frustration, and become *fatter* than you were before you started the damn diet. One desperate approach to weight management is the bulimic route. As I'm sure you know, that's when you eat and then clean out your system by regularly throwing up or using laxatives, enemas and diuretics, and sometimes, at the same time, exercising to excess. By continually abusing your lower GI tract, you lose the ability to eliminate normally, and if you throw up enough your esophagus becomes inflamed and your glands swell."

"Jolie can tell you about the throwing up."

I turn to him. Why am I not surprised? "I didn't know."

"She's over it now, but she went through that when she was a teenager."

We walk on for a few minutes without speaking.

"In the worst-case scenario," I say, "purging can lead to heart failure because you're losing life-sustaining minerals like potassium. If the disorder is anorexia, you simply starve yourself to death. Although these women—and most are women—have a tremendous fear of food and gaining weight—they're preoccupied with food, sometimes even hoarding it and making a great show of collecting recipes. A lot of these women are also depressed, irritable, withdrawn and have little interest in sex. When weight loss continues to advance, they may find it hard to concentrate, have memory loss and withdraw. It's really like a slow death. And some women are bulimic and anorexic.

"In some of the worst cases of anorexia, sufferers subsist on as little as a couple of hundred calories a day. Imagine eating nothing more during the day—and for days at a time—than a yogurt and a couple of bananas."

"Well at least my patients will love me, right?" Taylor says, trying to puff out his chest.

"No, actually, they'll be afraid of you and be distrustful. You're the guy who'll make them eat all of those fattening foods they've been avoiding."

"So what do I do?"

"Try to convince them that you want to see them grow healthy, not fat."

He weighs that one for a while, then shakes his head.

"Don't think I was cut out for medicine," he says. "So what else is involved?"

"You use your degree in psychotherapy in addition to bariatric medicine because this group needs intensive counseling first—individual and family counseling, lots of support and sometimes medication. The most serious cases end up hospitalized. Basically, all your women will feel so frustrated that they'll sink into depression, or worse, feel as though they'd like to kill themselves."

I take an envelope out of my bag and hand it to him. "I thought this would interest you. She doesn't have anorexia, but it's typical of the kind of letters I get. This woman thinks she's the only one in the world who feels this way."

Dear Maggie:

This is hard for me, but I can't keep it in any longer. You know the old joke about the fat girl with the pretty face? Well, that's me, I swear. I hate the way my body looks, so all the clothes I buy are coverups. But the real problem is that I can't hide my body from my boyfriend. Every time I get into bed with him, I dread the thought of him seeing me naked, so I resort to turning out the lights before I get undressed, and telling him that I like to make love in the dark. (I'm not the only one who acts this way, am I?) Otherwise, I wear a robe, and slip it off under the blanket. Can you possibly understand how awful I feel? I want to enjoy sex, but I feel so trapped by what I look like. Help, please.

Taylor frowns. "They really let their hair down with you."

I nod. "Those are your patients. So what are you going to do to help them?"

"I start by seducing them with my compassion, my un-

derstanding, my warmth—at least according to the script.
A lot of their motivation to change comes from wanting
to look good to please me."

That's familiar. "How does it turn out?"

"Four drop out, three make some progress, one kills herself, and one falls in love with me and becomes thin, turns
into this dynamite dish and I fall for her. We leave the place
together to set up our own clinic."

"Gee, how realistic. I can't wait to see it."

Taylor raises an eyebrow. "Maybe they can give you a
cameo role."

"As what, the stiff?"

He half smiles. "Maybe the journalist who comes to do
a story on me."

"Is she thin or fat?"

"You tell me," Taylor says.

I don't answer.

"So is that *your* life?" Taylor asks. "Losing and gaining,
anger, frustration?"

"I've been there, but I hope not anymore."

"What's your secret?"

"I'm a Taurus—bullheaded. When I want something,
I make it happen. At least for now, I've got the body beat.
I worked out like a demon, I ate less and I lost the weight.
I feel good about that."

"Do you usually get what you want?"

"How did the conversation get turned around to me?
Why don't we stick to the script?"

He slips his arm under mine. "I want to know what
makes you tick."

"You do," I say mockingly. Not knowing what else to
do, I imitate one of his crazed fans, madly pulling at my

hair, "Mike, you're so gorgeous, I can't stand it…" I break into hysterics, pretending to stick a paper in his face. "Here, give me your autograph, sign this…PUHLEEZ!"

"You want it right now?" he asks, pulling me toward him.

"Taylor," I say, pushing him away. "You're in the right profession."

Secrets of Successful Weight Loss

Thanks to an extensive new study on the secrets of successful weight loss, I now know exactly how those who have lost weight have managed—against the odds—to keep it off.

Have I got your attention?

Good. But now, dear hearts, I'm sorry to say that I'm not going to report on a herbal potion that comes from Katmandu, or a new diet drink or exercise guru extraordinaire. The secrets are enough to put you to sleep, but, here goes, anyway.

The largest survey ever on long-term weight loss, done by Consumer Reports, found that those who had success keeping weight off didn't credit diet drugs, special programs, supplements or even special diet foods.

The survey polled 32,000 dieters and found that 83 percent who kept the lost weight off for more than a year didn't rely on gimmicks. What most did rely on was exercise. For eight out of ten people who kept the weight off, working out three or more times a week was ranked as their number one strategy. While walking made first place as the most popular type of exercise to keep pounds at bay, almost

30 percent lifted weights to boost calorie-burning muscle mass.

Want to know their other success secrets?

* Control the spikes in blood sugar levels caused by eating refined carbohydrates by substituting complex carbs like whole grains and high fiber foods.
* Get enough lean protein to help you feel satisfied.
* Opt for high-volume foods to trick your sense of satiety—for example, pureed vegetables turned into soup, rather than the plain vegetable, or a whole orange vs. a glass of OJ.
* Eat enough fat so that you feel satisfied. Allow up to thirty percent a day, just make sure it's the healthy kind such as olive and canola, or from fatty fish and nuts.
* Think nutrition on a daily basis. The dieters who were successful said they used these principles every day.

It turns out the photo of Marcus Camby made the cover of the *Daily Record:* "DOWN AND OUT." The picture credit: Tamara Brown. I make a note to send her a bottle of Dom. Ty sends roses. Everyone in her family called, she says in a voice that I barely recognize. The last time that happened, her uncle died.

Just one picture, one flick of the shutter, and the photograph opens up the promise of a new life for her. *That* shot might have been a fluke, but from now, if I know Tamara, her shots will be informed, calculated.

Valentine's Day is coming up and at 6:00 a.m. L.A. time, Tamara's in chat mode and brings me up to date. She

complains that with me out of town, she had to go to the
library for help.

"So I ask the white-haired librarian for the section on
aphrodisiacs, and she looks at me like I'm from another
planet. 'There is none,' she says, and points me toward food
science instead."

Am I hearing right?

"Medicine comes from plants, so somewhere inside one
of those books, there had to be tips for a cook interested
in heating up romance."

I'm laughing so hard that I'm sure I'm waking up the
whole house. I can envision her thumbing through books
methodically, pausing to scan sections on cayenne pepper,
rump roasts, and crème fraîche. Tamara's idea, of course,
was to come up with the ultimate seduction meal. The
plan is for Ty to start reading her book that is set at a
weight-loss center. And then...he could forget about
going home.

But he's divorced. She has to go slowly. "He's probably
scared," she says, "doesn't want to be a two-time loser."
Then there's the business of working in the same office. If
it didn't work out, it would be awkward to keep running
into each other.

But what to make? She decides on oysters to start, but
then? "Listen to this," Tamara says. She's flipping through
a book called *Foods for Love, The Complete Guide to Aphrodisiac Edibles* by Robert Hendrickson, and his possible
main courses including phallic-armed octopi, the repro-
ductive organs of jellyfish, scorpion fish and pickled beaver
tails. And if those don't fit the bill, Hendrickson describes
other exotic and/or disgusting turn-ons such as salted
crocodile semen, the orange-colored roe of prickly sea

urchins, considered by the Japanese and French to be an aphrodisiac either raw or pickled, and swan's pizzle, the immense elongated muscle of the four-foot tridoca clam, the tails of blowfish…

Was it something in my drink from last night?

"So what do you think?" she says finally.

"Swan's pizzle."

"What?

"Just KID-DING. Let's see…to fuel his carnal instincts, go carnal—steak. I never met a man who didn't like beef. Creamy mashed potatoes, and maybe spinach for the token vegetable. And if you're going to hell anyway, cheesecake for dessert or a fruit tart. Either you'll turn him on or you'll kill him."

"What about oysters to start?" she says.

"Tricky, but if he likes them…lots of phosphorus."

"What would I do without you, Maggie?"

"You started doing better the day I left."

"Pure luck."

"Fat chance."

She has her menu. Oysters, filet mignon, mashed potatoes and fresh spinach. I turn over and go back to sleep.

fourteen

I'm up hours later, mulling over the night before. There seems to be more than just a kinship between us now, but whenever I'm emotionally involved with someone, my vision is blocked and I can't scope things out. Was Taylor coming on to me? Or is he just naturally flirty? He wants my help and being attentive can only help him secure it. Safer to feign disinterest, I decide, and continue playing consultant, rather than starstruck fan. It wouldn't be the first time I was way off base.

As I'm about to go downstairs for coffee, I open the door and spot a folded blue note wedged under it.

Morning M.—
   Had to go to Houston for two days of exterior shooting—last-minute change in the sked. Enjoy house, take car—keys on kitchen counter near yogurt maker. We'll pick up where we left off—
   M.

Ugh! Two fewer days together. The gardener, the pool man, two maids, a security guard and Jolie would be my only company. What better motivation to work out. I grab my sweats and am about to change when I see the flickering red light of the answering machine— probably the office, a world that I was happier forgetting at the moment. I press Play and sit on the edge of the bed.

"Mah name is Tex, I'm a big-time jerk in New York. I'm thinking about starting a new career as a food critic, but I don't have friends at work to go out with anymore and damn, it can take forever to write a review if you're only ordering for one. So I wondered now if you could help me get my buddy back. I'm not good at that kind of thing. I'm used to pushing around copy, organizing stories, not my own life. Have your people call my people."

Had Alan Barsky sneezed on him? The impersonation virus was spreading. Tex had always had a humorous touch. He knew how to tweak a situation, to soften it. He spent his days dissecting people's work. If he couldn't handle *them* he'd have been lobotomized by now. I dial his home number to answer his recording with one of my own.

"Before I'd even consider helping you get your lunch pal back, I'd have to know more. What's so special about long lunches out anyway? Think about brown-bagging it sometime." *I'd resist making a crack about Sharon preparing lunch.* "Instead of food, splurge on an expensive haircut, say, or a well-cut Italian suit. Put yourself behind the wheel of a sports car. Live out *your* fantasies, Tex, and see if they hold up. Let's compare notes."

I exercise for two hours. Muscle burns more calories than fat, and I worked religiously to convert.

I have the jitters about taking his car. *It's only a car.* But the alternative is to stay housebound and for what? I ease it out of the garage, lurching a bit at first, and head for Rodeo Drive, probably the world's most exclusive place to shop. Behind the wheel I'm feeling like a Judith Krantz heroine, *sans* poodle.

I stroll into Giorgio's and examine a luscious pink cashmere cardigan with a matching camisole—but HELLO, the Manolos—then I drop the sweater like it's hot. American Express has probably sent out a nationwide alert on my name. Instead, I pay cash for a pair of gorgeously obscene red ribbon string bikini panties, so scant that I can tuck them in the change purse of my wallet—probably just the point. Equally brief, I must say, is the measly Cobb salad posing as an entrée that I have for lunch in a salad boutique down the street.

I eye the Rolls Royces as I walk. From close range, this world doesn't look as crazy as it appears from New York. Could just two weeks out here distort my perceptions that way?

I walk back toward the car, eyeing the passersby, when my eyes fix on a familiar sight. It *couldn't* be. Absolutely not. Nuh-nuh-nuh. But indeed it is, and he's waddling into Bijan with a curious look on his face. Bijan? Maybe the world's most expensive men's store where you shopped by appointment only?

I stand outside and wait. Where was Tamara when I needed her? Forty-five minutes later, he emerges, hands clutching two glossy shopping bags. I'm on his tail, surreptitiously narrowing the distance between us. I'm inches from his back, about to tap him on the shoulder when Wharton spins around suspiciously.

"Maggie, my word! I don't believe it. What a coincidence."

"Bill!" I smack his shoulder affectionately. "I guess business is better than I thought. What are you doing in these parts?"

"I took a day off from the editorial convention in Palm Desert," he says, guiltily. "I decided against a lecture called 'Catastrophes in the newsroom.' Too real life." Proudly he opens the bag to show me ordinary-looking ties he has just bought in mottled shades of yellow and green.

"Unusual," I say, "amazing," then leave it at that for lack of anything else to say.

"And who's paying for *your* shopping?" he says, noticing the yellow-striped Giorgio bag. "Me or Mike Taylor?"

"Got a gift certificate to Giorgio's with my last purchase of Red."

"How are you doing out here?" Wharton asks, narrowing his eyes.

"Not bad. It's a change though, isn't it?"

"Nice for a week," he says, then lowers his voice conspiratorially, adding, "but I wouldn't want to live here, would you?"

"I miss the city," I say, realizing that I mean it. "We're different stock, you know?" Are his eyes getting moist?

"Can I give you a lift? I hired a car. It's right down the street. Or we could stop for some decadent dessert, how about it?"

"Thanks, but I have to get back. I'm parked nearby."

We stroll down the street, and I stop in front of the car.

"Yours?"

"A loaner." I have to admit I'm enjoying his incredulity. "Well, I gotta run. See you at work in another week and a half, Bill."

"Yes, well keep enjoying yourself." He walks ahead, then suddenly turns and calls out. "Any restaurants you recommend?"

"Morton's is great, so are Jar and Spago."

"Spago? I couldn't get a reservation!"

I watch him amble off. Decadent dessert, indeed. Diet saboteurs come in all guises.

Weight-Loss Saboteurs

Your boyfriend—or father—mother—best friend— or husband—applauds your weight loss one moment, and the next brings you a ten-layer chocolate cake to celebrate your success. What is he or she? A weight-loss saboteur.

Your mother has you over for dinner every Sunday, and even though she knows you're watching your weight, insists that you take home the leftover lasagna. What is she? A weight-loss saboteur.

You pass that fabulous new Belgian bakery every day on your way home from work. What is the bakery? A weight-loss saboteur.

Your weekend tennis partners always insist that after the game the group has dessert at the charming neighborhood ice-cream parlor. What do you call the shop? A trap.

Saboteurs come in all sizes and shapes—both human and inanimate. What they all have in common is that they work against you, creating tension in your life, anxiety and binge eating. What to do?

* Know the enemy. If a particular person seems to delight in offering you the kinds of foods that you're trying desperately to avoid, rehearse your strategies in advance. Go over the script. "I know Kevin will ask me out to my favorite French restaurant. This time I'll decline or tell him where I'd like to go. I'll be in charge."

* If the neighborhood bakery is hard to walk past, change your route or put on headphones and a favorite tape and play it loud so that your mind is distracted.

* If your tennis group always hits the pastry shop after the game, leave and wish them well. For me, at least, it's easier to pass up on dessert altogether than to have just a taste or watch someone else who's indulging.

The click of the front door sends my heart racing. Does the house come with a defibrillator? Taylor slips the overnight bag off his shoulder, and tosses his leather jacket onto a chair. He's wearing a white T-shirt and jeans. He walks toward me, flips down on the couch, extending his legs over the arm. He drains my iced tea.

"So how's my favorite rocket scientist. Spaced out?"

"Cloud nine," he says, eyes closed. *Okay, not very original.* "What did I miss?"

"I went to Rodeo Drive and ran into my publisher. I had a great time driving your car, and I even thought about making off with it and heading to New York...you wouldn't press charges, would you...? Let's see, what else...

I accidentally tripped the alarm when I opened my window. Security came…I was questioned by two gorillas with tattoos…now at least I know how to disengage it so I can get unfiltered air…. Other than that, nothing much."

"Where's Jolie?"

"*Je ne sais pas.* I haven't seen much of her."

"Our time's getting short," he says, smiling slightly. "How about we go over some of your—"

"There's a folder on your desk with a year's worth of my columns and some journal articles. Enjoy your afternoon."

He hangs his head down off the side of the couch, pretending to be dead. "Can't I get the Spark notes?"

I give him a withering look.

"I'll fail the final without them."

"How could I look Spielberg in the eye again?"

"Well, if I ever finish we can celebrate 'cause there's a party tonight—the one that was supposed to have been two days ago. Wanna go?"

"If you'd rather just see your friends on your own, I'll be fine here—"

"The party's at ten," he says, jumping up and messing my hair. "You're going."

I'm about to start some research for another column when I look up. Taylor is standing there with a pathetic look on his face. What was I thinking? Did I really expect him to start wading through one hundred and fifty-six columns? More likely he'd hand them over to someone at the studio who would boil everything down to three paragraphs.

"Yes?" I say, feigning ignorance.

"Let's go over some of these," he says, shaking his head. I welcome the juicy excuse to leave my own work behind and follow him to his office like a compliant puppy. There are two couches, facing each other. Should I sit facing him, or next to him? This isn't psychotherapy, so I sit next to him, and for the next hour and a half, we go over some of the main points of my work.

I'm pretty proud of what I've done, now that I read it all again. There's a column on portion size with the basic premise "Forget about dieting—if you want to lose weight all you have to do is slash portion size."

"Look at the palm of your hand," I tell Taylor. "That's about the size your steak or chicken breast should be."

"What?" he says, staring at his hand in disbelief.

"You wouldn't believe what the rubber food models we used in nutrition class looked like. An appropriate portion of mashed potatoes is smaller than a B-cup bra," I tell him. That gets his attention.

To give him some historical perspective, I offer these tidbits:

"When McDonald's started out if you had a burger, fries and a twelve-ounce Coke, it came to 590 calories. Today, if you order an Extra Value Meal, which consists of a Quarter Pounder with cheese, Super Size fries and a Super Size Coke, you're taking in a whopping 1550 calories, about the total number that the average diet offers in an entire day."

And another example—"Back in the 1950s, what was considered a family-size bottle of Coke held 26 ounces. Today, a single-serve bottle is 20 ounces.

"America has increased the amount of food that they eat, thanks not only to jumbo restaurant-size portions but also to mass-quantity-size items bought from stores such as Costco and Sam's Club in order to save money. Except, while you keep your wallet fat, you keep your waistline the same way."

"So what do you do, order in?"

Spoken like a true movie star. "No, people in small-town America don't order in. You divide up the three-pound salmon, for example, into four- or six-ounce portions, cook one and freeze the others. In a restaurant, you and a friend share one steak, or ask for an extra plate and cut away half of the portion to take home. Instead of the second half of the twelve-ounce steak, have a large green salad or fruit salad for dessert."

"Gulag diet," Taylor says glumly.

"No, just reorienting yourself."

To offer more evidence of how America has changed, all you have to do is compare the average weights of men and women from the early '60s to today. Back then, the average man weighed 168 pounds and the average woman 142. Today, the average man weighs almost 180, and the average female 152.

We move on to a column called "Forget About Fat." This one talks about being more concerned about the number of calories you're eating rather than the grams of fat because I'm convinced Americans think that the words *low-fat* on a package gives them a license to eat all they want.

"So you pig out on regular chocolate chip cookies instead of the low-fat ones?" Taylor says.

"No, you eat the yummy ones, and enjoy every bite. You just limit the number you eat. It's better than eating twenty low-fat cookies because you're not saving calories at all, you're just sacrificing flavor."

Then I look back at a column that I did on consumer products growing in size in recognition of Americans' widening waists. Taylor gives me a blank look. He's oblivious, as are most people who've never had a weight problem. We start with the size of seats in Ford's Lincoln Navigator that were roomy to begin with, but were widened by an inch in the 2003 model. In addition, the area between the driver and steering wheel was opened up as well. The seats also got wider in Ford's 2003 Focus compact.

"Mattress sizes are growing, too," I say. "Simmons increased the size of the box springs under its queen-size mattresses to 66 inches. The wider mattress is dubbed the Olympic Queen."

"Sounds like a cruise ship," Taylor says, smirking.

I ignore that.

"Chairs are getting wider and selling better because of it," I say, giving him some background. There's even a 500-pound lift recliner that lifts and tilts forward to help an obese person get out of the chair. He groans, and I begin telling him about clothing. "Many of the major retailers are now catering to plus-size women. JCPenney began a new division in 1999 catering to full-figured women, and Kmart not only increased the area devoted to plus-size clothes by 25 percent but also introduced a junior-plus-size department in 400 of its stores. So has Hot Topic. They have a chain called Torrid aimed at plus-size teenagers. According to one estimate I read, plus-size clothing sales are a $17-billion-a-year business, outperforming the rest of the garment industry. Overweight women can now buy better-quality underwear, lingerie and wedding gowns. And the best news is that now there are even online dating sites so that heavier women don't have to compete with model types for men."

"Wow," Taylor says. "I had no idea."

"Most people don't, and you just don't see it in California," I tell him, "and you don't see it in New York City. But travel around the country, and you see the problem of obesity when you walk down the street. According to some statistics, half of all American women today wear a size 14 or larger. In 1985, the average size was 8."

I don't even go into the medical field, where obese patients have special needs, including larger wheelchairs, beds, special air-circulation mattresses to prevent bedsores, and on and on, or in the travel field where an obese person has to buy two airline tickets.

We segue into more familiar ground: food tricks instead of diets. I start with the obvious: having fresh fruit instead of juice because it has more fiber and higher satiety value. We talk about heating V8 and sipping it slowly as a soup, instead of downing a chilled glass of it in a second. For whatever reason, when it's hot—and you can add some cut-up vegetables—it seems to be more filling and satisfying. The same goes for pureeing vegetables into a soup instead of eating them cooked or raw. Another trick is to buy plastic ice pop containers and make your own ice pops using plain old water, or diet soda instead of sugary juice.

"Water pops?" Taylor find this funny.

"Believe it or not, it helps to just have something in your mouth," I say, and then, oh God, start to blush. He turns toward me and smiles. Now we're talking about something that Taylor can relate to. He leans over and kisses me so softly that I'm not even sure that he did, and for some reason, the sweetness of it, especially in the middle of the late afternoon with the warm sun bathing the office in sunlight, turns me on more than anything else he could have done.

"Something in your mouth, huh?" he says softly. I lean back and nod, very slightly. And then, as if on cue, the mood is broken as the phone rings. He doesn't answer it, but a moment later, there's a voice on the answering machine—the head of production at his studio—saying that he needs to talk to him, right away. Taylor exhales and gets up, looking down at me on the couch, with my head resting back on the cushion. He smiles and shrugs his shoulders, helplessly, then walks to his desk to make the call.

fifteen

Later on that evening, we're off to the party. It's in a beach house that's within swallowing distance of a giant tsunami, and once in the door the walls feel like sausage casing squeezing all of Hollywood together. All intimate friends, all familiar to Taylor. Very. Was his mouth sore from hello-kissing so many pumped-up lips? My guess is that most of the group is from TV, but I watch so little that I can't tell a soap opera vixen from a surgeon on *ER*.

This is Taylor's extended family. Women are flashed his full throttle smile, hugged, smooched, whispered to. This is no place for the insecure at heart. Wondrous cleavages abound. So do pert asses, great legs, perfect cheekbones and twenty-thousand-dollar smiles. Taylor introduces me around, but after the polite smiles, I fade into the crowd like an extra. Everyone wants a part of Taylor. Women and gay men want to sleep with him, and the straights want to meet him for golf. If he minds being a body pillow, he hides it well. My leading man is a born party animal.

The room gets smoky, close, and I need air. I ease away from him, averting my eyes from the buffet table, cognizant of the fact that neither the giant pyramid of bite-sized quiches nor the mound of golden crab cakes has been touched—*what else did you have to know about this group?* Do you know how wild I am about crab cakes, especially when they're made with chopped red pepper and lots of dill? And what better to go with them than the nearby pot of golden lemon mayonnaise!

I snag one and walk out to the beach, glancing back at the party through the picture window. Planet Hollywood. Faces that I have no interest in meeting, or talking to. I mostly avoid parties, uncomfortable with keeping up the forced banter, steering oneself from one group to another, chatting with one eye fixed on the door to monitor flow. Another future column—the pain of being out and on display?

Maybe it all brings me back to grade school proms, hugging the side of the room near the windows and sitting in a folding chair for the entire junior high school prom when my mother convinced me to go even though I didn't have a date. How clearly I recall crossing the great room with all the couples dancing when I had to go to the bathroom. One of the greatest things in life for me is knowing that now that school is over, I never again have to wonder if someone is going to ask me to the prom.

Through the window I see a curvaceous blonde howling with laughter. Well, this was nirvana for any celluloid wanna-be—producers, directors, cameramen, studio heads, stars. But for an ink-stained wretch from the Big Apple? And talk about accepting fat? It was a nonissue at this party, if you didn't count the kind that's taken from your rear and injected into your face.

Tex would know the feeling. If he were here we'd be exchanging glances, and I'd see it in his glazed look. Oceanic boredom. I feel as though I'm looking at him through a giant zoom lens. Where was he now, with Sharon having feijoada with black beans at Casa Brazil? Scarfing down a three-pound lobster at The Palm? Maybe he was just home watching the news. If I was with him, we'd be twittering about a breaking story, bad-mouthing some government official, laughing over a correction. Or a correction of a correction. He'd be on the phone with the office, opening his eyes to me in exasperation. Life seemed more sharply focused at home. Edited of excess. At the moment, it seemed like a warm bathrobe, instead of a snug, scratchy, organza dress.

I reach for my cell phone and almost automatically start dialing the New York area code, 212. I'm not even certain if I want the call to go through, but when I hear it ring, I reason that fate has ruled me.

"Metro."

It's Larry, and in a heartbeat I've got to decide whether to ask for Tex or just hang up.

"Hey, Lar, it's Maggie. How's it going?"

"Fair to middlin', *et tu?*"

"Good, good," I say, hastily.

"Hold on, the Texan's on the horn."

I'm walking deeper into the ocean and wallowing in the thought of my solitary existence here, knee-deep in the ocean under a moonlit sky, while on the other side of the country, my colleagues are sitting in a neon-lit newsroom trying to shoehorn copy into too little space.

"How's the California dreamer?" Tex says.

"Oh, you know, working hard. It's a rotten job, but someone's got to do it."

"So where are you now?" he says.

"In the ocean."

"Watch out for Jaws."

"The killer sharks out here don't swim in the sea, they work in the studios."

"I wouldn't know about things like that," Tex says. "I'm a country boy, remember?"

"So ya starving to death without me?"

"Well, let's put it this way," Tex says. "I had lunch with Justine yesterday, and she left over half of her food."

"Sounds like the perfect lunch partner. You paid for one lunch and got two for the price."

"But then she dragged me to a fashion show. Wanted a man's perspective on a new collection."

Hmmm, that gave me pause for thought. "So did you trade in your football jerseys for black silk shirts?"

"Nah, just a black opera cape and a white silk aviator's scarf, why?"

"I'm on the next plane home."

"So you've come to your senses."

"Don't bet on that."

"So what are you cookin' up out there?" Tex says.

I'm not sure how to handle that question. "Oh, you know, just spreading the overweight gospel to the uninitiated."

"We need your help more than they do," Tex says.

"And why is that?"

"Justine's threatening to get the Atkins police after me."

"Send her to Paris. Make up a new designer, make up a scandal. Hemlines are going up to the navel."

"Hmmm, now that's a thought."

Then there's a call waiting for him, and another one after that, and after a quick "Don't forget us," he hangs up.

I call Tamara. Turns out she's spending more and more time with Ty—in his West Side apartment that looks as if it was done by a decorator from the Sports Channel. She's told him about her novel. Apparently she's finished it and mailed it off to one of the leading publishers. It's about two women, a writer and a photographer, who meet at a weight loss center. I wonder what the romantic angle is, and it occurs to me that it could be Taylor's next movie.

I slip the phone back into my bag as I walk up toward the house. I spot Taylor through the window—a romantic film star of the silent screen. The only thing missing is the plonkety piano. He's telling a story. Everyone is enthralled, then they're in hysterics. This is his town, and I'm the bag lady who comes over from Ireland. I walk farther from the house, down toward the water, kicking off my shoes and lifting my dress. The wind blows at my back, ballooning out the front of my skirt. I turn the other way, feeling the force of it wrapping the fabric tightly around my legs. Fat, thin. At the whim of nature.

A milky glow surrounds the full moon and casts a haze on the slate black water. It's almost 80 degrees here and below freezing at home. I want to imprint this moment in time in my memory, a visual souvenir of a perfect winter night in Southern California.

I use these memories like a life raft to spirit me away from reality's disappointments because they testify to the existence of a higher life. I call upon my mental scrapbook of memories when I want to catalog my life's most poignant moments. Waking up in the Texas hill country in the early-morning chill with a sky nonstop blue; walking along an empty beach on private Palm Island in the Grenadines. The manicured gardens of the Villa Borghese in Rome, the air perfumed with flowers as I walked with a dark-haired Italian boy. These were gifts in the montage of memories, experiences when life reveals itself at its best, awing you with its raw beauty.

I try to memorize everything I see as I stand ankle-deep in swirling water. It would all be pushed aside when I was home. Tamara would move up at the paper, and I'd have to find another support person. I'll miss having her sitting outside of my office every day. I don't like to lose people. But to see it happening to Tamara doesn't surprise me. Life is all about serendipity. You just have to be open to it.

Like Taylor's call, and the changes in my life that it set in motion. And it wasn't just the weight. It was the stimulus for getting me to the point of shaking up the status quo and trying to make things better in my life. It gave me the boost to say that I would try to do better for myself. That I was worth it. That I would strive to be the best Maggie that I could. And that whether I failed or not, I would know that I tried—that I dieted, that I exercised, that I was ready to take responsibility for myself and help determine the course that I would follow rather than bemoaning my fate and throwing up my hands in surrender.

For that alone, I owed Taylor. And now that I'm exercising, I'm convinced that it's the perpetual motion that is largely responsible for keeping the weight off. That's definitely a column. I savor the last bite of the crab cake and lick my fingers.

The Fidget Factor

Think you're fat because you had twice as much for dinner as your thin neighbor? Think again. Take note of this tidbit that I found in a textbook:

"One is hard-pressed for evidence that groups of overweight individuals actually eat more on the average than people of normal weight."

What it comes down to, the experts say, is remaining in motion. Thinner people move more. I call it "the fidget factor." A more recent study held that thin people start to fidget more after they overeat, as if their bodies were instinctively battling the weight gain.

So what's holding you back? When you're cooking in the kitchen, turn on the radio and sway in time to the music while you're mashing potatoes. Move your upper body while you're sitting at the computer waiting to download a program. Get up during TV commercials and walk to the kitchen for a snack instead of keeping the bowl next to you. If you want ice cream for dessert, walk to the store, don't drive. Get moving…anywhere…anytime.

I glance back at the house. Was he doing some coke in a back bedroom now? Behind a closed door with some leading lady? Nothing would surprise me. He seemed pretty relaxed about everything.

Why don't I take lessons from him? Breathe, ease my choke hold on life. It's hard to do if you live in New York. Everyone wears body armor, assumes a sense of entitlement, a self-preservation mind-set. City life calls for being a strategist, figuring your way around the crowds, traffic, sealing out noise, adapting to tight spaces, getting by with less. I'm gazing at the water when a hand on my shoulder makes me jump.

"BOO! It's only me." Taylor laughs, kissing me on top of my head.

I turn abruptly. "You scared me. I guess my mind was someplace else."

He nuzzles my shoulder. "You're just having a great ole time, right?"

"No, it's fine, I just don't know anybody. Anyway," I say, gesturing around me, "I usually don't get a chance to spend my nights like this so—"

"Guess I should have realized you wouldn't exactly feel at home here." He slips an arm around my waist.

A male voice calls Taylor from the house. The words carry against the wind… "Hey, Mike, get back here, there's somebody who has something nice for you." Then a high-pitched woman's laugh.

"You're wanted."

He frowns and shakes his head. "I don't think I'll be missed. Everybody's half-wasted in there, anyway."

"How's your blood chemistry?"

He tilts his hand back and forth. "C'mon, let's go home."

"Going home." That was a wild thought. We walk to his car only to find an offering parked on the hood: a sad blonde in a black cat suit who's also ready to go home with him.

"Michael." She slides down, pressing herself up to him. I, of course, am invisible.

I stare with disgust and sympathy... *Great, another Venus flytrap.*

"Melanie, I think you need to go home, babe," he says softly. He looks at me, his eyes widening in desperation.

"Take me with you, Michael, I want to go home with you."

He puts his arm over her shoulder. "I'll walk you back to the house." He tosses me the keys. "Prepare for launch."

Melanie snuggles against him as they walk. Her slurred words trail after them... "Remember how good it was with us that night, Michael, remember?"

I start the car and drive slowly toward the house. The headlights blind him when he comes toward me. He holds up his arm to shade his eyes.

"Get in, Taylor. I'm your designated driver."

He walks around to the passenger seat. "I don't know who I'd put my money on, me half in the bag, or you sober."

"Taylor," I say, brushing white powder from his top lip. "You need to chill."

I could never have imagined myself being seduced by a car. Maybe it was a California *thang,* something in the air you breathed that gave you a 911 turbo high. I hold the wheel loosely as it snakes along the curving road. I glance at Taylor, who has his head back against the seat, eyes closed.

"Where's Jolie tonight?" I ask lightly.

His eyes open and he squeezes them for a moment, as if to focus, then shakes his head.

"She was in a pissy mood, and decided to do a magazine shoot they offered her in Phoenix. She'll be back next week." He rubs his eyes. Had the drug cocktails gotten to him, or was there something on his mind? I couldn't tell.

"Listen, for whatever it's worth…she's not the love of my life. It's more of a convenience thing, for me at least. It's probably more to her…I don't know, but for me…" He shakes his head.

Was that his spin on "my bedmate doesn't understand me"? I'm not sure what to say so I'm silent as I drive up the hill and punch in the codes. I know them by heart now. I pull into the garage and turn off the ignition. Neither of us moves. Finally, I reach for the door, but he leans over and holds my arm.

"Wait." Then his mouth is on mine and I'm yielding to the pressure of his lips as his fingers gently knead the base of my neck. If his work is as good below the waist…The car is steaming up like a Turkish bath. I ease back from him, taking a breath.

"Maybe we shouldn't start this now, you're so wasted."

"Mmmm." He's kissing me again.

"Taylor."

He looks as though I've startled him. "What?"

I close my eyes, exasperated and get out of the car. He follows me to the kitchen door and starts to open it, and then stops. The lights are on, but there are no sounds. He looks at me warily, then cautiously steps in. And there, at the kitchen counter, is Jolie, flipping through French *Vogue*.

"Oh, hey, well, what are you doing home?" Taylor asks, with sudden sobriety and an easy charm developed in fifteen years of theatrical training.

"Everything went wrong and the shoot was canceled. I tried to call you *mais* nobody was home."

"Oh man," he exhales, involuntarily raking his hand through his hair.

"Bummer, yeah," I say, badly squelching an eruption of

laughter. The magazine pages keep flipping. Someone has to break the strained silence.

"Well, I'll let you guys catch up," I say. "See y'all in the morning."

Taylor gives me a sheepish grin. "Sleep tight."

I climb the stairs, obsessed suddenly with biting away a ragged sliver of a cuticle, knowing I will end up drawing blood. I storm into my room, slip off my shoes and fling them toward the closet. One inadvertently misses its mark, and ricochets out of the open window. SHIT! If I had only left the damn windows sealed. Now I'd have to go downstairs again, and outside to search. I wasn't about to leave a snakeskin Manolo out in the damp night to get moldy.

I lie back in bed waiting for them to go up to sleep before I tiptoe back downstairs. My eyes are closing, I can't help it, and then I'm drifting, dreaming of seeing Tex and Justine going into an eyeglass boutique.

She laughs off his selections. Her eyes sweep the hundreds of frames and in a nanosecond, she snatches up three pairs. She extends her hand.

"Try."

Before he has time to look at himself, she picks out the ones that "they" would take.

He jumps back involuntarily. "They're six hundred dollars! And that's without the lenses."

"Or the brown tint," she says.

"Tint?"

Then she leads him by the nose to Barneys, and ooh, Joseph Abboud.

He doesn't know what she's talking about. She shakes

her head in despair. "Joseph Abboud," she repeats. "We're going to dress you in him."

I see them emerging together, weighted down with garment bags bulging with Scottish cashmere sweaters and jackets, tropical wool gabardine slacks, sea island cotton shirts and a dozen coordinating silk ties, all in muted tones of mahogany, rust, tan, camel and beige. Then they're in the gym, working out side by side. He's got a gorgeous body, and she's reed-slim, dressed in a thong leotard. I wake up, startled, and remember where I am.

Slowly, I ease open the bedroom door and slip down the staircase toward the front door. Whew! They've already gone up. I tiptoe out to the area that I judge to lie directly beneath my window. My eyes scan the grounds, but I don't see it. Not having exactly a handle on the laws of aerodynamics, I'm not quite certain where to look for an airborne Manolo that has been propelled out the window and down two stories.

I walk farther from the house, pushing aside bushes, stepping over plants. Just my luck I have to plow through the Garden of Eden, hedge by hedge. Why the hell couldn't he have a Japanese rock garden? A serenity garden with sand and smooth stones. I look and look but don't see anything. It couldn't have vanished, not unless the ground is made of quicksand. My toe catches something hard and for a minute I think that it might be the shoe, but then realize that it's either a sleeping rattlesnake or a garden hose. No sound or movement, so I assume it's inanimate or dead. I keep searching and suddenly spot the heel jutting up from the ground close to the house. Aha! I take a step and am about to lean over and pick it up when an ear-splitting alarm pierces my heart like a spike.

OH MY GOD! CHRIST ALMIGHTY. I start to bolt, then duck, then try to run. A moment later, a brilliant bath of light streams down from an overhead flood, blinding me. I creep closer to the house, paralyzed by fear, expecting a pair of burly arms to throw me up against the house and pat me down. What should I do? Hold my hands up till the cops come? How the hell do I turn everything off? This must be what it feels like to be part of a botched prison escape. My heart is beating as though it's breaking out of my chest.

"HEY, WHO'S THERE?" It's Taylor. I look up and see him leaning out the window.

"WHO THE HELL'S OUT THERE?"

I close my eyes. "It's only me, Taylor," I say in a small mouse voice. "Jesus, your alarm system scared the shit out of me."

"Maggie? What are you *doing* outside now? Wait, I'll come down."

I stand still, holding the stiletto in my hand like a talisman to ward off evil spirits. If only I could be someplace else! I would take a nuclear testing site in the Nevada desert, Easter Island, anyplace. And why isn't the old San Andreas fault lending me a hand here? But no such luck. Not a tremor, not a shudder. In a minute, Taylor walks up to me, clad only in black silk boxers, a taut, tanned Adonis.

"What's going on?" he says, bewildered. "What in the world were you doing out here?"

"Testing ground-level security. Wanted to make sure that you were safe from invaders."

He doesn't say anything.

"The shoe, the shoe," I say, finally, holding it up to his face. "It somehow got out of my grasp and took a nosedive out of the window."

"You are somethin' else, babe," he says, shaking his head. He takes my hand and starts leading me toward the front door, but then he turns back to me. "C'mere," he says, guiding me into the gardening shed. I follow him, and in the darkness he leans up against me, covering my mouth with his.

"This is what we should have been doing," he says, working his mouth down to my neck. His hands are slowly tracing the outlines of my body and I'm pressing against him and moaning. There's a cushion on the floor and he edges me back down onto it. My skirt is being tugged slowly up my thighs and my breathing is getting short. He's so warm against me, pressing, hungry, his body hard. In just a minute I won't be able to stop things. His hand is beginning to slide up between my legs, and I pull back from him sharply.

"Wait, no, I can't. I feel like we're sixteen-year-olds tiptoeing around back behind the garage while my parents are upstairs. A minute ago you were upstairs in bed with Jolie, and now you're sneaking around here with me."

"So what? I want you," he says, not separating himself from me. I push his shoulder back.

"But this is so sordid, really. I can't do this—the furtive fuck in the—ahem—'tool shed.'"

He presses his forehead against me, and waits until his breathing slows. "Okay, okay, you're right. I don't know what I'm doing." He looks down at himself and smiles shyly.

"Give me a minute, okay? I'll walk you up." He stands there, eyes closed. Finally, pulled together, he helps me up and leads me back into the house. I follow him up the stairs, and work hard to pretend that I'm not short of breath. I have a sudden memory of being six years old and excitedly playing red light, green light. When we get to my bedroom door, I barely look at him.

"G'night," I say, quickly slipping inside. I undress and then get into bed, lying there unable to sleep. Instead of being flattered by his attention, it depresses me. Groping in the dark, that's the only way I can think of it. He was high, and he was horny. It didn't feel like there was any more to it. I'm the other woman in the house. What kind of move could he make that would be honest, open and caring? However you looked at it, he was sneaking around. But even if he wasn't, is he really interested in me? Or am I just another conquest, living—off-limits in a sense—in another part of his house? Maybe the duplicity of it turns him on. Maybe he really is like the sexy sleaze he plays on TV. Maybe… Oh, what does it matter? I drift off into a fitful sleep.

sixteen

When the call comes in the wee hours of morning, it doesn't surprise me. Tamara has been living the life already. In addition to shots of Camby, that together formed a basketball ballet, she has candids of the staff: Wharton spilling coffee on his lap in the cafeteria; Ty tossing a wad of paper in a garbage pail as if he were shooting a basket; Tex giving the coffeepot a menacing look; Justine studying her profile in the ladies' room mirror.

Ever since she started keeping her camera with her, she'd been capturing intimate slivers of life. Outside accounting she'd talk with the secretary, while keeping her eye on people opening their paychecks. In the cafeteria she'd shoot people taking first bites of the daily special. It didn't win her popularity contests with her colleagues, except for Wharton.

"Give me your best shots," he told her again and again.

"I'd like to see what you've got." Obviously he didn't mind being included in her rogues' gallery.

"So the telephone rings and Wharton's secretary asks me to come up to see him," Tamara says, continuing her update, "and I panic."

"Why?"

"The first thing I'm thinking is that it's something that you've done, Maggie."

That wakes me up. "I do have a lot of skeletons in my closet."

"Then I'm thinking that I'm spending too much time away taking pictures," Tamara says. "Okay, maybe I'm slacking off a bit while you're gone, Maggie, but so what? There really isn't that much to do when you're not around. So I go up to his office, and his secretary waves me in. Big Daddy is sitting behind his desk, smiling at me."

"Then?" She has a way of taking forever before she cuts to the chase.

"'Sit down, Tamara,' he says, 'I have your portfolio right here.' He looks through it and says, 'You've certainly been busy with your camera, haven't you?'

"Maggie, that's when I'm sure that he's canning me."

She's secure. It takes one to know one.

"Then he says, 'Have you thought much about where you'd like to go with your picture taking?' So then I'm positive I'm being canned. I mean, 'Where you'd like to go'?"

"What did you say?"

"'For now, I'm just practicing, hoping to get good shots, but I haven't really planned anything beyond that.'"

"Okay."

"Then, listen to this. He says, 'I have a proposition for you. For a while now, I've been thinking about doing a weekly photo column called *Whoops.* It would consist of pictures of celebrities caught unawares—like Ralph Fiennes walking down Broadway pulling up his fly, or a Ford model emerging from a secluded nightspot, on the arm of someone else's husband. What do you think?'"

"Unbelievable. What did you tell him?"

"Maggie, I still didn't realize he was offering me something. I looked at him and said, 'Well, readers would love it.'

"And he says, 'Think you could handle it?'"

I start clapping my hands.

"A little peep came out of my throat," Tamara says, laughing. "'Me?'

"And he looks at me and says, 'I thought that was obvious.'"

My eyes are filling with tears, but I don't want her to know this. I'm going to cry, but I'm praying it doesn't happen until I hang up. "So what did you say," I say, pretending to cough, as if that's why my voice is growing deeper.

"I jumped up from my chair and flung myself in front of him. 'I will not disappoint you. I promise. I'll spend every second of my life getting pictures.'"

"There's nobody who deserves a break more," I say. "I'm so thrilled for you, I don't know what to say."

I know that Tamara picks up the emotion in my voice and is touched by it. I hear her voice getting softer and ragged too.

"Can I tell you something, Maggie?" Tamara says, not waiting for my answer.

"This is the first time in my life that hard work has paid off. I'm being judged for what I did, not the color of my skin, my sex, or where I went to school. For once, I got a break, a chance to make it. Quantum leap out of the ghetto. And with no one's help. No handicaps, no deals. A break!"

I've never heard her talk like this, and the tears are welling up in my eyes.

All I can croak out is "I know, I know," and we leave it at that, promising to speak again the day after Valentine's Day.

In the early-morning sun, the bedroom is washed with piercing white light, like an overexposed photograph. No wonder New York is so often gray, the sun here is doing double shifts. Perfect weather or not, I'm on my own today. Taylor's in the studio. Then I remember promising to cook for him on Valentine's Day.

But what? Eggs? Eggs and caviar, or eggs and smoked salmon? Eggs were foods of love, and what more apt symbol of fertility, fecundity? Or maybe just a big ole tin of caviar and shrimps diavolo. Or bouillabaisse, lighter fare. Always keep the dog a little hungry. I don't dwell on where this love feast may lead.

It would be a switch from last Valentine's Day when I spent the night at home alone and was tucked into bed with a book by 9:00 p.m., wearing a flannel nightgown that had been a sweet-sixteen gift. Just as I was setting the alarm, the phone rang.

"Turn on CNN," Tex said. "They're doing a report on—"

"The Valentine's Day massacre?"

"Awful date, huh?"

So I lied. A woman had her pride. "I don't want to talk about it."

"Guys are assholes, Maggie...so what happened?"

Safer not to embellish the falsehood. "There are no

words…" Half an hour later, he arrived at my door, unannounced, with a red fur teddy bear slung over his shoulder. It was almost as tall as I am.

"I'm getting a hernia," Tex said, brushing my face with the bear's arm.

I'm not surprised he's back from his V-Day dinner with Sharon. She got up early on weekdays to talk with her financial clients, and Tex couldn't handle the alarm clock beeping at 5:00 a.m.

"You'll have to rent him an apartment of his own."

"We can share custody."

Before the night was over, we traded Valentine's Day stories and finished a bottle of Merlot.

"I took out a girl from Goldman Sachs a couple of years ago," Tex said, nodding his head glumly. "As soon as we sat down to dinner, I knew it was a mistake. She started out by telling me that she had to be home by nine. 'I work out with my trainer at four-thirty, and get to the office by five-thirty, then I'm putting together these billion-dollar mergers in Silicon Valley until ten at night,'" Tex said, parroting her nasal voice.

"'Tex, you wouldn't believe…Microsoft's *fate* hanging on issues of credibility…the SEC halting trade in the shares of five Internet-related companies…the astronomical force of deals in the global economy.' I sat there, fixated on the size of her teeth—long, white, convex, predatory," he said. "And then the clincher was when she said she'd be thirty in three months and that her income for the year was almost a quarter of a mil more than the last."

"So you ordered champagne?"

"No, I slid her the check."

I can't remember many Valentine's Days when the night lived up to some magical level of romanticism.

"In college, a girlfriend fixed me up with a cousin who was visiting from out of town," I tell him. "I looked at him and wondered whether all the men in Wheeling were five foot four and sold insurance or whether I had just gotten lucky."

Tex smirks.

"You just know how our dinner conversation started."

"'Term or life?'" he says.

"Yeah, it was Valentine's Day and he was trying to sell me life insurance. So do you sell more of the term or the whole life policies? Oh, oh, I see. And then you can convert them? Really! We weren't even finished with the appetizers. Then he bragged about how he saved money by buying chuck instead of filet mignon, because with enough pounding you could tenderize it so that no one would know the difference."

He also had a system for saving money on toilet paper by counting the sheets he used each time he went to the bathroom, but I didn't share that with Tex.

That was the last time I ever dated by default, especially on Valentine's Day.

It's not that I'm after a night of endless sex or treacle romance, it's just that I want to be with the right person. I hate the requisite roses or satin hearts filled with gummy chocolates, or the tacky gift of lingerie. (Men rarely splurge on the luscious French or Italian stuff, anyway—it never crosses their minds that there's a difference.) And for lack of knowing what else to do, most guys seem to fall victim to cliché and mass marketing, making the occasion even more painful than if they just showed up with some great take-out food, a good movie, and a smile that would tell you that there was no other place on earth that they'd rather be.

But now here I am three thousand miles from home, and I'm faced with cooking up a menu to make L.A.'s sexiest bachelor sizzle.

I'm walking through the aisles of the grocery store to buy the Valentine's Day menu, and I get an idea for my next column based on what's being done to our food supply.

Food-Ceuticals

Why can't they leave plain old food alone?

Every time I go to the grocery store, I notice that the food has been adulterated. The orange juice has added calcium. The cold cereals seem to be filled with ground-up multivitamins. And now I read that the new generation of comestibles coming your way will contain hidden medicines. Would you believe bananas that produce a cholera vaccine? Genetically engineered corn that contains oral vaccines for travellers' diarrhea?

We already have genetically engineered foods to fight off insects, but where are we headed with this new generation of "agriceuticals," as they are dubbed? Frankly, the whole business of messing with nature this way scares me. What's ahead? A phone call to the local pharmacist to make sure that there are no drug interactions between foods every time we eat a meal?

As I'm stirring a pot, he sidles up to me, resting his hands on my hips.

"What's cooking?" Taylor says, sniffing the air.

"Swan's pizzle."

"Run that past me again."

"Don't ask…" I take a spoon of bouillabaisse, blow on it, then hold it up to his lips.

"Mmmm…I'm yours!"

I blush. Leave that alone. I lean over and kiss his cheek. "Happy Valentine's Day, Taylor."

"Same to you, O'Leary." He hoists himself up on the kitchen counter. "So this is my aphrodisiac special, right? Gonna drive me out of my gourd?"

"Possibly. Of course there's always the chance that it could have a reverse pharmacological effect."

"I'll take my chances."

I take a caviar pie out of the refrigerator and gently slide a knife through the layers—a topping of shimmering black Beluga pearls resting on a bed of cream cheese and egg salad. I cut a thick wedge for him and a wobbly sliver for myself.

"Should I cut a third for—?" *Why do I hate to say her name?*

He shakes his head. "She's staying with someone in Beverly Hills tonight. She wants to show me…"

"I hope I didn't screw things up for you—especially since I'm clearing out in a few days."

"You don't have to. Camp out here for a while." He eases me in between his open knees. "Give L.A. a shot. What do you think?"

"Taste the pie."

I watch him taste it and see the corners of his mouth curl. I sweep a tiny pearl from the side of his lip with my finger. He reaches for my finger, and licks it off.

I cut two more pieces and we move to the table, eating without speaking. The blood rises to my face. I hate that!

My stupid, pale Irish complexion always gives me away. I glance over at him, then lower my eyes the moment he catches my gaze. I follow his tanned fingers guiding the fork up to his lips, then look back at his eyes.

"Good?"

His head moves up and down slowly.

It's a game now. But who is the fish, who is the fisherman? Whichever, carpe diem!

I rise from the table and stir the vermilion-red broth, inhaling the pungent bouquet of simmering clams, mussels, scallops, lobster and red snapper. I set the steaming pot before us and ladle it into two bowls, then serve salad and French bread.

"Maybe we should just sniff this," Taylor says. "Get high on the scent."

"I'd like to invent a dish that you could inhale instead of eat. Wouldn't that make me the health guru of all gurus? Please the senses, satisfy the stomach, without touching a drop. We could go into business. I'd cook it and you'd serve it. We'd be rich. I could even write the screenplay."

Taylor shakes his finger admonishingly. "Careful. If you're thinking about screenplays, you're becoming one of us. Soon you'll get silicon breasts and cheek implants." He pushes his chair back, as if in horror.

"Yeah, then I'll never get out of this roach motel."

He tears off some French bread. "You'd miss New York. You wouldn't feel comfortable here, would you?"

"Not unless I sent for my Testarosa and my furs," I intone theatrically. "I live a lavish lifestyle in the city." I look around, feigning disgust. "How could someone like me rough it in a place like this?" I say, lapsing into Bette Davis. "What a dump."

Taylor stares back at me. "You scared of me, or just hostile?"

I'm silent for a moment, looking down at the table. "Both."

"Don't be." He lifts the champagne flute and takes a sip, watching me over the rim. "The meal's working," he says, holding my gaze.

I smile, then unconsciously swallow. "Dessert?"

He just smiles, takes my hand and leads me up the stairs. This feels so surreal. I'd imagined it over and over again, heading to the bedroom I was about to see for the first time. It's as if I'm watching a trailer, but the picture has never gotten made. I picture the king-size bed swathed in gray, see myself lying down, him above me…propping himself up with those arms.

He pushes open the white lacquered door, and there it is, shadowed by night. Opposite the bed is a glass wall and beyond it only blackness and twinkling lights and the bleached yellow of a three-quarter moon. In the daylight, the view will sharpen into focus, like a developing photo, to show an endless panorama of sunlight and blue ocean. He turns on a small steel wall lamp, and then kneels and lights three thick white candles on a red lacquer tray on the bedside table. I watch his lips come together to blow out the match.

"C'mere, sex symbol."

He stretches out next to me, pushing back hair from my face and blowing off stray strands with a puff of breath. "Nobody can live up to that."

"Try."

He runs his fingers lightly over the outside of my dress, easing each button open, and then slowly sliding the silky fabric down until it reaches my waist. His lips brush my bare shoulders, and a hand slips behind me. With just a touch, my bra loosens. Does everything go easily for this man? His lips run along the hollow of my shoulders and down toward my breasts. I lean into him, and moan.

"Who taught you how to do…that?"

"This?"

"Umm…yes…"

"Or this?"

"Yes…God…"

"What if I stop?"

"I'll…oh…kill you…"

The mouth stops. So does the slow stroking finger playing on the outside of my panties. "No, you won't," he whispers.

My arms tighten around his neck, but he eases back. Payback. I try again to pull him toward me, but he resists. A slow grin spreads over his face.

"What?" I whisper, pleading.

"Want to throw your fuck-me pumps out the window again?"

I bite his lip suddenly. "Only if you crawl around with me to look for them."

"Mmmm, sounds like fun." He lifts my shoes from the floor and arches his arm back as if to hurl them out of the window.

"Taylor…please…" He wrestles me down to the bed, dangling them high above my head with one hand, while the other pins my wrists together over my head. I push against him, fighting to reach them.

But with a learned cool, he leans over, caresses my ear with his lips, taunting me. Then, pressing himself against me, he whispers, "Put them on…"

★ ★ ★

"The dinner went perfectly, by eleven we were in bed, and then, in the middle of the night, I heard the moan."

"The what?" I'm sitting up in Taylor's bed now and checking my watch. Fortunately, he isn't awakened by the ring of my cell from the room down the hall from his. It's 4:00 a.m., and Tamara is calling me from the hospital. It doesn't help that she's whispering from the opposite end of the country, and I'm half-dead.

"The moan. I ran to the bathroom door and called him, Maggie, and there was no answer. Finally, there was this terrible croak. 'I'm dying,' he said. 'It must have been something I ate.'"

I know what's coming.

"So he stumbles out of the bathroom looking like he's dying. Says he lost half the fluid in him, so we dash down and jump into a cab to the emergency room. Ty's lying back in his chair in the E.R., looking pale and faint. Finally they call us and ask him what he ate."

"The oysters," I say, so low that I think she can't hear me.

"Uh-huh," she says, "uh-huh. A bad oyster. 'Happens every year on Valentine's Day,' the doctors says, glaring at me. 'Why don't people ever realize what a dumb idea it is to eat raw shellfish?' he says. Do you know how guilty I felt, Maggie?"

"How's he doing now?"

"He's going to be okay," Tamara says, glumly, "no thanks to—"

"Don't blame yourself. Millions of people eat oysters, and it just happens that some of them are bad." I turn and look at Taylor, who's slept through this, so far. Thank God I didn't make him oysters.

I hear her breathing. She's sitting in the No Smoking lounge now, she says, watching a gray-haired woman in a hospital gown with spongy slippers who's attached to an IV pole. "Sitting right under the No Smoking sign," Tamara whispers. "The red tip of her cigarette is glowing like she's radioactive."

I've never felt so glad to be so far away.

It's Valentine's Day, and Tamara is now in the least romantic spot in the universe. For some reason, that makes both of us laugh.

"If you weren't sick enough when you came in," she says, "the sight of people moaning, being wheeled from ambulances with heart attacks, strokes, gunshot wounds—and one bum oyster—could make you keel over."

"Sick," I say, starting to laugh.

"You know, Maggie, there have been a few men in my life who I could imagine myself killing—shooting them, or maybe strangling them. But in my wildest dreams, it never occurred to me to use an oyster!"

How refined a murder, how deft. "One swallow of the soft, gray, slimy little bivalve, and the deed is done."

"Oh God," Tamara says, hysterical now. "If he pulls through, I'll do all I can to make it up to him."

"Everything," I say, "except cook."

seventeen

"Still afraid of me?" Taylor asks, leaning on one elbow on his Hollywood bed. When I first heard about Hollywood-size beds, I assumed it was a joke. Then I found out that there really was such a size. Inches longer, naturally.

No, I'm not afraid of you, Taylor, I'm afraid of every woman you're going to meet who's sexier, thinner, younger, prettier...

"Afraid of *you?* You should be afraid of me now," I say, pulling the sheet around me. "You sleep with a journalist and you run the risk of reading about it in the gossip rags the next day." I trace my finger along the swell of his shoulder. Just those arms...

Taylor exhales hard. "It's been done. Don't remind me."

"I trust you didn't get a high score. Well, not to worry. My account will do wonders for your image. You'll need to install one of those infrared sensors right down here." I reach down and tease him with my fingers, tracing an *X*.

"To change the subject, what happens when Jolie comes

back? Does *she* get the guest room? Do we play musical beds? Am I relegated to the tool shed? How are you going to mastermind this, Taylor?"

"Actually, I thought I'd invite a new girl over that I just met and put you both in the guest room," he says, running his fingers through my hair. "She's different than anyone I know—very hot, a little overweight, a great cook, and all she thinks about is sex. Heavy chicks like to get it more—betcha didn't know that."

"Mmmm.... Dangerous lies."

Taylor smiles, then his face turns serious. "I'm going to talk to Jolie today, and tell her—"

"Shhh. Don't tell me..." What did he want from a woman? Maybe Jolie wasn't the one, but was he capable of commitment to someone else? *Him* monogamous? And if he was, how could anyone handle the tidal wave of fans?

Hard to imagine spending your life clinging to a movie star's coattails as his success soared upward or spiraled down, forever anxious about what his next project would be, where it would take him, or if his female costar would take him.

No, I'm totally cool about you spending three months in the Amazon with Kim Basinger, in Adam and Eve, *shooting and reshooting the procreation scenes. Verisimilitude.*

"You're off in space." He turns my face toward his. "Talk to me."

"I was just writing the article for the *Star* in my head," I say, slipping my hand around the back of his neck and pulling him down on me. "I have to check some more details though."

After a perfunctory kiss, he pulls away. "You're thinking about going home, right?'

"Not right now, I'm not."

"Stay. Let's see what happens with us."

"I'm not from here, it's so—"

"What? It's so what?" he says, shaking his head. "And what is so fucking *great* about New York?"

"All I can tell you is that when I hear Frank Sinatra sing 'New York, New York'—and I've heard it a hundred and fifty times—it still brings tears to my eyes. When I see someone wearing a T-shirt that says New York Fucking City, it always makes me laugh. And the longer I stay there, and the worse it gets—and it does—the more I know that I can't leave for more than a few weeks at a time because it's a part of me. So that's my nonanswer. New Yorkers are like an extended dysfunctional family—everybody's screwed up, so we're in good company. You're where you belong."

"You're not normal."

"Normal people are the ones that you don't know very well."

He laughs and I trace my finger along his ribs. "You're not real to me, movie-star man. I keep thinking of you on the billboard."

"I can't live up to that, Maggie. Reality doesn't cut it the way fantasies do."

"It's pretty close." Then I stop smiling. "Maybe it's the challenge of seeing if you can get me to move here to start my life over for you...of course, if you threw in the caaaaar..."

Every day, Tamara says, she sits bedside and watches the IV dripping into Ty's limp arm, praying that he will suddenly rise up, as if reborn, throw down the covers and go home. But three days have gone by already, and the insidious little bivalve still hasn't released its virulent grip.

By day four, he starts showing signs of life again. Would he turn into a vegan, or maybe a fruitarian and live on trail mix or granola from now on? Would the poor man, ever in this lifetime, be willing to look at a morsel of shell-fish again?

She makes the mistake of asking him how he feels.

"Like a truck ran over me. I have a new respect for the power of nature."

"I can't tell you how awful that made me feel, Maggie. I told him that I wished it was me, instead of him."

"What did he say?"

"When he gets out he'll cook for me and even the score."

"He'll get over it."

"He'll forgive, but not forget, he said. But in the mean-time," Tamara says, brightening, "I did get a great shot of a Broadway actress leaving here after a face-lift, thanks to my night-vision glasses."

"Your what?"

"I bought them in a spy shop." I let that register. Is she just a trifle too committed to the new column?

"In a million years you won't guess who picked her up?"

"Picked *who* up?"

"The actress with the face-lift."

"Don't tell me. I do not want to know. And if you don't watch who you take pictures of, somebody's gonna put a bad oyster in your lunch...."

Bill is looking forward to your return, the e-mail from his secretary says. *Shots of you and Mike Taylor in papers here— readers fascinated by your exploits yet confused about appear-ance changes—tout le monde asking, "What's going on with Maggie? Losing weight purposely? Hunk related? Is Maggie abandoning readers now that she's thinner?" Questions abound. Advise.*

Readers' questions would have to be addressed, but what would I tell them? But more important, spies in financial told me, the whole mess was boosting readership. That explained Wharton's note with a forwarded invitation to a food-tasting dedicated to everything chocolate.

Maybe You're Not To Blame

If you follow the news as closely as I do, you get to the point where you feel it's only a matter of time until science confirms what you already know. Today, for instance, there was a front page story in the *New York Times* about how they've discovered a hormone that's apparently to blame for why the overweight can't stay slim after they diet and lose weight. The name of the chemical villain is *ghrelin*. Before meals, levels of ghrelin shoot up. After eating, they drop. And when you give someone a shot of ghrelin, they basically pig out, eating about thirty percent more than normal.

And here's the worst part: People who diet and lose weight produce more ghrelin than they did before they dieted. What does that tell you? That after you diet, your body is working against you, trying to get you to go back to your old chubby weight. The explanation being that the body was designed to protect you from starvation in times of famine, and one way was to slow metabolism and perk up appetite.

The new studies, reported in the *New England Journal of Medicine,* also describe how after grossly obese people have gastric bypass surgery, they end up with very little of the hormone which explains why they report a decrease in their appetites.

So where does that leave us? Well, maybe since ghrelin is the first appetite-stimulating hormone found to be produced not by the brain—although it acts on it—but by cells in the stomach and the upper small intestine, maybe clever scientists can come up with a drug that will block the hormone, cutting appetite. The other side of the picture is that for those with cancer, suffering from extreme weight loss, the hormone may help stimulate appetite. Stay tuned. Meanwhile, research is concentrating on chubby rats.

In my absence, Tamara's book has been rejected. It's about a photographer and a newspaper columnist who both give up on trying to lose weight on their own and decide to go to an in-patient weight management program together. They struggle together, bond, and emerge convinced that they will forever be in control of their lives and content with who they are. She'd apparently also told Ty. It hits him as off. He tells her to revise it and then send it out again.

"He thinks it's 'too easy,'" Tamara tells me.

"Why?"

"After they leave, they team up to do stories about the American way of losing weight, and start their own anti-dieting magazine, they both find guys and fall in love."

"So?"

"He thinks that they like themselves too fast. Thinks they don't suffer enough."

"In the real world, yes, most people do, but this is made

up," I say. You can tell that my career as a novelist is going nowhere. Why should she make her poor heroines suffer, didn't women suffer enough in real life?

"He thinks I'm taking women back in time, offering them an unreal image."

"These women lost the weight by *not* dieting, *that's* the point."

"Exactly," Tamara says. "It's a lifestyle…and the book's a romance…reality doesn't sell. And then I said, 'Anyway, you'll find out that when they set up their own antidieting magazine, they're so friggin' overworked they don't have time to eat. And if you can forget to eat, you're cured. You're not obsessed with food anymore. You find something else to fill you up.'"

"I'll publish the book," I say. "I can't wait to read it."

"Men don't get it," Tamara says. "Anyway, two publishers called to see if you want to write a tell-all book."

Thunk. I drop the phone, laughing out loud.

"Why is that so funny? There's a forty-billion-dollar diet industry out there, Maggie. Maybe instead of just shooting holes in it, you should consider using it to build up your retirement fund."

But I can't stop laughing. "If Taylor's fans alone bought it, it would be a bestseller."

Dear Ms. Brown:

Thank you for giving us a chance to read New Beginnings. *We've looked it over and also gave it to another editor who read the entire book. In the end, while we found it lively, we also felt it would be a midlist book for us and difficult to publish as well as we'd like to. With regrets, I'm re-*

turning the manuscript, but grateful that you gave us the opportunity to review it.

And she thought she was tough. I look at the fax and shake my head. Poor Tamara. She was so convinced that the book was good. I call her to commiserate.

"You can't get too cocky in this world, because life has a way of smacking you in the head and tamping you down," Tamara says.

I hear Ty in the background. "Everyone gets rejected," he says. "It means nothing. It's a rite of passage."

"He's right," I say.

"You gotta stick with it," Ty yells. "You know what a publisher once said about Kon-Tiki? 'Who in hell wants to read about a bunch of crazy Scandinavians floating around the ocean on a raft?'"

Now I know I like Ty.

"I put my heart and soul into that book, Maggie. And you know, every time I reread it, I can't stop. I mean, it is a page-turner, isn't it?"

"That's not it, Tamara. Maybe it's just not what that particular publisher was looking for at the time."

"That particular publisher is behind half the bestsellers on the list."

"Onward," I say for lack of something better.

"So what do I do? Keep sending it out?"

"Absolutely. By the time they get around to answering you there's a new crop of editors anyway."

"Won't the word spread that there's this bum manuscript going around and around?"

"It's not a bum manuscript," I say. "You may have to do some rewriting, but you've got a good story."

"I don't know," she says, sounding dejected. "Maybe I deluded myself into thinking that when I got the column I'd be living a different kind of life from then on, that rejection was behind me."

"Sometimes it looks like one step forward, two steps back," I say, "but you got to keep at it."

"Maybe writing's like weight loss," Tamara says. "You succeed for a while, but then you inevitably slide back. Success is just a bump now and then in a long continuum of failure."

"That's not the Tamara that I know talking. I know you don't believe that."

"Maybe I just can't do it," Tamara says. "Maybe it's just too hard. I don't have the talent. I'm a fraud."

"If you start to think that way you become paralyzed," Ty says. "Right, Maggie?" he says, yelling into the phone.

I hate three-way conversations, but he's right. "Yeah," I yell. "Everything's hard, especially taking the first step."

"But I don't want to keep failing, goddammit."

"Look at me," Ty says. I hear him come and sit next to her. "Have you ever failed before?" he says.

"Of course I've failed before, Jesus!"

"You still alive?"

She doesn't answer for a minute. Then I hear her laugh.

"Okay then," he says.

"Maggie, I gotta go," Tamara says. "I got a pile of letters to tear up."

I hang up. I don't think she notices.

"Your last day," Taylor says, slipping his arm around my waist as we walk to the car.

I glance at him, then look away. I woke up this morning with no appetite. Don't remember the last time that happened. At my worst, I breakfasted on Coke and potato chips. But now there was only this hollow feeling.

He dangles the keys in front of me. "Want to drive?"

I shake my head. We drive up the Pacific Coast Highway. He left the studio early so we could spend the afternoon together. I turn and stare out the window at the ocean as the waves break against the rocky coastline, glittering like faceted stones—the *second* perfect thing my eyes feasted on when I woke up in his bed. I open the window to breathe in the cool, salty air.

I hate goodbyes—that gnawing fear that the harsh winds of fate might change your life from that moment on, separating you forever. The air charged with the unspoken. Airports were the worst, particularly after September 11th.

To relieve the discomfort I'm feeling, I start blathering on endlessly about weight loss. "…the absurdity of looking at a weight chart and finding your ideal weight. I mean there are fifty different tables, some take into account frame size, sex and age, others don't. They don't distinguish between excess fat and muscle. You can look fat but have a high percentage of…" *I'm boring myself to death, but I can't tell what he's thinking. He seems to be caught up in driving.* I catch my breath and stop in midsentence. I don't think he notices.

"So now you're an expert. Maybe you should take over the column for me."

"What would *you* do, act?"

"I can't act, I can't even lie—well, not for long. And my problem now is that my readers want to know how the hell I lost weight and what's happening to me. A lot of them are going to hate me now. My message is going to get a lot more complicated." I shake my head. "I just have to sort out what to tell them."

"Tell them you had a crush on a movie star and wanted to test out the fantasy, but it passed and you realized that in real life fantasies burst like soap bubbles, but you decided to stay thin anyway, and you ran back to your New York life to pick up the pieces."

"That's not my story."

"So what is?"

I shrug.

Taylor's watching me stare ahead. "So what is?" he says, reaching over and holding my arm. "You've got to figure out your moves pretty soon, you know."

His face is so close to mine that I don't move. I can almost feel the warmth of his skin. I want to touch it, but I don't. I shift in my seat, uncomfortable.

"Maybe the New York columnist goes home, and before her plane lands, the movie star starts living with another leggy blonde who weighs ninety-five pounds and wears a size four, and they live happily—and then unhappily—ever after until he meets a sexier one with a different accent who wears a size two. The actress du jour, or maybe a Scandinavian cover girl this time—"

"You don't give me much credit do you? Or yourself for that matter."

Why am I doing this? Do I have to test out his allegiance to me? And why am I putting myself down like that?

"Maybe you're right," I say in a whisper. "Guess it comes with the territory." Neither of us knows what to say, but I'm getting edgy as he starts racing around the turns as though he wants to permanently imprint his tire tracks on the road.

"Are you trying to smash us both up? Would that solve things?"

"No, but some coke might help. Want some?"

"I prefer Pepsi."

"You're always on, right? I can't get through to you." He drives faster, turning up the radio.

"I'd prefer not to be cremated in your car just now," I shout above Aerosmith, "so would you mind slowing down—no, pulling over?" He doesn't seem to hear, then suddenly swerves off the road. I pitch forward in my seat— glad that I didn't have lunch—and feel the seat belt stretch and snap back on me. I reach for the radio and turn it down. It seems like such a long time ago that we were heading to his house for the first time. I'll never forget how he stopped—more slowly then—to teach me how to drive a stick.

"Okay, let's run off to Vegas. How many times have you been proposed to before, anyway?"

He shrugs. *No one could accuse him of being a braggart.*

"Is that what you want—to tie yourself down to one guy for the rest of your life?"

"I've never thought about it in those terms, but at some point…I guess you meet someone and…you can't imagine life without them. You don't feel like you're giving anything up or losing anything…just the opposite."

"But that's not what's going on here."

"It's so different here for me," I say, shaking my head. "I'm facing the wrong ocean. And the prices on Rodeo Drive are starting to look normal to me…."

He smiles. "I don't know of too many girls who make me laugh," he says, running his hand along my chin. "I'm going to miss that."

"It's a survival tool of the overweight…anyway a good friend of mine is getting married. I have to be there."

"So send her a solid gold fondue pot—on me."

"It's a him…."

"Him." He nods, exaggeratedly. "He's not marrying *you*, is he?"

"No, smart-ass. But I've known him for a long time…."

"You really like the guy."

"He's just a *friend* at work…. I'm crazy about *you*, Taylor, but—"

"It'll pass—"

"Don't say that. It's just that I can't run away forever. I have to go back to my column, my life…. Does that make any sense?"

"I don't know," he says, tapping the wheel nervously. "I'm no expert. I skipped out on one bad marriage, and I've slept with an awful lot of women that I haven't loved—"

"Slut."

"You got it. Aside from my three-month marriage, I've only been crazy in love once maybe. She was nineteen, and I was twenty-two. But then she moved a thousand miles away and I lost her. And now I meet Maggie O'Leary from New York who broke the mold, and got to my heart through my stomach. And what do I get?"

"Indigestion?"

"No, dumped for some—"

"Stop—"

"Anyway, I got you a going-away present." He pulls a small red velvet box out of his hip pocket and places it in my lap. Cartier. I look at him warily and slowly open it. I lift up a shimmering gold chain with a charm hanging from it in the shape of an open book. There are emerald-cut diamonds running along the spine. *Dangerous Lies* is engraved on the cover. I flip it over and see the engraved words: *With love, Mike.*

"You're making going home very hard, you know?" I don't want him to see my eyes, but he does. I open the chain and he lifts my hair and closes it behind my neck. I get a shiver as I feel the teasing touch of his fingertips on my neck. He looks at the necklace, then turns and stares out the driver's window.

"Well, there is a positive side to everything," he says, rhythmically tapping the heel of his hand on the steering wheel for the second time. "At least you won't be stripping the damn gears of my car anymore."

"I'll miss this car," I say, closing my hand over his on the wheel. "I really will."

eighteen

In atmospheric colic, the 747 from Los Angeles to New York swoops, dips and ricochets through the atmosphere. From a world of sunshine, I'm hurled into a raging nor'easter.

I stare out the window, taking deep relaxing breaths to overcome my nausea and chills. Are we even going to make it? On top of everything, I feel like I'm coming down with the flu. Is this Mother Nature's way of punishing me for flying off to L.A.? Adding to my malaise is the haunting vision of Taylor's face growing fainter and fainter as I walked from the gate. "It was a sweet time, Maggie." No, it was more. I was leaving wonderland.

But there was no time to nurse my misery—I had a column to write. Offer the hug, the Band-Aid, another shot in the arm. I needed a shot all right—curare maybe—to stop my own heart. I glare at the screen of the laptop.

Three false starts, and after two hours in the air, all of

the words I've written have been dragged into the electronic trash bin. Have my writing skills evaporated? Where was that warm, caring, intimate voice with readers? Maybe now that I had become thin—or thinner—I had grown cold, angry, strident and unfeeling. I could see the letters. *When you lost the weight, you lost your heart.*

No, my heart was still there, but I had changed. Things hadn't turned out the way I figured. I never imagined my boy-toy fantasy would warm to me. Actually, I hadn't thought about *his* feelings at all—how liberating!

I finger the necklace. *Dangerous Lies.* Loaded words. I had been given the rare chance to walk into the cotton-candy clouds of imagination and explore blind longing. Maybe *blind* was the operative word. It reminded me of a cartoon that a friend had on her refrigerator: A princess is sitting, eyes closed, dreaming of her Prince Charming and just at that moment, he passes by her on horseback.

The flight smooths out and we begin to descend. I recognize the lights of Queens, the gray waters off Long Island. I look over Manhattan, spotting the Empire State Building, and the glittering 59th Street Bridge, and am haunted, like every New Yorker, by the absence of the twin towers of the World Trade Center.

I look for glimmering swimming pools and mosaics of twinkling turquoise, but there are none. Just tall buildings, and traffic-snaked roads. Tie-ups on the Cross Island Parkway, the glamorous Gowanus. The plane gets closer and closer to land, and finally, the reassuring BUMP as it hits the ground. I'm thrust back in my seat, feeling the rush of speed as it approaches the terminal. Tear-size rain pellets pound the glass. The northern half of the sky is a swath of charcoal gray. Home.

I zip the laptop case and reach for my handbag, then sit while others file out first. They move like cattle, lugging heavy bags that pound the sides of the seats as they amble down the narrow aisle. The plane is nearly empty when I get up. I slip on my jacket and head for the terminal with my swollen suitcase. It feels as though I'm dragging home a corpse.

I'm looking toward the taxi line when I spot him. Six foot five, always high above the crowd. But this Tex…has a look. Not newsroom anymore. Downtown. Sleek hair-cut, faint outline of a sandy beard along the jaw, steel-framed sunglasses, weathered-leather bomber jacket. He has that "just back from St. Bart's" glow that blends with the clothes, and I'm wondering if he went so far as to visit a tanning parlor. I look him over, head to toe. Was he even trimmer? Whose hands had remodeled him, some Fash-ion Institute ingenue? Couldn't have been Sharon—she could use some updating herself. He waves.

I hesitate, then wave back, walking closer. He's leaning up against a railing, smiling expectantly.

"What did you do with Tex?"

He points to the ground. "Down there with the old Maggie."

I run my hand over the sleeve of his jacket. "Sample sale?"

"You underestimate me."

Under the jacket he's wearing a tan cashmere turtleneck instead of his usual standard-issue blue pinpoint oxford shirt and poly tie. I feel the sweater. "Nice, but what's going on around here? I go away for a lousy two weeks and you become Richard Gere?"

"Not 'You look good, Tex, I like the clothes. You lost weight.' Just 'What's going on here?'"

I catch myself. "Okay. You look good, Tex. I'm impressed. Stunned actually. Mr. *GQ.*"

"Jesus, you're something."

"Sorry, I was in California, remember? I guess I lost some of my brain cells. They're airheads out there, you know? The state flower is the golden poppy, a natural source of opiates, you believe that?"

He looks at me without saying anything for a minute, then shakes his head disapprovingly. "Well, the endearing personality is intact."

"Thank you." *Bastard.*

I know I shouldn't, but I can't help myself. "Next, you're going to tell me you have a part in a TV series."

"No, I'm still Metro editor, very happy with my job. I know who *I* am."

I open my mouth to reply but before I do, I see his eye on the necklace. He reaches out for the charm, lifts it, then turns it over. For a split second a look of incredulity passes over his face, and he snorts and shakes his head.

I want to kill.

"Don't tell me you had a love affair with that clown."

"First of all," I say, cocking my head to the side. "He's not a *clown,* as you so articulately phrased it. He's a world-famous actor. And second of all, it's really none of *your* goddamn business what *I* did."

"No, you're right," he says, shaking his head in agreement, talking loud enough for people around us to halt their own conversations and start staring. "You are free to mess up your own lousy life. But if your sweet, private life is nobody's business, then don't hang a sign around your neck advertising it, okay?"

Everyone around us seems to turn into an audience, watching to see how the play will end.

"Actually, it's not a sign at all," I say as haughtily as possible. "It's an eighteen-karat gold charm with diamonds made-to-order by Cartier. And you can just go screw yourself." I viciously pull my bag from his hand, nearly toppling him. "You know what? I'd really rather take a cab with a kamikaze driver than have to endure spending another second with you."

"Well, that's just fahn with me." He's yelling now, and thanks to the high ceilings, the sound waves are echoing throughout the terminal. "I don't know wha I wasted mah whole afternoon coming out he-ah anyway." The accent again. Stupid hick. Why didn't he just go back to the armpit of Texas where he came from? Maybe because where *he* came from they probably didn't have newspapers, just notices of cattle auctions. The nerve of *him* to humiliate me.

I run out into the pouring rain, throw my bag into the back seat of the first cab that stops and bark, "Manhattan."

I slam the door and am a victim to an air supply that's been beamed by the cloying vapors of bottled air freshener suctioned to the driver's dashboard. Imagine jasmine, bathroom deodorant, B.O. and decay, all together inside a dark bottle. I know the fetid molecules are invading the fibers of my clothes like cigarette smoke in a crowded bar. I start to gag, and lower the window as far as it will go, welcoming the rain that lashes my face. I sit back and listen to the driver whispering into a cell phone for the entire fifty-minute ride, convinced that I'm being driven by someone who has now plotted a new terrorist attack against my city.

In my elevator lobby, I stab the button for my floor and ride up to my apartment. I turn the key and enter an apartment that looks strange and unfamiliar as though I'm reentering somebody else's old life. I throw open the living room windows and stare out blankly at the view. Concrete and steel. Bad enough that I left the sun-soaked world of California, I've come back to a city that now seems like it was shoehorned inside a dark, drafty elevator shaft. I strip off my clothes and toss them into a pile on the floor. As I walk into the bedroom, I glance at the row of plants along the window sill that my elderly neighbor promised to take care of. The edges of the leaves are black and drooping. Even the poor resilient cactus looks as though it's succumbed to dehydration. My tiny teardrop of a New York garden has perished in my absence, starved of the few pathetic droplets of water, all it needed just to simply stay alive.

The next morning, just as I'm about to enter my office, I hear the click of a camera.

"Got ya," Tamara says, grinning. I give her a small smile. The gossipmongers quickly congregate around me. "How was your pupil?" a secretary from Foreign giggles. "An A-plus?"

"So is he really like the character he plays in *The High Life?*" *Well, he gets high.* I look at Tamara. She knows something's amiss, but we don't have time to talk. There are candidates waiting to be interviewed for her job. I want to cut through the stereotypes and hire a male, but few apply. One of the most promising is a gorgeous acting student, grounds for immediate rejection.

Meanwhile, I dismantle the gallery of hunk posters with the solemnity afforded a series of shining presidential hopefuls who, through no shortcomings of their own, drop by the wayside. I stare at a blank wall, studying the hairline cracks as if they are seismic fissures in a planet that is about to implode.

"Redecorating?" Tamara says.

"Huh?"

"How about a poster of some really wanted dudes." She holds up the FBI's "Most Wanted."

I wave it away. "Unwanted." I look back down at the desk as if I'm lobotomized, skimming letter after letter. Readers are keenly aware of my weight loss, image change and the trip. I don't have secrets. Now I know what it's like to be running from the bulls at Pamplona. I try to concentrate on the column, but everything I write is garbage. Finally I bat something out.

Dangerous Lies

In my own life I've been living some dangerous lies. *[I had to get that in somewhere, the phrase was now etched in my brain.]* I thought that I would never again attempt to lose weight, never even put myself on an exercise program. Then, challenged by an assignment that would take me to the center of celebrity, I decided to tackle some major lifestyle changes. *[No, admitting my infatuation with Taylor is going just a wee bit too far. Anyway, none of their damn business.]*

I began eating three small meals a day and two smaller, healthy snacks. I drank water instead of soda, juice or alcohol, and worked out regularly. So far, I have kept off all but five of the thirty-five lost pounds. Can I maintain the rest of what I lost? Who knows? Biology is destiny and the deck is stacked against me.

But more important, I now have a new sensibility about that predisposition that will affect my food choices. Be assured, however, that I will never cut myself off from the joys of eating—there's a reason why food tastes good. These days I think of food as a spiritual offering. I will never again use it as a weapon against myself, because that would demean the preciousness of life, of survival.

As for exercise, who can afford not to, now that a new study shows that mice who exercised grew twice as many brain cells as those who didn't. We're running out of excuses.

Before I press Send, it goes to Wharton with a note: "I hope this addresses all of the questions and concerns. Glad to be back, Maggie."

He messages back: "Liked the column. Happy you're back. Just one thought: Should we change the name of the column now to 'Slim Chance'?"

"Bill. I've changed enough. Let's leave *something* the same."

No party in Santa Monica tonight, and no lobster spring rolls and black bass. Instead the choice is a carton of take-out stir-fry shrimp and broccoli from the Tang Dynasty Palace or a tin-foil pan filled with tomatoes, black olives, iceberg lettuce and chunks of feta—the Parthenon salad—from Niko's Diner.

I stop at Blockbuster Video first and eyeball the Mike Taylor section, pulling out a copy of *Super Sleuth,* then look for his first movie, *The Trainer.*

"He's so hot," a girl standing behind me says when she sees the cover of the video. I turn around. She has long, straight hair and is wearing tight jeans and high-heeled boots. A college freshman, maybe.

"I heard he's gay," I say, shoving the box back into the shelf.

"Really?"

"Hard to believe, huh?"

I take out *Leaving Las Vegas.* Halfway into it, I press Stop. What a downer. Home for two days, and nothing more from Tex. What exactly was eating him?

As well as I thought I knew him, he remained something of an enigma. Here was a guy who took comfort in editing—cleaning up other people's messes, making life neater, cleaner, more comprehensible, more to the point. And he was good at it. When parts of a story didn't read smoothly or make sense, bells went off in his head. He was familiar with the language, its clarity, its subtlety, the various shades of mood and meaning each word had the exquisite power to convey. It served his needs, really. It made sense out of the jumble of life. But aside from the way he performed at work, how finely honed was his own life? Was his smug, self-satisfaction really a cover-up?

I'm feeling frustrated, out of control, but instead of going into the kitchen and seeking fulfillment in a pint of Rocky Road, I head to a corner of the bedroom closet where I keep the free weights. Biceps curls. I lift the weights up angrily, pumping, heaving hard. Whatever his motivation, he could have opened up, told me how he felt, not just show up at the airport, think he had it all figured out because he glanced at the charm, then put Taylor and me down at the same time.

While he was getting his doctorate in sartorial splendor, maybe someone gave him a tutorial on being a prick. I flew back from L.A., back to the job, ready to pick up my old life, and his reaction to a few harmless, cynical comments on my part was the Antarctica freeze.

I put the weights down and think of food again. One expert suggested that if you got the urge to binge, you should force yourself to wait five minutes before doing anything. The next time you should wait ten minutes, finally working your way up to waiting half an hour before you touched food. Eventually, the theory went, if you were able to delay eating by half an hour, you would be able to think rationally about how destructive the behavior was, and substitute something else. Of course, you could always try this home remedy for reducing hunger pangs that I picked up from a Harvard University newsletter, although I can't say that I tried it, or plan to: Dissolve a gelatin packet in water, stirring it well and quaffing it 2 to 3 hours after a meal to reduce appetite for the next meal. This can be done two to three times a day.

But what I do is grab a handful of air-popped popcorn, sprinkle it with salt substitute and force myself to go for a walk, vowing that I'll walk until I drop. Park Avenue is ideal—building after boring building, none of them home to delis or pizza parlors where the scent of toasted garlic knots might lure me in. I go home too exhausted to eat anyway, my body too tired to trouble my mind with stress.

But at sunrise that ends. Now it's time to work the body and ease the mind. Not bothering to dress, I step aboard Mr. Ed in my spinster pink flannel nightgown and begin the rhythmic slide. It's calming, like cradle rocking. After a shower and a cup of French roast, I leave for the office.

I work until lunch, then walk out to Tamara's desk, grab

a Milky Way sitting there and devour it. Tamara takes this in, silently. Then I turn to her.

"Can I borrow your shoes?"

"My shoes." She repeats it as more of a statement than a question.

"My Manolos are at the shoemaker. I need to be taller."

She looks at me strangely as she slips them off. "Going out?"

"Just to the newsroom."

I ignore her look and with head held high, shoulders back, pupils dilated, I take long strides down the wide center aisle, past a maze of computers. With adrenal hormones flooding my veins, I feel my blood electrified, roiled by a surging power that turns me into a walking Vesuvius, my eyes focused on the Metro desk. I march purposefully, stopping just inches from Tex's shoulder, and wait. Seconds pass. Nothing.

Am I invisible? Apparently. With an inhalation of breath, I give voice and heft to the apparition. I lean toward him slightly, my arrestingly calm voice barely above an icy whisper.

"So, you're just going to ignore me? Is that it?" I watch him continuing to type, undeterred. I'm ready to reach behind his terminal and disembowel it. In a nanosecond, I fly into an uncontrollable rage, drawing my hands into tight fists. I resist the urge to pummel the back of his head. I *am* a lady.

"I JUST WANT YOU TO KNOW, TEX RAMSEY," I shout, "THAT I LEFT A WORLD-CLASS LAY, A MAN WITH ABS SO ROCK HARD THAT A MISSILE WOULDN'T PIERCE THEM, TO COME BACK HERE TO ATTEND *YOUR* WEDDING, DO

YOU KNOW THAT? ALTHOUGH I NOW CAN-NOT I-M-A-G-I-N-E IN MY WILDEST DREAMS WHY ANYONE IN THEIR RIGHT MIND WOULD WANT TO BE SUBJECTED TO BEING MARRIED TO **YOU,** YOU INGRATE, SO DON'T YOU DARE, **DARE** IGNORE **ME.**"

The entire newsroom falls into a dead hush. All eyes are on me. Finally Tex closes the screen and glances up, over his shoulder at me. Just a flicker of annoyance crosses his face.

"Will you please just shut up?"

He stands, and looks out over the newsroom, address-ing the sea of frozen faces fixed on us.

"We're trying to put out a newspaper here," he says, with an annoying smirk on his face. "Deadline is approaching. Will everyone go back to work?" At once, a sea of eyes look down.

He grabs my upper arm, like a probation officer who suddenly takes custody of someone who has violated pa-role, and leads me through the door of his glass-walled of-fice, shutting it behind him. He leans against his desk, arms crossed over his chest, eyeing me with a practiced cool. He gestures toward the couch. "Siddown." He studies me for a minute, saying nothing. Then the head shakes slightly.

"You want to turn yourself into a self-parody and run off to L.A. to screw movie stars, go right ahead. Play play-mate of the hour and act like a gushing fan out of *People* magazine—you go right ahead, that's just fahn with me. But don't expect me to stand by and cheer while you get seduced by celebrity bullshit and make a horse's ass out of yourself on your so-called assignment. Your real mistake was coming back—because whatever it is that's missing in your life, it's clear you weren't finding it here. Now, if you'll excuse me, I've got a paper to put out." There's a breeze as he strides past me.

I sit there, stunned, immobile, then look up, aware now of my glaring visibility through the glass wall. I stand, head high, and begin to walk out, purposely letting a swinging arm slam into an oversize University of Texas beer stein, sending it crashing to the floor and splintering, spewing pens and pencils through the air like shrapnel. Don't mess with Texas, huh?

nineteen

"I know you're wondering where I am."

"So where are you?" Tamara says.

"Over Pennsylvania, I think, heading west."

"*What?* You're in a plane?"

"Well, how else would I be over Pennsylvania?"

"Whoa, Maggie, what about your job?"

That's the last thing I'm thinking about at the moment. All I know is that I had to get out of the office, out of Manhattan, out of New York. I know that Tamara is now taking the heat, trying to field calls and put off everybody who's after me, but how she'd handle things was the last thing on my mind when I got back from the newsroom and fled.

"What about the column?" Tamara says, her voice distorted by the phone on the plane that makes everyone sound inebriated.

"I'm not leaving that," I shout. "You'll get the columns…I had to see Taylor, it's complicated, I can't explain now, but I have to see things through out there. It was a mistake to leave…that's obvious now…"

"Taylor? Maggie…what can I say?"

"Say you'll cover for me. I'll be sending you the columns. Gotta go, Tamara…you're the only one I'll miss, babe. Talk to you later."

The line dissolves in static as she shouts, "Wait…but I didn't get…what should I tell Wharton?"

After hanging up, I sit back in the airplane seat and press my thumb on the inside of my wrist to take my pulse. I didn't need a second hand to tell me that my heart was speeding. Shattered nerves? Lack of sleep? Or the plane vibrating? I summon the stewardess, order coffee, then wave it away when it comes. I don't need caffeine, what I need is a Xanax. I reach inside the side pocket of my purse for the small brown plastic bottle, and immediately have trouble coordinating the delicate maneuver—pressing down with the heel of my hand and unscrewing the cap—simultaneously. Kidproof? More likely everyone-proof. Finally, hands quivering, I shake out a precious white oval. A half usually worked, but not today. I pop a whole one, and then another.

The scene in the newsroom is playing over and over in my head and I'm fuming all over again. The nerve of him to humiliate me by ignoring me. Then, after reducing me to shrieking at the top of my lungs like a crazed harridan, and making a spectacle of myself, to be coolly led into his office, dissed and then abandoned because he disapproved of who I chose to sleep with. Did that Texas jerk with the monumental ego think he was in Mike Taylor's league?

And HELLO, who was *he* to judge *me?* If I critiqued every broad that he had gone to bed with I'd be slim just from flapping my jaws. And to think of all the things I con-fided in him. The manic premenstrual moments when I called and asked him if I'd ever be happy. I cringed at the thought of how I had spoken openly to him of my fears of never meeting anyone. Growing old in my one-bedroom apartment, sleeping alone in the double bed, still interested in *Cosmopolitan* magazine at age forty or fifty (*Get Him and Keep Him In Bed!*) and shaving off a good five years of my age, and far more off my weight (c'mon, everyone does it) if I connected with someone promising in a romance room chat.

Sharing intimate conversations with him came easy then, but now I was in a lather thinking of how I had trusted him and unburdened myself to him. And big brother would just sit there and listen mostly. Except for one time when I complained about a guy standing me up and he jumped to my defense.

"Where does he live?"

"Why?"

"I'll go punch his face in."

Sometimes he offered advice, but more often he was just a sympathetic presence. I was the same way with him. But lately, there was Sharon. Even when I sensed they might have had an argument, he tended to keep it to himself. Men did that...they didn't lift the phone and call a friend.

But now, God, I'd be a complete laughingstock at the paper. The answer was to never go back to that place. How could I ever hold up my head? I never want to look at that SOB again. Let the paper go under, him with it. I'm going to be syndicated, I'd survive.

At least the Xanax is starting to work. I could feel it filtering through my blood, calming it, soothing me, like liquid sleep infusing my tissues. Maybe the '90s answer to opium. I thought of Taylor waiting for me when I got off the plane…his beautiful face, that cut, sinewy torso, the way he held me, being in bed with him, being held in his arms, the house, the gardens. He would take me back, take care of me, give me anything I wanted. I'd be happy with him, he was strong, famous, accepting of me. He'd never throw me out, he'd help me. I'd put New York behind me…and I'd be happy…at last. My eyelids fluttered as I slipped under a thick narcotic blanket. I wanted to sleep that way forever.

I had no idea how long the flight attendant had been tapping on my shoulder. In the dream someone was saying, "Miss, miss…" I was lost, immobile, there were gardens, the blue Pacific, somewhere in the background a movie projector….

"We've landed."

"I drifted off…I…"

"Are you all right? You look a little pale."

"Fine…oh…just wiped out…" I reach into my bag for a compact, and then look at my face. Cadaver chic. I dust on blusher and then more, and then stop and quickly wipe it off. What was I thinking? Full faces didn't need blusher, I knew that. I switch to lipstick, add mascara, then pinch my cheeks. Wake up! The sun was shining, why not? I get myself up and pull my bag over my shoulder. One last look around, and I walk down the aisle.

It's so odd to be returning now. Would I drop into his arms like nothing happened? What would we talk about? Where would I sleep? Was Jolie out for good? I didn't hate the girl. I wanted to at first, but I didn't. How could I? Not enough there to hate, really. Aside from her packaging, she didn't lead an enviable life. She was an unhappy model, a bulimia graduate in love with a guy who didn't love her back. She had the looks, nothing more. What was to envy? *How was your day, Jolie? Was the lighting bright? How many rolls of film did the photographer go through? Did you wear coral lipstick? Pink?*

My mind is shutting on and off. I'm trying to stay alert, figure things out, but my body is leaden, oblivious, opting to float off. The sun blinds my eyes, and I try sunglasses. God, just to sit down again, rest. I don't see him now. Where *is* he? Couldn't he even get here on time to pick me up? I think of the cartoon I had on my refrigerator— a bride and groom coming out of the church and she turns to him: "You know, you're really starting to get on my nerves."

I head toward the waiting line of cars, weaving in front of a midnight-blue Jaguar, then stepping aside to avoid a red Range Rover that comes to a screeching halt.

Then, in the distance, I spot the T-shirt with the *High Life* logo. Its model wears it well, of course. The relaxed posture, and the tanned face warming as he smiles. I step toward him, my ankle inadvertently twisting slightly due to the weight of the bag. "Dammit!" I wobble to the side, nearly tripping, then catch myself and regain my balance. This is not going as planned.

He bolts toward me, reaching out for support. "I recognize you now."

"Déjà vu all over again."

He takes my face in his hands and studies it. "You okay?"

"Mildly tranquilized, otherwise terrific." I'm trying for upbeat. "Didn't get much sleep in the last twenty-four hours. So one—no two—measly little Xanax hit me like a grenade." He leads me to the car, throws my bag in the back, and holds the door open.

"Well, forget the pharmaceuticals, and just sit back and enjoy the ride."

I am not the kind who does impulsive things. No one would ever describe me as "flighty." Sober, more likely. Levelheaded. I'm a list maker, I use lined yellow legal pads, every item numbered according to priority. I have a collection of highlighters so that key items are neon green or creamsicle-orange. I also have Filofaxes with business cards in plastic sleeves, "to do" lists, subway maps, street address locators, area code directories. I do research. I'm methodical about checking with multiple sources for every new theory committed to paper. The corrections column rarely, if ever, includes items about inaccuracies in my column unless they result from hasty surgery made by editors on deadline who, in effect, removed the wrong kidney. Millions of readers go over my copy, the topics I write about are painfully familiar to so many that I can't afford to be sloppy, or worse, wrong. I could do bodily harm. I make a point of following that old rule of journalism: If your mother says she loves you, check it out. So I always take the time to make that last call. I'm conscientious, methodical.

So how does a person like that, who, except of late, buys Ferragamos that you can actually walk in, who buys all-purpose Nike cross-trainers, who wears black jackets instead of white ones that would show food stains board a plane without giving a second thought to terrorism, hijacking, engine failure or simply the obscene price of a plane ticket purchased last-minute? Well, maybe that was the old me, the one who was plodding and predictable.

The new one would be free of those kind of restraints. From this day forth, I would be carefree, devil-may-care. I'd live life on a whim. Go wherever the urge took me.

Taylor glances over at me. "HELLO! You're miles away."

"No, I'm here," I say, reaching out and rubbing his hard shoulder. What better reality check?

"Let me guess," he says. "You're reexamining your life right about now."

"Is this the Edgar Cayce Airport pick-up special? You're now going to play clairvoyant and see into my mind?"

"That's right," he says. "Here goes: You're going over the past twenty-four hours of your life, and now wondering what the hell you're doing here."

"Thank you, I already have a shrink for that."

"You know what my advice is? Enjoy the moment. That's all we have."

"And today's the first day of the rest of my life." I close my eyes. Did Hallmark cards sponsor his series? I turn and stare out the window.

He swerves the car over to the side of the road and sits there looking straight ahead of him. Slowly he turns to me.

"Where are we going, Maggie?"

Unconsciously, I draw a hand up to my mouth like a prepubescent kid and bite at a hangnail, only, this one's on the end of a perfectly painted scarlet fingernail. Why was there always a wily nub that defied all your efforts to nip it off?

I reach over to him and lift his sunglasses slightly, peering into his eyes. "I don't know, Taylor." His expression softens and his face breaks into a smile.

"So is my house gonna become a shelter for runaway journalists?"

"Mmm…a safe haven where you keep lost souls until someone comes to claim them and give them a proper home."

He shakes his head in despair. "You're screwed up, baby."

"Don't just beat around the bush, Taylor. Come out and say what you think."

twenty

The beach is a barren landscape that belongs just to us in the late afternoon. We sit wrapped in a blanket, drinking champagne. Lucky for us he had a bottle stashed in the trunk. There are no cups so we pass the bottle back and forth.

"I never chug-a-lugged champagne."

"It's the best way to get drunk," Taylor says.

"Is that what we're trying to do?"

He shrugs. "It helps to break through the reality barrier. French truth serum," he says, hoisting the bottle. "You start speaking your mind, but it comes out in French so no one can understand what the hell you're saying."

That strikes me as the funniest thing I've ever heard. I laugh so hard that tears well up in my eyes, and Taylor leans over and licks them away. We're lying under a blanket tent, blotto.

"We can't drive home like this."

"Let's nap here for a while," he says groggily. I move closer to him and never see the sun set. When I wake up, not really out of my fog, it's one in the morning and there's a brisk wind. I lay back, listening to the comforting rhythm of the water slapping against the sand. Taylor's curled up in a fetal position, dead asleep. It feels like we're on some lunar landscape away from civilization.

"Taylor," I whisper. "We have to go. It's late."

He doesn't move.

"Taylor." I nudge him.

He opens his eyes and looks at his watch. "I was comatose," he says, rubbing his eyes. "Not used to the fresh air."

Slowly we get to our feet, dragging the blanket and the empty bottle. In the darkness, we weave toward the parking lot.

"I left it around here, didn't I?" he says, scratching his head. No one has a worse sense of direction than I do. Whenever my instincts tell me to go left, I go the opposite way, and I'm usually right.

"I thought so," I say. "But it is probably further down." We walk another few hundred feet or so, afraid to look at each other, and then continue walking. Finally, we're at the end of the lot, with nothing but the ocean on one side and the highway on the other. There isn't a car in sight. We look at each other without saying anything. There's no way to get back.

It's one thing to lose your car, and another to lose your identity. Whoever took the car now has the registration, Taylor's wallet, his license, money, credit cards and his phone. The only thing in his pocket is a used tissue and about thirty-five cents in change.

"Just great," he mutters.

I know better than to say anything when a man is furious. Fortunately, I have my bag with me, with a phone and some money. I hand it to him.

"Call the police," I say, hoping that we won't have to hike home. Why the hell had I worn high heels?

He shakes his head. "We're both shit-faced, we look like we slept here for a week. It's not the most opportune moment to report a theft. Let me see if my agent's around."

His agent was in New York. "Shit," he mutters.

He punches in another number and waits while it rings. "Shit."

Then another and another.

After the eighth call, something about our situation strikes me as funny. No, hysterical. I start laughing and can't stop.

"I'm glad you think this is so hilarious, sweetheart," Taylor says. "I have to be at the studio at the fucking crack of dawn."

"I'm sorry, it's just that this is so surreal. I mean, just stand away from it." I wave my hand in a wide arc. "Water water everywhere and not a drop to drink. We're literally at sea." I laugh even harder.

"You lost me," he says. He picks up the phone again.

I wait while the phone rings and finally hear a soft female voice.

"Nicole, it's Mike… I'm okay, sweetheart, yeah. I know it's two in the morning. Listen, I need a favor."

There are times when you need a handful of cookies for comfort. And other times when the whole bag won't be enough.

Nicole Cervantes was a redheaded, nubile Brazilian sex

kitten with breasts as big as Corcovado. Hollywood took a liking to her on sight, and within months she had a three-picture contract with Miramax. Somewhere along the way, hers became one of the phone numbers that Taylor knew by heart.

"She's just a friend," he says, dismissing the question. The dreaded *f* word. I take his answer as a conversation stopper, and sit on the roadside, hugging my knees, wondering what kind of car the savior from Ipanema will be driving. The answer flies around a curve coming to a hair-raising screech that creates a cloud of dust. She is behind the wheel of a fire-engine-red Mercedes with white leather upholstery.

"Get in," she yells, "I can't get out, I'm not dressed."

Where was Tamara when I needed her? Taylor offers me the front seat, but I shake my head and climb into the back.

"Only for you," Nicole says, flinging her orange Hermès Kelly bag from the front seat over into the back, barely missing my thigh as it barrels to the floor.

"I was about to go to sleep," she says, reaching over to pull Taylor toward her by the back of his neck. She brushes his lips.

"Mmmm," she says, licking her lips.

A moment later, she flicks on the ignition.

"Thanks for saving us," Taylor says, patting her shoulder. "My car disappeared." He turns back and introduces me.

Nicole nods perfunctorily without fully turning her head.

"Your place?"

"Thanks," he says, nodding hastily.

I cross my legs and stare out the window. Did this man know any normal woman, except for me? His life was a fucking Victoria's Secret runway show. I'm furious at myself for being mad. Why was it that these bimbos always brought out the worst in me? Ten years of therapy vitiated, without a trace. I was back in junior high school, watching the cheerleaders as I hid myself in the last row of the gym.

On the hill, Taylor jumps out and punches in the code. I glance at Nicole through the space between the seats. Is it my imagination or has the terry bathrobe inched down her shoulder? I catch a glimpse of a small heart-shaped tattoo, and then follow the drape of the robe and notice that it's not doing a great job of covering her thighs. God, I hate this. I turn back to the landscape. Taylor is rambling on about who was cast in his new movie, and something about that is funny to Nicole, who offers a rich throaty laugh. I keep my finger pressed on the button to lower the window as far as it'll go.

In front of the house, I climb out first. Taylor lingers a moment, turning to Nicole. "I really appreciate this. I owe you," he says.

God, just slip her a twenty.

"I'll remember that," Nicole says, fucking him with her eyes.

I head toward the house. I better get used to it.

Should I call the office? It was overdue. I lift the receiver and hold it against my chest, staring off. Slowly, as though I'm coddling a Fabergé egg, I put it back in the cradle. What was there to say?

I heard Taylor leave for the studio after what seemed to be fifteen minutes, not a night's sleep, and when I get up hours later, I walk around the house trying to acclimate myself again to where I'm now…staying? Living? I peer into room after room, trying to imagine that it's mine. But that entails envisioning the accompanying lifestyle, and my imagination doesn't stretch that far. I dream about a second bedroom or maybe or a third. New countertops. A suede couch. No sane person imagines relocating to San Simeon.

I walk into the kitchen and yank open the heavy door. I stand bathed in the heavy blast of frigid air, and pick through the fruit bin until I find a firm apple. Should I take it upon myself to clean out all the now-aged gourmet treats, or was that something to jot down on the maid's to-do list? I slam the door and walk upstairs to the desk where I left the laptop. I start making calls, but when the secretaries of sources ask for my number, I'm evasive.

There was the gym, and no excuse to not work out, so I spend New York's lunch hour exercising. When it's L.A. time for lunch, I start a column and make a note to check a few facts before sending it in. Now what? No office buddies to chat with. No Bloomingdale's a cab ride away to buy mood-lifting cosmetics. So I do what everyone in L.A. does. Taylor's castoff Lexus is parked in the Siberia section of his garage, and the keys, conveniently, are in the ignition.

The traffic on the Los Angeles Freeway is gridlocked due to a collision that seems to be a quarter of a mile ahead. Three or four cars have crashed into each other and there are flashing lights and the sirens of approaching police. If only I had the company of a book on tape. I check the glove compartment, but it's empty, except for a half-empty bottle of Poland Springs and a pair of sunglasses.

I think back to my conversation with Tex, just after Taylor first called. The freeway, the freeway, what an oxy-

moron. Was this what I had to face every time I had to go
somewhere? After ten minutes of immobility, with cars
lined up all around, I'm growing more and more aware that
I have to find a bathroom, and that any minute now the
achy sensation I'm feeling below my waist could mean my
period. Suddenly it feels as though a vise is tightening
around my neck.

I have to get out of this, but how? I can't just change my
mind and make a U-turn. Absentmindedly, I turn on the
radio. The sports reporter is giving the scores of college
football games nationwide. One after another. Were they
covering every damn game? Who cared if Delaware's Blue
Hens lost? I change the station—hating the damn digital
dial—looking for music, calming music, but there is only
rock, then country twanging about a lost love and the
heartache. I switch it off and try to pay attention to the road.
Nothing to get excited about, this is only temporary, the
cars would be moving soon, but my heart isn't buying it.
What if it took hours? Could you airlift cars to get them
out of the way?

All of a sudden I'm feeling these electronic pings in the
middle of my chest that are like misguided bleeps on a
heart monitor. I've never had this before. Is it PMS? Cardiac arrest? I see myself lying in an intensive care unit with
only a black screen at my side; on it, a white electronic
line is making scribbles that defy a predictable pattern.
Wild needle lines. Next to that machine would be another
that looks like the bowl of a Cuisinart with an air pump
inside it, and a black screen with a pulsating needle that
scribbled the kind of cardiac graffiti that would summon
the entire staff if they needed to jump-start my ailing
heart.

Take it easy, take it easy. This is probably what every-body out here goes through. It's the workday version of their tension headache. So why is a film of sweat soaking my blouse? Even my armpits are stinging, as though the deodorant is acid, eating into my pores. Did I even re-member to put it on this morning? I can't remember now. I grope for some tissues in my purse and start mopping my forehead with a shredded, disintegrating wad, lint float-ing in the air like anthrax spores. Why didn't I buy the nice neat pack of Kleenex? Why do I always end up with a wad? Is it my imagination or am I short of breath?

A wave of panic sweeps over me. Was this a heart attack, or just fear? The odds were against it being a heart attack, but why not? Things happened. Eighteen-year-old con-ditioned athletes keeled over inexplicably, even junior high school kids who were never sick in their lives. Heart valve problems, preexisting conditions, who knew what else? I start talking to myself as though I'm a small child. Do I look crazy to people in the next lane? Who cares, anyway, they probably think that I'm just on the phone. "You're fine, you're just fine," I say out loud. "Just a little scared, that's all. It will pass. You're fifteen minutes from Taylor's house, as soon as you're there you'll be fine. It has just been a tense week. It's the Xanax, the lack of the sleep, the tension.... You can handle it, it will be over soon. You'll have dinner with Taylor, wine, and everything will be fine."

But then the questions. What would happen to me now? My throat tightens. What would my life be like here? Was this it? What kind of life would it be? And what about my mother? She was so far away. Who would take care of her? That tremor, oh God, what if she was devel-oping Parkinson's disease? It never occurred to me before.

At a time like this, I leave New York and fly across the country? How selfish. What if she had to be moved to a home? And some of those places were so awful. The neglect. My heart starts to pound harder. To calm myself, I try to take deep breaths. In through the nose, out through the mouth. Relaxing breath. Does that nonsense do any good anyway?

When traffic finally starts to move, I get off at the next exit and at the first turn, I swerve the car to the curb. A sign says Dead End.

I reach frantically into my purse for my phone, throwing aside mints, a tampon, a compact. I dial Tamara, then start over. I forgot to punch in the area code. The battery is low. Did I even pack the charger? I must be losing my mind. Why the hell hadn't I at least charged the phone overnight? I dial again.

"Maggie O'Leary's office."

At the sound of Tamara's voice, I try to speak, but all the tension rises up into my throat. Tears well up in my eyes, and the only sound that comes out is an odd cry, like the croak of some wounded creature. Then it turns into a sob.

"Maggie? MAGGIE? IS THAT YOU?"

Somehow, I get the word *yes* out.

"WHAT IS IT? WHAT IS IT, BABE? TAKE IT EASY, TAKE IT EASY."

"I— I—" More crying.

"Maggie, TAKE A DEEP BREATH. CALM DOWN. YOU'RE OKAY. I'M HERE WITH YOU… Maggie? I don't know if it's the connection or you that's breakin' up."

I catch my breath. "I'm okay, really." Deep breath. "I think I was just having a meltdown."

"Maggie, get on the next plane and come home. I never

understood what the hell you left this place for anyway. Go directly to the airport and just wait for the next plane out. There's gotta be fifty a day. Just book the first one and—"

"I'm okay, really. I can't come home now…. I just can't."

"Why not?"

"It doesn't make sense. I just got here, I…we…have to give it time…. I can't just go flying from one city to another like an unguided missile…"

"Yes, you can, Maggie. What are you saying? You have a life here…you'll find another job…."

"What? I'll find another what? WHAT DID YOU SAY?"

"Maggie, you missed the column. There was nothing in the paper where your column was supposed to be."

"You didn't get the column I filed?"

"You heard me."

"But I sent it, it went through…. I never got anything back from you."

"Maggie, your head is somewhere else. There was a black hole where your column should have been. You haven't returned Wharton's thousand phone calls, and now the column's kaput. Finito."

"But I SENT IT, Tamara, I swear."

"Wharton is thinking of having Justine write it and renaming it 'Thin Chance'—"

"Did you hear me? I SENT—"

"Maggie, any day now, he's going to put the announcement in the paper."

"WHAT? WHAT? WHAT ARE YOU TALKING ABOUT?"

"He gave up on you, babe. Maybe you filed, but he never got it, and that did it. He was fed up. You're out of touch, nowhere to be found and...." The line filled with static and went dead.

"You're breakin' up again," Tamara said. "Maggie? Maggie, you there?"

I don't remember starting the car, but I find myself driving along the Pacific Coast Highway, staring out at the ocean. Like an automaton, I turn off the ignition and walk down to the beach where Taylor and I had spent the afternoon. It's familiar turf, like a tiny safe haven, only, now it's just me. The weather is perfect, as if in ironic direct defiance of my state of being. As usual, I'm out of sync, living in some parallel universe. But I'm grateful that very few people are around. I don't want to pretend to act normal.

Whenever I have to sort out my feelings, I write them down. It forces me to concretize the angst, gives it form, substance. I'm carrying a pen and paper and now it seems like a luxury to see my words on real paper instead of an electronic screen. There's more comfort in the deliberation of the effort. It's like sweeping a floor with a broom rather than using an electronic vacuum. More soothing, less mechanical. And if you didn't get the words down on paper right, there was a certain satisfaction in crumpling up the sheet rather than deleting words as if there never was a paper trail of false starts at all.

SOS

This won't be a comforting column, or one offering counseling or advice. It isn't written with a steady hand in a sane frame of mind.

It's a column about needing help in sorting out my life.

There are times when the body is smarter and quicker than the mind. It stops you in your tracks by sending out Mayday signs: Flashing red lights in the form of a quickened heart rate and an erratic beat. Biomechanical sirens like body sweat, nausea, pressure in the chest. A feeling of being cornered, panic-stricken and overwhelmed by the sensation of impending doom that cuts into your gut. It's a biological meltdown, better known as a panic attack.

I was driving on the Los Angeles Freeway, trapped in my car, in a gridlock of traffic. I was overtired and overstressed, just a few days after crossing three time zones on the way from New York. I live a life based on deadlines and watching the clock, consumed with the world of being overweight, and negotiating a path to happiness and fulfillment despite the burden of such a handicap. No one knows better than me that bouncing between the worlds of the possible and the impossible is a rocky road.

I tried to radically change my life three months ago. I wanted to get rid of all my excess weight. I wanted to look thinner, prettier, sexier and more appealing. I wanted to get to the point where I could attract a gorgeous-looking man. So I turned myself inside out. Every day, for three months, 24/7, I ate differently, exercised, tried every beauty treatment known to man, denied my body chemistry and vowed to triumph over nature. I thought that I had a new body and that made me a different person. That invincible new me sought to start a new life, and forget about the past. But you can't deny who you are, and if you do, it will eventually come back to bite you.

I tried to run from myself and my problems by taking refuge somewhere else, but rather than saving myself, I was more lost than ever. My body knew that before my mind did.

What happened? I panicked.

I felt lost, abandoned, filled with a fear that was greater than any I ever felt before. I saw myself living in a world of imagination, an observer of the real world outside of myself.

Panic attacks don't last forever, but they last long enough to give you a message that you can't ignore. I can't run away from who I am or where I live. That sounds so simple now, but it took me a three-thousand-mile trip that ended inside myself to see that.

My life started out like a windshield with a small crack in it. But rather than attending to that tiny fissure, I ignored it, and the crack wormed its way up, down and around until the damage was so widespread that just a final tap—a traffic jam on the freeway—was enough to shatter my fragile self to smithereens. But I've got the inner resources to survive a panic attack and learn from it. I'm

stronger for it. And whatever else happens, the memory of it will be there to remind me of what happens when I'm at war with myself and I'm losing the battle.

I tear off the piece of paper, fold it up and wedge it into my pocket. It's calming to just stroll along the beach, watching the water glittering in the sunlight. There's an old discarded beer bottle sticking out of the wet sand and I pick it up. The glass is smooth as beach glass from the gritty wash of being pelted over and over and over by the wet sand. Beaten up by life. I hold it by the neck, then reach into my pocket and take out the paper. I wedge it down into the neck of the bottle, and then lift my arm into an arc and pitch it out to sea with as much power as a Roger Clemens fastball. It soars through the sky before dropping down into the water, disappearing below the surface.

Dear Mike:

I hate long portal goodbyes and anyway we did that. Thanks for the temporary safe haven, for the affection, and the willingness to put up with me. My job's on the line in New York and if I'm not back by the morning, the only place my name will be appearing will be on unemployment checks. I'll never forget the champagne on the beach, but I'll try to forget Nicole and the disappearing bathrobe. I never was one to share my toys.

Love,
Maggie

P.S. I can't wait to see Dangerous Lies. *(Do I get a screen credit?)*

P.P.S. Clean out your refrigerator before it turns to gourmet penicillin.

twenty-one

I head up to his office without stopping at my desk—if it's still mine—and barge in. The shocked expression on his face makes it painfully clear I'm the last person on earth he expected to see.

"THIN CHANCE?" I blurt out in disbelief as I'm dropping into the Christmas-plaid chair directly facing Wharton. "You were going to give away MY column—or should I say OUR column—and call it 'Thin Chance'?" I'm hyperventilating, pressing my hand at the base of my neck. What have I got to lose, either he'll hire me back or call security and have me handcuffed. Wharton stares for a moment, a mixture of amazement giving way to relief. Finally his stern expression softens.

"Are you staying here now or have you become, in the jargon of the day, 'bicoastal'?"

"I love this city, for God's sake, you know me better than that, I would never ever leave."

"Well, you could have fooled me. I tried to reach you over and over again but—"

"I'm back, Bill, back. I was exhausted. Back and forth over the time zones was just…the lines got crossed." I wave my hand as if to clear the air.

"Lines got crossed? Maggie, we were waiting for a column—"

"Anyway that was then and this is now," I say, not letting him finish because I couldn't own up to the realization that I was so distracted that for the first time in my career I forgot to file. "And I'm so anxious to—"

"I don't know, Maggie, I've started to set things in motion now to replace the column. I don't know if I can just reverse—"

"Bill, you've been like a father to me, a mentor. If *you* hadn't originally conceived of this column and shaped it—practically laid it out from *A* to *Z*—we wouldn't be leading the papers in this city, and probably the country, in health coverage."

His color is rising—what man didn't succumb to shameless flattery? "So why sabotage that success by changing the whole gestalt of our column? America doesn't need to kill more trees to read about the thin perspective. The news is fat. It's spreading worldwide—Christ, obesity is rearing its ugly head in New Guinea, even the Cook Islands. Nobody was fat there twenty years ago. It's a global issue! How could you possibly turn the clock back and change the entire focus of your brilliantly conceived column that could well set us up for a Pulitzer—"

"Well, I haven't put anything into the paper yet…" He looks off as if he's trying to come up with some face-saving proposal. "If you're truly through traveling, and ready to put in the time again—even more time now to right things—I suppose I could reinstate the column." His round face slowly wrinkles into a smile.

"Great, great, done." I jump to my feet. "Why don't we have lunch. I feel like celebrating. God, I'm so starved already. What time is it?"

Wharton looks at his watch. "It's only ten-thirty. Why don't we say twelve?"

"Great," I say nine more times before walking out. "We'll celebrate the rebirth of the column and the rest of my life." I turn and see him cocking his head to the side, not sure of what he just heard.

Weightier Issues

While my weight is sure to go up and down, because of my odyssey I'm now more certain than ever before of who I am. I feel that I truly like the person inside me.

The weight matters less than my personality, my soul, my spirit. I accept myself more, and so I feel closer to my readers—heavy or thin—in their daily struggles with obsessive eating, and the emotions that surround it. Yes, I do love food, I always will. But I also love the body that it goes into, and I now promise to respect it more. I vow to move more, exercise, work the machine because it was created that way. Left immobile, the body would wither away, like a vestigial organ.

You'll also hear more from me now about the very real dangers of obesity. That said, I still feel strongly that the health risks should not push the overweight to suffer through punishing regimens that doom them to short-lived successes and long-term weight cycling. It makes far more sense to forget about dieting, and simply make modest but long-lasting changes in lifestyle that you can live with. (And yes, you can replace sodas with just plain mineral water.) Your body is your physical reality, you have to live inside it, in peace and serenity.

And, lastly, don't forget—you don't have to be perfect to be loved.

I sign off and call out to Tamara. I haven't seen her since I came back.

"Tamara? T A M A R A? Hey—anyone around here know what happened to my sidekick?"

Justine is passing my door and sticks her head in, staring at me incredulously. "You're here?" she says.

"Obviously."

"You should have told your secretary," she says snootily.

"What do you mean?" I'm getting nervous now.

"She's on her way to L.A.," Connors says coolly.

"What? What for?"

"To rescue you, my dear. She said you needed help, and she left here with fifty dollars she borrowed from *me,* and a bran muffin from the coffee cart." I stare back at her, not knowing what the hell to do now. Then it hits me and I start dialing Taylor's private line.

He answers the phone, but he doesn't sound like himself. Is he coming down with a cold? Did I just wake him out of a dead sleep?

"You gotta friend named Tamara?" He's pissed.

"Mmm," I say. *"Pourquoi?"*

"The *pourquoi* is that she just punched me out, and I can't stop my goddamn nose from bleeding."

"What?"

"I answered the door in the middle of the night and this girl with a camera is standing there. She says she's looking for you."

"Oh no." My eyes are closed.

"Oh yes. She seemed to think I wronged you in some awful way."

"There were all these crossed signals, Taylor. I am sooo sorry." I'm afraid to ask my next question, but do anyway. "It's not broken, is it?"

"No," he says. "I guess I should be thankful."

"You should be thankful that I'm gone."

"Well, you've got devoted friends," he says. "She called you the sweetest lady on the face of the earth, and then called me a miserable son of a bitch for making you so upset."

"She didn't quite get the full story," I say, pushing out my cheek with my tongue.

"Listen, I gotta get more ice," Taylor says. "I'll talk to you later, Maggie."

I hang up and get into a cab.

Tamara looks as if she hasn't slept for days as she stumbles through the front door of her building, barely nodding hello to the doorman. She approaches the elevator, then she stops in her tracks and does a double take. I'm sitting on the lobby couch, where I've been parked for the past three hours.

"Maggie. *Maggie?*"

"Welcome home." I'm up on my feet and we're looking at each other eye to eye.

"I figured out how to get thin," she says, letting her bag drop.

"Oh?"

"You live on plane food."

"That so?"

"Yes, ma'am. The economy-class diet—limp vegetables, soggy pasta, tough meat. You take a bite of each then leave the rest over. It couldn't add up to more than a hundred calories, according to my calculations."

"I'll use that." My toe starts tapping then, the culmination of a three-hour anxiety fit. Tamara and I just look at each other. "So, ah, been anywhere interesting?" I say, cocking my head to the side.

"Yes, I've been chasing down movie stars.… Wait till you see the pictures. Bloody great. Living color."

"And why is that?"

"Money, fame…no," she says, stamping her feet. "For you, Maggie. I…you're my best friend, Maggie. And I couldn't stand the idea of losing you, and you losing yourself. I went out there to help…to bring you back."

"Oh God. To what?"

"To…your senses?"

"You're the only one left who thinks I have any." I'm smoothing the lapels of Tamara's jacket, nodding my head, and then I throw my arms around her neck and hug her. We're both crying, and I'm not sure why, but then it hits me that there isn't anyone else in the world that I know who would do what she did—not counting the punch in the nose.

"So which one of us is crazier?"

I'm carrying Tamara's bag and we ride up to her apartment. It's almost lunchtime and we're both starving. I go

through her refrigerator, opening up the fruit and vegetable bins and looking behind the cartons to the back of
the shelves.

"In the old days we would have eaten now, right?"

"And how," she says.

"We probably would have boiled up a pot of spaghetti,
thrown together a tomato-and-pepper sauce with some
pepperoni, made an arugula and radicchio salad, cut open
some Italian bread and slathered it with butter and tons of
garlic and toasted it to perfection. And for dessert, we
would have had some coffee Häagen-Dazs, with crumbled
chocolate chip cookies on top."

"That's right," Tamara said. "In the old days."

"What the hell, you want to eat?"

She starts to laugh. "You don't have to ask me twice."

"I mean after all we've gone through, at least we deserve
a decent meal, right?"

"Nobody ever got fat on just one meal," Tamara says.

"Who said that?"

"You did."

"Don't quote me to me." I take a bottle of white wine
out of the refrigerator, pour it into two glasses and offer a
toast: "To what happens to the best-laid plans."

If readers were interested in my personal life before
California, afterward, it reached a new high. The major-
ity of letters applauded my honesty and openness. (They
should only know.) I showed myself to be as vulnerable to
the desire to be thin as they were, they said. (A good share
of readers said they only wished that they had the same
gorgeous motivation as I did to change.) Many were eager
to follow my lead and said that they would consider ex-

ercising. But now I also had a little hate cabal out there, and those letters were mean-spirited, vitriolic and bitter. One was cc'd to the Catholic Archdiocese. So much for sainthood.

I filed the hate mail away. Maybe Tex was behind it. Probably had a voodoo doll made in my image with a charm around its neck. I hadn't seen him since I was back. It would be interesting to see how he would react to me if we ran into each other in the elevator. I thought about calling him, and then decided against it. Did I dare go to see him? Repeat the mortifying walk I had made up to his desk? Why not? No one at the paper would ever say, "Maggie? Maggie who? No, I don't recall ever meeting her." Whatever else they would engrave on my tombstone, they'd never put the word *anonymous*.

I pad softly to the back of the newsroom and crane my neck. This time I wish I'd worn a chador. I couldn't bear the thought of getting the same reception again. Well, whatever. I walk closer, only to come up behind an empty chair. There's a small needlepoint pillow on it: "Out align." *Meant for me?*

"Where's Tex?" I ask offhandedly.

"Tex-as," Larry says. "His mother died."

"Oh." I can't help biting my bottom lip. "I didn't know."

"Yeah," Larry says. "Out of the blue."

"Do you have a number for him?"

"Yeah, except I don't think you'll be able to reach him. After the funeral he's traveling around for a week or so."

"Where?"

He shrugs. "He doesn't always make a point of explaining his whereabouts."

"Sharon with him?"

"Legs? I guess."

Legs? Why do they all have to act like such jerks? "Good to see you, Lar."

"Hey, Maggie," he yells after I start to walk off. "How was California?"

"Out of this world." I get back to my office, grab my coat and decide to take myself out to lunch. Nobody else was offering.

twenty-two

Maybe I'm never going to *not* think of eating and gratification in the same breath, but at least when I go out to eat now, I feel as though I'm holding the reins. I wanted to have an elegant lunch, and since there was no one to share the table with (I passed on lunch with the publicist for Godiva) I decide to enjoy my own company.

Going out to lunch alone at a restaurant that has starched white tablecloths and fresh flowers and waiters who keep their eye on the level of water in your glass, however, means assuming a role. You need to appear confident, secure, using body language that tells everyone around you that you're glad to be by yourself, you enjoy your own company and relish the privacy—isn't it such a rarity? Your carriage makes it clear that you are alone by design, not sheer desperation.

So I make a reservation at a favorite Italian restaurant where the maître d' is savvy enough to greet me with a warm smile instead of the dreaded "table for one?" I stride

back to a banquette along the wall, casually spread my napkin over my lap and raise my eyebrow to signal for the
waiter. No, I didn't bring a book. I wasn't going to bury
my head or distract myself. I was going to stay in the present. I order a mineral water, and then sit back and look
around. Couples mostly, or groups of four. Business meet-
ings, and one pair of starry-eyed hand-holders.

I think about Taylor—his face, then his body—and
then push the thought out of my mind. I did the right
thing leaving. No matter how I looked at it, I couldn't cast
off the image of myself as a Mike Taylor groupie. (He's so
hot!) There could never be equal footing between us.
The celebrity mythology was just too cosmic to go away.
It would always feel like another world to me. And his fans
would always have a greater claim on him than I would.
How many women could he share himself with? The distance between us now helped my perspective.

I scan the menu. Clever eater that I am now, I took the
bite out of my appetite before I left the office by having a
large Granny Smith apple. Sanity would govern my choices.
Salad to start, then chicken lemone with roasted potatoes.
I close the menu. No need to dwell on the options. One
of my pet peeves, in fact, is when people agonize over the
choices, wringing their hands over what to have.

With one hand shielding the spray, I squeeze a wedge
of lime into the sparkling water. The table looks art di-
rected. The lime coordinates with the petite green-and-
yellow pottery pitcher filled with yellow tulips, and next
to it, a tall rectangular bottle of grass-green olive oil. I driz-
zle some out into a little platter, sprinkle it with chips of
coarse salt, and then dip a wedge of thick-crusted Italian
bread into the fragrant oil. A perfect marriage of tastes.

Then, as if a magic spell had been cast over me, I sit back and feel immensely happy.

I'm transported by the surroundings to a small Tuscan hill town—a cerulean-blue-painted ceiling, terra-cotta floor tiles, and ochre walls. Businesses are closed for three hours—it's time for lunch and then siesta with work behind me. Such balance in one's life, such harmony.

I step out of my life and put things in perspective wondering how fate will resolve the conflicts in my life. I remember being a child and plucking a daisy—he loves me, he loves me not, he loves me. Now, though, I'm not sure how I want the game of chance to come out. Still, at this moment, it doesn't matter. I love myself, and there's no one I want to change places with. Being Maggie O'Leary is just fine. Today, in fact, it feels terrific.

I think of my father and the unconditional love that only a parent can offer. He died two years ago, and I carry a little of him around in me. I was special to him. He never said it, but I just knew. Aside from my crazy love life, I knew that he would be proud of what I had done with my life, and how it had turned out. He always believed in me, and it made me believe in myself.

Now, not only has my career skyrocketed, I've come to know a lot more about myself over the past few months, and it had nothing to do with years of therapy. It's from life lessons. I've grown smarter about health, and am unafraid of writing about that, even if it contradicts a lot of the thinking that originally made me popular.

Okay, so I had done a colossally stupid thing by flying to L.A., imagining that I could escape my problems by getting back into Taylor's arms, but there were worse things I could have done. At least I now knew that movie-star looks might be the starting point in a relationship, but not the basis for one.

The waiter arrives with the salad, a massive pyramid of tangled greens, lightly dressed with a vinaigrette dressing. It was a brilliant mix of sweet and bitter greens, as crisp and flavorful as any salad I could imagine. Then the chicken: tender scallops with a lemony glaze. Bite by bite, I eat each golden piece. When the dessert menu is placed before me, I eye it, admire it, and then close the leather-bound book. I sign the check, leave a generous tip and walk out into the midafternoon sun. I decide that I'll start a column, and then visit my mother.

Weight Loss Pays Off

Now there's an economic incentive for losing weight—it pays. The IRS recently weighed in with new sympathy for the overweight. Next time you do your taxes, make sure to deduct your weight-loss expenses as a medical deduction.

This new IRS ruling could well point the way to other institutions—such as insurance companies and federal programs such as Medicare—to foot the bill for weight-loss related expenses as well. But that doesn't mean you can deduct expenses for a fancy health club or a week at the Golden Door. The only accepted deductions will be for weight-loss programs for medically valid reasons.

What does this really mean? For the first time— hooray—the government recognizes being overweight, and the problems that go with it, as a disease.

I turn back into a child every time I climb the stairs to the brownstone. My memories are drawn back to the warm summer nights when neighbors sat out on their patios on aluminum folding chairs with glasses of tea or iced coffee, and dishes of ice cream.

The women, dressed in snap-front housedresses, would gossip about the neighbors, or local merchants. "Ever since they sold Sal's, it's gone downhill," Mrs. McAlary would decree as she held out her leg and studied the varicose veins that crisscrossed it like purple ropes. "They give you less manicotti, and now they charge you for the salads."

I think back to the time the man in the adjoining brownstone died. Mr. Katz. Everyone in the neighborhood, including Sal, came over to Mrs. Katz's house with covered dishes of food. That confused me. Someone had died. Why were they having a party?

I ring the bell and wait. Finally, my mother opens the door and greets me. She's wearing a pink flowered housecoat and matching pink plastic slippers that flap against the back of her callused heels when she walks. She's wearing bright pink lipstick, powder, too. All those times, when I was a child, I remember opening the medicine cabinet and examining my mother's powder like it was some magical beauty dust that only adults were privy to. I liked the smell of it, and the design of the white-and-coral box. It was made by Coty. The puff was caked with pinky beige powder. Rachel. The color sounded like the name of a beautiful girl.

Next to the powder there was a red Maybelline eyebrow pencil—"light"—tweezers, and a deep pink lipstick with a sweet smell. I think it cost about a dollar twenty-nine and came from Woolworth's. I hadn't looked into the medicine cabinet in years, but I was sure that it would look the same, except, maybe, for a new puff.

"Nice surprise," my mother says. I kiss her and smell the powder on her soft cheek.

"I took the afternoon off."

"Come in, I just made coffee, and I have some delicious cookies. There's a lot, I brought home extra for you to take home."

"It's fine, Ma, I don't need them. Just the coffee."

"What do you mean? These are our best cookies."

I'm annoyed already. I walk in and sit at the kitchen table. Nothing ever gets worn or beaten up in my mother's house. Except for a tiny burn on the white Formica table—where I once started to put down a hot pot of soup—nothing was different. I see the familiar plastic bottle of yellow dish detergent on the sink next to a soap pad container that looks like a hollowed-out tomato. I never got the point of that. The dish drainer is white, made by Rubbermaid. How did my mother keep hers clean? Mine inevitably turned yellow.

"So how are things at work?"

"Oh, you know, the same. The column's doing really well. I—"

That makes her laugh. "So now America's happy to be fat?"

"No one's happy about it," I say, shaking my head at her like she's a small child. "But it's a fact of life, and you can make yourself miserable or not. *That's* the point."

She just nods and stirs her coffee, adding one sugar, another, then a third. "Oh, if it were just that easy...."

I look back at her. "Did you ever diet, Ma? Did you ever

want to get thinner so that you'd look sexier so that more boys would like you?"

She looks up and smiles. "In the eighth grade, I came home from school and crawled into bed. I was bawling. I had a crush on a ninth-grader. Vincent DeMayo. Funny how you remember names a lifetime later. Anyway, I was walking with my friend Linda, and somebody whistled. We both turned around, and Vincent looked at me and yelled, 'Not you, tub of lard.' I wanted to die. I went home and all I ate for the next three days was lettuce."

I smile. "And then?"

"After all that I didn't even lose a whole pound. I was furious."

"So what did you do?"

"I told Vincent that if he ever said a mean thing to me again, I'd have my uncle, the butcher, cut him in half with his meat cleaver. And you know what? From then on, he was afraid to look at me."

Maybe we were more alike than I thought.

"Then I met your father." She's sixteen again, remembering. I'm studying her face as it softens, fascinated. I don't remember ever having this kind of conversation with her before.

"He heard what Vincent said and how I threatened him. He came over one day and said he liked women who stood up for themselves. He asked me to go to the movies with him. He said he respected me for that. My character."

"Your character? A tenth-grader said that?"

"Well, he really liked my red hair, but he said something about my personality, too."

I taste a cookie. "Good. Actually, it's not good, it's great."

"We're the best bakery in the neighborhood, no, in

Brooklyn." She looks at me closely. "So why weren't you at work when I called?"

"Oh, it's a long story." I look at her and realize that for the first time, in a long time, I want to tell her. Need to. I want comforting words. "I know you're going to think I'm crazy, but here goes."

"You're pregnant?"

"No, Mother, I'm not pregnant." I stop biting the corner of my nail. I tell her the whole story about Tex, and then about Taylor.

She doesn't respond. Did she hear me? "Mother, I—"

"You're dizzy, Maggie." She starts drumming her fingers on the table, her sign that she's deep in thought.

I look at her and purse my lips. "No, I met Taylor when I was out on the coast. He's very handsome, hard to resist. He's a big star. Then I had this blowup with Tex. I needed to get away…one thing led to another…"

She folds her hands in her lap and just sits there, staring off. "So you run from one, go to another, come back… I don't understand the whole thing." She's holding one hand in the other. "This is the actor from the television show?"

I get up to pour myself some more coffee. "Yeah."

"Is he Catholic?"

I roll my eyes. I don't believe it. "Zen Buddhist. I don't know what he is. Who cares?"

She stares back at me. "You did the right thing to come back," she says, shaking her head. "You're too good for him, Maggie. You can't throw yourself away like that."

"You never said anything like that to me before." I don't know why, but at this moment even platitudes from my own mother are reassuring.

"You'll get your life together," she says, smoothing her

apron. "You're a smart girl, you always were. For some women it just takes more time."

She stands up then and starts putting the dishes into the sink. My family never spent time sitting around at the table. "I have an appointment at the lawyer, Maggie. I have to get ready."

"Why do you have to see the lawyer?"

"I'm closing the business and selling the property."

I just look at her.

"I'm too tired to manage it anymore."

"Who's buying it?"

"A group of Koreans. They own all these nail parlors and—"

"Another stupid nail parlor? Mom, my God, we're like…a fixture in the neighborhood. You can't get a loaf of Wheaten bread anywhere in the world that tastes likes ours and—"

"There's nobody to run the business, Maggie. You girls don't want to run a bakery. What am I going to do with it?"

It feels as though someone were forcing me out of my family house. I stare off into the distance. "I remember growing up in that back room. I had a playpen there, right?"

She shakes her head. "Yes."

"And the back table, that butcher-block table, where we used to eat ham with Velveeta cheese sandwiches for lunch, and cherry scones with milk after school." I shake my head. "I'll never forget how on the holidays they formed a line outside waiting to pick up their orders. Those Irish whiskey cakes, the soda breads, the Cadbury chocolate cookies. I remember loading the boxes the night before. Everyone was exhausted, but it felt good. It was our family business, we were prospering, and after all the work we would close on Christmas Day and stay home together as a family."

"The holidays," my mother says, shaking her head. "It's always such a crazy time."

"We were never home, I was raised in the bakery. All our birthday cakes. Remember Danny, the college kid who helped on weekends? I had such a crush on him. And the time I got mad at Kelly and poured flour over her head? I remember how it landed on her eyelashes. She looked like a snow angel. Daddy wanted to kill me."

"You were a handful."

"That place was like the ying and yang of who I am. I wish I could think of a way to save that place."

"It's been forty years," she says, holding out her hands in resignation. "It's over. I can't work that way anymore. It takes too much energy."

"Do you feel terrible, Ma? I mean, it was your *whole life.*"

"There's a time when you have to let go."

"I was never good at that." There's a stinging in my eyes. I look at the pale wrinkled skin on her face, the mottled skin on her hands and the slight tremor now. "First Daddy, and now this. I don't want to lose that... It's...it's everything." My hands shoot up to my mouth.

"You grow up, Maggie. Things change."

"Were you happy there?" I ask finally.

"Happy?" She contemplates that like it's a new concept. "We worked around the clock, there was no other life." She reaches for a plate and rinses it off before putting it into the dishwasher. "I don't think I ever asked myself if I was happy. Happy? What does that mean? We built up a good business. We had more than our parents ever did." She lets her voice trail off. "But we didn't live in the stars, Maggie. There's…there's no point to it. You have to just live."

"Just live? I'm not sure I know what that means. I want the best kind of life that I can make for myself. I'm right to expect that, aren't I?"

"Well…as long as it doesn't blind you, Maggie, and get in the way of you being happy with everything around you, everything that you have."

I stare out the window, watching plumes of golden light through the gnarled branches of the trees. It was a sight that I had seen so many times before, but now, for the first time, it holds such intense, fleeting beauty that it's almost too painful to look at.

"Yes, you're right," I whisper, "so right." I put my arms around my mother and feel the comfort of her soft, warm skin. "I'm sorry for always giving you such a hard time with everything… I miss you. I miss this house and everything here. I'm so lucky to have this…and to have you. I'm sorry that I take things for granted, Ma…."

"I'm glad you came to visit," my mother says, kissing me on the cheek. "Remember what your grandmother used to say?"

I look at her and smile. "Seeing you makes me rich." I always loved that.

"Go back now before the subways get crowded," she says, looking at me with a concerned expression. I pick up my bag and walk toward the door. I open it, and kiss her one last time. My mother starts to close the door, and then opens it up again.

"So, when are you finally going to bring someone here for me to meet?"

twenty-three

The thick down comforter envelops me like a feathery co-coon. I love down blankets. There's something irresistibly opulent about surrounding yourself with a billowy pillow of feathers. After an hour on the NordicTrack, I've been reading in bed with CNN on the TV, muted, like electronic wallpaper. No matter what I do, at this moment in time my body resists fatigue. I've already taken a hot bath and sprin-kled lavender oil on my pillow. It's supposed to relax you, induce sleep. Maybe I should move on to chloroform.

Truth is, even after my visit to see my mother, I still need to talk. But Tex? Would he still be so pissed at me? Would he care anymore, particularly at a time like this? I wish I knew if he was close to his mother. While women needed to talk out their feelings, men usually clammed up. They went drinking with their buddies, and vented their thwarted emotions by talking loudly about sports, cars or girls. Their shrink was Dr. Bud.

I put my hand on the phone and then hesitate. I try to imagine what I might be interrupting. He's from a small desert town near Odessa, surrounded by miles of dusty roads heading nowhere. His father died years before, so this was the end of the parental buffer that keeps death a generation away. Being around three married sisters didn't necessarily help. In fact, all that noise could make you feel more alone, especially if you were single. Of course he wouldn't be for long. I dial the number, and wait as it rings.

"Hello." Not Tex. Whoever he was had a thick drawl. I hear talking in the background. At least I didn't wake the whole house.

"I'm sorry to disturb you, but I'm trying to reach Tex. I'm a friend of his from New York."

"Hang on there, young lady." I hear a door open and the voice yell, "T E H X." A few moments later, he picks up.

"I'm so sorry, Tex."

There's a silence on the other end for a long minute. "Thanks."

"How long you staying?"

"Not sure."

"Tex. I'm so sorry…about your mother…and everything…I miss you—"

"It's okay, Maggie, I—"

"No, no, it's not. I know this is a bad time for you and I don't want to think that we're not even speaking—"

"Sounds like we are—"

"You know what I mean. I don't want there to be bad feelings between us anymore, I couldn't stand that. I just had so much anger in me for such a long time…." I stop, not sure of what to say. I don't want to go off about me and my problems right now. I can hear him breathing. "I don't know what to say… I'm…different now…"

"So you're saying that you're finally sane?" I can hear a smile in his words.

"Not nearly."

"Well, that's good… I couldn't stand a lobotomized Maggie O'Leary."

"You're my *friend,* Tex. I love you, really…. When are you coming back?"

"I don't know," he says, sounding lost. "I'm seeing this place differently this time. The quiet…the desert…all the space. The roads are so quiet you can drive blindfolded. I didn't know how badly I…I forgot what it was like not to have somebody yelling over my shoulder. And the snakes here are the real kind."

"I wish I could see it," I blurt out, surprising myself.

"Come on out."

"Just like that."

"Why not?"

"I just got back from Los Angeles…. I…I don't know."

"The movie star?"

"Yeah."

"You really stuck on him?"

"I don't know….nnnno."

"Jesus, Maggie, you're even a sicker puppy than I thought."

"Don't be mad at me."

"What difference does that make?"

"You're my friend."

"Is it over?"

"I don't know. Life's complicated…." I slide down in bed

and pull the cover over my head. We're like two kids now, hiding in our tent. "These things happen."

He doesn't say anything.

"Tex, you still there?"

"He's not with you *now*, is he?" he says, in a hoarse whisper.

"He's in L.A."

"He couldn't even pick himself up and fly back with you?"

I just hold the phone, listening to him breathe. Then the tears start, and I can't stop myself.

"Aw, Maggie, stop. C'mon, baby."

I'm sobbing now. "I can't. I know I have a real talent for screwing up my life, Tex, but..." I stop to blow my nose. "But I didn't even have a life before...and I was so messed up and just seething with anger—"

"Maggie?"

"What?"

"I...I gotta go now...Jesus, Sharon's calling me...the priest's here...I'll call you back, darlin'."

"Tex—wait—"

But he's gone. Slowly, I put the receiver back.

It's 4:00 a.m., and I'm lying awake, haunted by thoughts of *Leaving Las Vegas,* a movie about despair, broken dreams and drinking yourself to death. It makes me think about how alcohol is just one addiction on the illusory path to fulfillment, and how food is simply another. Maybe Taylor, a movie star, is cut from the same cloth. A piece of chocolate cake in a human body. I get up and make coffee—strong, espresso—then sit in front of the computer.

Various combinations of those 26 keys of the alphabet inevitably help me get to the root of what I'm feeling.

Dear Taylor:

I owe you more than the scribbled note that I stuck on your refrigerator (under L.A. Lakers magnet) after I suddenly cleared out. You really never had a chance to find out much about your fat tutor/houseguest/short-term bedmate, and probably (why not brag here?) the best cook, I'll venture, who will ever take over your kitchen. The crazy journalist who zigzagged back and forth from New York is a girl who has spent her life wishing on stars (no pun intended). As hard as I try to hide it, I'm easily seduced by fantasy, love stories, romance novels—the cheaper the better. Maybe to some degree that description fits every woman who's vulnerable and emotionally fragile. But I have to confess that I think it also has to do with being a woman who, for her entire life, has punished herself for being fat and unpopular, a woman who suffers from terminally low self-esteem. Clearly, I'm not alone—exhibit A, my decent paycheck for the column.

When your life is perpetually darkened by sadness, disappointment and unpopularity, what do you do? Create a better world that you inhabit in your dreams, a world where roadblocks become opportunities. You become a Victoria's Secret model (with bureau drawers overflowing with lemon-and-lime-colored demibras and matching silk thongs. A world without discolored cotton briefs with full-coverage backs). Men with bodies and faces like firemen—like yours, actually—are everywhere, willing to be seduced. But that fantasy world is actually a trap. Because if real people in this lesser world keep measuring reality against that fantasy, they're boomeranging their chances of ever becoming happy.

Now I know for sure that even men like you drop dirty socks on the bathroom floor, leave the toilet seat up and hair in the bathtub. They turn deaf in front of football games and belch after drinking beer. Like all mortal creatures, they have their limitations. I fell hard for you, or my fantasy of you, Taylor. But I know that we come from different worlds. In truth, I can't summon much interest in the day-to-day world of making movies. My interest is in writing, and getting better at it, not necessarily being more popular. I would be crushed by the full-time scrutiny of the paparazzi. And, Taylor, if I had to contend with screaming fans swarming around you every time we walked out the door, I'd go postal.

That's my side of it, of course. As to how you'd stand me? You probably wouldn't be able to. My body image will probably never change appreciatively, and ultimately, I think that in your rarified world where everyone looks retouched, my wailings about my perpetual failure to live up would start to grate.

Also, at heart, since I'm the type who's attracted to less of a glossy life, what would you do with yourself while I was home researching columns? Go out partying. You realize our percentages for success then, right, gorgeous one?

Then, even though this is a sensitive area, there's the business of marriage and raising a family. I'm getting up there, Taylor, and don't take this personally, but I just couldn't imagine you as the guy who I would want to be the father of my kids. Although you're off the charts when it comes to the DNA for good looks, when it comes to the burden of parenting, where would you be? A back lot in the Philippines filming the next great World War II movie? How would you read the kids a story—over your international cell phone? Am I starting to sound angry and cynical? You see how it's always there, just seething below the surface?

Any way I look at it, Taylor, I think my fantasy world with you would end the moment it began for real. Maybe, in fact, it did. (That second, full-price ticket to L.A. turned out to be cheap at the price.)

Have a wonderful life, Taylor, and I can't tell you how much it means to me to remember that you asked me to stay. Love, Maggie.

I stare at the screen. "Thank you, Michael Dell, for the therapy machine." I press Delete, and the screen goes blank.

At 6:00 a.m. the black sky is slowly fading to gray and then indigo. I climb back into bed and wake three hours later with the sun streaming through the window. I look out at the city sprawled before me. Inexplicably, I look forward to the rest of my life.

Obesity: A Disease or Symptom?

There's no denying it. Thirty-five percent of Americans are overweight, and twenty-seven percent of them are obese. But that said, researchers are coming to the conclusion that obesity means different things for different people, and simply losing weight doesn't turn a fat person into a normal one. While, undoubtedly, many overweight people have the typical risk factors associated with diseases such as high blood pressure, higher than normal blood sugar levels, and high cholesterol, many overweight people do not.

What's more, while it is commonly held that simply losing weight will make one healthier and live longer, studies have shown repeatedly those overweight people who managed to not only lose weight, but also keep it off had—I know this is hard to believe—SUFFERED MORE FROM HEART DISEASE AND A HIGHER DEATH RATE THAN FAT PEOPLE WHO SIMPLY REMAINED FAT! The only question mark, researchers say, is whether the people who lost the weight did so by dieting, or simply lost the weight because they became ill. This is something that the studies don't reveal, and that's why new recruits are being sought by the Institute of Diabetes and Digestive and Kidney Diseases.

I had ignored the calls from the William Morris agent, but they didn't stop. When I picked up my own phone one afternoon, Slim Sharkey was on the other end. The name alone should have put me on alert. But his voice was so smooth that before I could think of a reason to say no, yes came out. He was attractive, I had seen his picture in *New York Magazine,* and he was famous for his high-end deals, so what the hell? The Samovar was hard to turn down, even if I was on a low-octane fitness plan.

Slim Sharkey wasn't his real name. According to the word in gossip circles, he was dubbed Sharkey by a Miramax executive following a lucrative book-movie deal he finagled with a reticent star. A name like Sharkey assumed a life of its own, and he quickly put Richard Millstein—Dick—out to pasture. As to Slim, well, he was, and it seemed to go well with Sharkey.

I spot him sipping mineral water with lime at a lipstick-red leather booth. When I walk in I'm immediately seduced by the opulent decor, styled after the famous Russian Tea Room. Deep red walls, gilded trim, red-pat-

terned carpeting, and chandeliers ringed with gold Christmas balls. What better setting for talking about potential
deals?

He's suited up in Armani—a steel-blue T-shirt under a
slate-gray suit. The second thing I notice is what my
grandmother used to call "a nice head of hair." Dark
brown, longish, carefully layered, with highlights more
subtle than my own, enlivening his tan. He stands and
smiles warmly, extending a hand. "Slim Sharkey." I almost
laugh out loud and think, momentarily, of replying with
"Fat Barracuda."

The requisite banter takes nearly an hour. I show amazing control, slowly enjoying my beet-red, hot borscht
with slivers of veal and beef with horseradish dumplings.
Casually, I bite into one of the caramelized bacon onion
potato pirozhki. Divine. I want thirty more. But no, this
will be my first and only course. No blini with caviar,
crème fraîche and melted butter. No Chicken Kiev that
oozes butter. But yes, I do have a peppery bloody Mary,
and it helps melt away the tension. So do Sharkey's soft
brown eyes that rarely leave mine. You don't stuff your face
when eyes like his are penetrating—or trying to—your
psyche, or something.

He tells me how much he admires my work, and how
I have become a role model for brash, honest reporting.
How my take is fresh, insightful, inspiring, unique. Oh-la-
la, this is tickling my ego. He's a master of the stroke job
and I let him stroke on, entertained.

"I've been around the block, Maggie, and you offer
readers a voice and a conscience like no one else on the
health scene today." He asks about my background, and I
return the questions.

"How long have you been at William Morris? What kind of projects have you worked on?" He talks about his "other" life too, lest I should be left with the impression that all he does is make deals and doesn't have a sensitive side. He keeps a place in St. Maarten for scuba diving, "To get away from the Hamptons scene," he says, and he likes to go up to the Cape.

"Do you know Truro? I hide out there to paint and go parasailing."

"Me, too."

"Really?"

I just laugh, and order another Bloody Mary. By the time I'm ready to lick the soup bowl, the conversation turns to "the deal."

"It struck me one day, after reading your column, after California, that you could do a phenomenal book on how a high-powered New York health columnist's world is transformed by coming together with a Hollywood superstar." He lets his voice slow down, and I'm not sure whether I heard a question mark at the end of the sentence or whether he was just taking a breath and judging my reaction. For lack of something else to do, I shake my head slightly, in acknowledgment. He goes on.

"Readers would love to know how the relationship affected you, how he influenced the way you live, your feelings about yourself...." He lets his voice trail off and, again without a reaction from me, he lowers his voice and looks me in the eyes as if he's about to pull me down under the table.

"It could be very big," he says, letting the edges of his lips curl up slightly.

"A book all about little ole me and Mike Taylor," I say,

with just a hint of a smile. I can't help running my hand back and forth over the leather of the banquette. It's as soft and sensuous as the interior of a Rolls Royce. I don't know if it's the drinks, but I'm suddenly imagining myself lying on the leather without my clothes on. I force my attention back to Sharkey.

"A tell-all book, right?"

He nods just slightly, as if fearful of breaking the mood with words, then adds in a voice so low I can hardly hear, "Any way you wanted to tell it, Maggie. It would be your book. Your *showcase.*"

I'm looking back at Slim, but actually staring through him. What could I tell readers about Taylor? That he was a sweet, decent guy with no pretensions? In the long run, maybe less than meets the eye? But the body—it should be recorded for posterity. Photographed, sculpted. A road map of muscles and strong curves. His presence was compelling, he had great charm, knew how to use his mouth, but? He welcomed Spark notes, cocaine?

Actually, I couldn't recall seeing a single book in his house, except for the coffee-table book on Native American jewelry with the cover color that coordinated with the leather upholstery. The Taylor library seemed to consist of *The Hollywood Reporter, Variety, Details,* the *L.A. Times* sports section and movie scripts.

As far as I could tell, he wasn't a guy, like Tex, who would ever become fascinated with the arcane aspects of a hobby, a story, a sport. Was he really like *The Trainer,* his first movie? The human exercise machine who got you into better shape? Maybe meeting him, and sleeping with him *had* muscled me up. But for what?

I turn to Sharkey. He's waiting for a reaction. I spot him glance, surreptitiously, at his watch under his cuff. It's thinner than a sheet of the pastry dough.

"I'll think about it," I say, finally. "I just don't know."

"That's fine," he says, looking directly at me. "Take the time you need. Just remember, this could be a blockbuster book. A book about diet, romance, celebrity glamour and changing your life. A book that would inspire American women, empower them."

Empower them? I want to punch out people who parrot the jargon of the day.

"Awesome," I say, sliding out of the booth.

---

twenty-four

There are times when work is your salvation. It fills a void in your life and helps remind you that while emotionally you may feel as though what keeps you together is not stronger than a fragile membrane, you continue to stake a claim as… a writer…an accountant…a teacher. You have a purpose beyond sucking wind, exfoliating skin cells, growing dark roots, exhaling carbon dioxide, consuming foodstuffs, and taking up a coveted seat at rush hour on the Lexington Avenue #6 train. At those times the deeper you can immerse yourself in your work, the greater the salvation it offers.

The idea of imparting nutritional guidance to readers, friendship in print, and serving as columnist/shrink, all included in the fifty-cent morning paper made me feel, at that moment, that my existence was justified. I had a purpose. And it was not to *empower* women, or write an account of my relationship with Taylor. It was to report, and act like a sifter—someone who sorted through scientific

material and helped shake it out for readers so that they could use what was new and pertinent.

So when the clock struck 10:00 a.m., I was behind my desk, journals piled neatly at my side, checking health Web sites, reading summaries of the latest research and trying to think of nothing but being a productive journalist. But I'm looking over statistics on the growing incidence of obesity and it doesn't take much to shatter my concentration. From the corner of my eye, I see movement and then I jump back as something saucerlike flies across the room and I nearly tumble to the floor. It's not an extraterrestrial object, however. It's a white Stetson, and it slices through a stack of papers, sending them flying as it comes to a smooth landing on the corner of my desk.

"Souvenir from the Mad Hatter," says a disembodied voice from outside the office door. I look up and wait, trying to hold back the smile that's going to give me away.

"Were you visiting Alice in Wonderland?"

He pokes his head through the door. "It's a hat store near Midland."

I pick it up and turn it around. "I love it." I glance up at him quickly, and then do a double take, as he drops down on the couch facing me. Was it the tan?

"You put it on whenever you're going to cry and you look in the mirror," Tex says. "You'll feel like an idiot and it'll stop you right away."

I hold it to my heart. "I'll wear it to lunch."

"Good," he says, jumping to his feet. "I'm starving, let go."

We head out into the afternoon sun and walk for bloc passing the Plaza Hotel and the towering trees and spray ing green lawns of Central Park that are bathed in the c

lemon glow of afternoon sunlight. Hours go by, and I
can't recall what we talk about, or even if we talk much at
all. I hold on to the sleeve of his jacket, and feel the pebbly grain of the leather brushing the side of my face. We
go into the zoo, and watch a family of monkeys sitting together, one adult picking obsessively at the fur of another,
grooming it, while the babies race around, pursuing each
other. If I had to describe the feeling that I had in just one
word it would be *anticipation.* We walk out of the park,
across to the West Side, past a field where boys in blue-
and-white uniforms play soccer, yelling out to each other
excitedly.

Eventually we end up in a small dim Italian restaurant
and sit across from each other at a corner table covered
with a starched white cloth. I gaze out a small leaded-glass
corner window and watch the world change when seen
through triangles of yellow-, blue- and then rose-colored
glass. After barely glancing at the menus, we order antipasto
and rigatoni. Pavarotti regales us with a sublimely lyrical
"Nessun Dorma" from *Turandot.* What would Calef's fate
be? Marriage to the princess or death?

"A lot has happened since we spoke on the phone," I
say finally. "You won't believe this."

"Try me."

I shake my head. I don't where to begin. "It's just
so...so—"

"I'm waiting..."

I run my hand lightly over the tablecloth and finally look
up, telling him about Taylor, his life, my infatuation and
the need to run away after the scene in the newsroom.

"I couldn't imagine how much being rejected by you
would hurt," I admit, surprising myself with my candid-

ness. Suddenly, I feel like I want to be totally open with him. I don't need to couch what I say in half truths for my own self-respect anymore. We're both past that.

He nods, wordlessly, staring into my eyes, his fingertips forming a tent, pressed against his mouth. He has incredible powerful hands. I think about arm wrestling him.

"You know the funniest thing?"

He shakes his head.

"I just got an e-mail from Taylor. They've delayed the film by six months. He's off to East Africa for a movie about a rubber baron." I shake my head. "My so-called life…. There's so much that I wanted to tell you. I felt so badly about what happened between us."

"Look, I was pretty cruel to you too, so it's okay—"

"No, it's not. Losing the weight was like the beginning of a healing process that I had repressed for so long. It opened up this volcano of emotion. When you lose all the weight you lose some of your identity. It's confusing to change that much. Everything gets harder. The fat excuse is gone and you have to confront new issues."

"You mean you don't just go from fat to happy?" he says teasingly.

"You just go from fat to less fat and still unhappy, but for different reasons. The problems are still there."

"Well, it's reassuring to know that you're still torturing yourself."

"I'm getting better though, but it's something you have to work through. There was just so much resentment that I carried around with me for so long. And I guess you were in the firing range…but it was so stupid. I'm so sorry. I mean, you changed too and I couldn't even give you a simple compliment—"

"I'm tough...don't worry about it."

And handsome, I almost say. I'm seeing that for the very first time. "But now, let's get to you, Romeo."

He closes his eyes.

"Tell me, what's happening with Sharon?" I'm biting my lip.

"Not a lot to tell," he says, shaking his head slowly. "She left Texas a few days after we got there. What she seemed most concerned about was getting up in the middle of the night to reach her global network of clients. I heard her talking one night, and I sat up in bed. Thought she was talking in her sleep, then I saw her whispering into the phone...." He widens his eyes. "She hated the heat, doesn't like the desert. Nothing to do. Couldn't stand barbecue...or outdoor life. First woman I ever met who couldn't even grill a steak. Maybe that should have told me something." I watch him as he looks off, lost in thought, and I wait for him to continue.

"I realized that I didn't want to go after her." He's looking into my eyes now, as if to judge the effects of his words. "I haven't called her since I'm back." He looks down and then back at me. "Remember all the cozy weekends we spent together cooking?" he says, reaching across the table and putting his hand over mine. I catch the glint in his eye and we just stare at each other.

I nod. That small kitchen, but we never got in each other's way. Some of our best conversations came over drinking wine, sautéing vegetables, drinking wine, altering the consistency of spaghetti sauce, drinking more wine. It was our intimate space, I see now, for the first time. Cooking was just a backdrop for us to be together. "We had good times."

"I always thought that we were just friends," Tex says.

"But after the fight and then losing my mother…there was only one person who I wanted to be with."

I'm holding my breath.

"What I'm saying is…we have something pretty special."

"Maybe you just saw me for the first time when I lost the weight."

Tex narrows his eyes. He sees right through me. "Give me more credit than that," he says.

That was familiar.

"That was your issue, not mine. I never cared whether you gained or lost. You were this real woman, and all I saw was a vulnerability that you worked hard at trying to hide."

"And here I thought you didn't understand anything about me except my appetite."

"Maybe that was just our cover."

His blue eyes are breaking my heart right then. He just stares, like a child with no pretenses.

"Well," I say, exhaling, "it's really a terrible idea to get involved with somebody you work with."

"Ma'am, I couldn't agree more."

I pull my hand back from him suddenly. "I'm scared, Tex," I say, hugging myself.

"Of what?"

"What if it doesn't work out?"

"After my aching heart mends I'll write the book *Eating My Heart Out: My short, tragic love affair with Maggie O'Leary,* quit my job and live on the royalties."

"See what happens when I let my guard down with you?"

"Let's get out of here," Tex says, dropping some bills on the table. We walk away from two plates of barely touched food. In the cab I lean against him.

"What did we learn from all this?" he says, lifting my chin so our lips meet.

"That I had the wrong dreams."

I slice an orange and press it down over the rotating blade of the juicer watching a cascade of pale yellow liquid, like watery gold. I use another half, and then another until a blue pottery pitcher is filled. In a copper omelette pan I pull down from the overhead pot rack, I melt a pat of butter and then pour in a bowl of scrambled eggs. French bread is warming in the oven, and I open a jar of thick blueberry preserves and carry it to the table with two tall white mugs filled with French roast coffee.

He comes in behind me and kisses me on the nape of the neck. "A woman in the kitchen making me breakfast," he whispers. "My day's starting out perfect."

"Don't get too comfortable with that."

"Why not?"

"I usually don't do breakfast."

"Well, that's fine, because I usually don't have time to eat it."

Then it occurs to me that I don't want our, now-eighteen hours together to end because we have to go to work. "Let's call in sick."

Tex snickers. "I *am* sick—of that place."

I go to the phone and lift it. "You have to leave the room while I'm calling."

"Why?"

"Because I'm going to crack up laughing."

"I'll sit here and be real serious." He grabs the paper, and I start to dial. When Science's secretary answers, I look up at him and start to laugh. I slam down the phone.

"Stop it."

"Stop what?" he says, pretending that he doesn't know.

"You were smiling! I'm trying to act sick, to make my voice sound heavy and you're sitting there smiling. You're going to get me fired."

"You gotta rehearse," Tex says. "Look in the mirror." He messes up his hair, and slouches toward the hall mirror where he studies himself. Meanwhile, I sneak into the bathroom and make the call. When I come out, he's still standing in front of the mirror.

"I don't feel well," he says. Then in a deeper basso, "I don't feel well today, I'm going to be staying home." He opens the front of his bathrobe revealing some chest hair and turns to the mirror at an angle. "I...I don't feel well today, I'm going to take the day. I'm kinda off today, I have this cough, I'm all congested, I'm going to take the day. I'm just outta sorts today, I'm going to take the day." He says it over and over, in different voices. I start with the giggles and ended up howling.

"Are you trying to sound like Mitchum, Clint Eastwood—or the Count on Sesame Street?"

"C'mon, it's good."

"So call Larry, tell him you're sick."

He starts to dial then collapses laughing, and hangs up. "Wait, wait."

"You can't, you cannot do it."

"'Course I can."

"You can't—so call him. Go ahead."

He dials again. "Larry, hey, how's it going? Yeah, I know, listen something came up, you man the fort today, man, I'll be in tomorrow...yeah, thanks." He exhales a huge boisterous bellow after slamming down the phone.

"You are such a fraud."

"No, I said something came up."

"Yeah, what?"

"God, you're so easy to set up," Tex says, grabbing me.

We wake up again at noon.

"This is like being twenty-one again," Tex says, rolling over. "I think that was the last time I slept this late."

"You can't keep up with me."

Almost unconsciously, I pull the sheet up over me.

"Ever dated a really skinny broad?"

"Oh sure, half the old Ford model agency have slept in this bed."

He's staring at my body, smiling, as though I'm a Renaissance goddess painted by Titian. And for once I'm feeling womanly, curvaceous, overripe, instead of the *F* word.

"I never did like boyish, skinny women," Tex said. "Bony jutting hipbones, small pert breasts. They look sickly to me, emaciated, underfed. No softness, no generous contours, no sexuality…"

He lies back on the pillow with the back of his hand resting on his forehead. He's staring at the ceiling.

"Tex?"

"What?"

Before I can think of what I'm saying, the words spill out. "Do you think you could love me?"

He puts his arm down and turns to me. "I never had a choice."

While deadline is encroaching for everyone else, the two of us are strolling up and down the aisles of Fairway, a West Side food market, examining the lettuce and arugula and squeezing red, yellow and orange peppers to find the firmest ones. We buy the peppers and greens, along with a chicken and asparagus, black olives, elephant garlic and a crusty Italian bread (for him). We're making Mediterranean roast chicken with asparagus and roasted peppers over mixed greens tossed with black olive aioli.

As soon as we walk into the kitchen, he reaches for the wine. "This is where it all started," he says.

"So the weight thing doesn't matter, huh?" I ask casually.

He checks the oven. "Not enough to pinch on skinny broads," he says, sliding the oven mitt along the length of my thigh. "They slip out of your grip."

"I may have met the only man on earth who likes fleshy women."

"You're wrong there, darlin'," he says, slicing up the bread and feeding me a piece. "All the hoopla about being thin comes from women. Real men love tits and ass."

"So eloquently put. Anyway, I still love you."

"Sure you do."

"God, you're so in love with yourself. I can't stand it. I mean, is there something in the soil or the air that makes Texans so plumb proud of themselves?" He grins, putting together the ingredients for the black olive aioli: mayonnaise, garlic, tapenade and lemon juice.

"A rich Texan's hard to resist."

I'm letting that sink in while I finish setting the table. Tex has Fiestaware in, I think, every color ever made. I put out a plum-colored plate for me, and one in lapis blue for him. The salad bowls are yellow and coral. Our wineglasses are made in Mexico and are heavy bubbly green glass that's splashed with streaks of yellow, orange, blue and green. Every time I set the table in Tex's apartment, I feel like I'm getting ready to party.

I walk back into the kitchen, take the asparagus out of the water, cut them up and toss them over the greens. I glance at him, but he isn't giving anything away. I turn to the roasted peppers, slicing them and mixing them in. Tex peeks into the oven to check the chicken, and I walk up behind him and put my hands on his shoulders.

"I'm waiting…."

He smiles, but says nothing.

"Don't tell me you got some huge inheritance."

"Pretty damn good."

"Oil?"

He pivots. "Oil? Did you say oil? Not anymore, darlin'. Those days are long gone." He fills a glass with water and holds it up. "Recognize this?"

I stare. "H2O."

"Yes, water. Water is Texas gold these days, and my daddy's dry, dusty land turns out to have huge underground aquifers."

I'm holding the edge of the kitchen counter to steady myself. "So, now you're going to be even more insufferable."

He takes my hand and we Texas two-step to the table. He lights the candles and we sit down facing each other in the flickering light.

"Want me to give it all away?" he says.

"Fat chance."

Epilogue

Doing It My Way

I can't avoid it forever. Readers are obsessed with how I lost the weight. So much for my success in getting them to accept their fate. Should I describe my methods straight out? Should I try to put all my crazy tips and cheating strategies into a program? Wharton wanted me to tell readers that I would soon publish, "Maggie's Diet." He wanted to sell it as a special pull-out section that they could stick up on their refrigerators. Newsstand circulation would soar, he said, and so would sales of back copies. He even thought about packaging it as a book. But, of course, foremost in his mind were dollar signs, not improving readers' blood lipid levels.

There was the issue of what to call it. Maggie's Mad-Woman Makeover Diet? Maggie's Celebrity-Stalker Diet and Exercise Plan? The Mike-Taylor-Made-Me-Do-It

Diet? Or simply, Cheating On the Job: How a Fat Columnist Lost Weight While Writing About Accepting It. No,
I could do better.

Maggie O'Leary's "Hollywood, Here I Come" Eating Plan and Exercise Guide
(A SPECIAL PULL-OUT SECTION)

Okay. Okay. I've been deluged by mail asking how I lost the weight.

Number one: I didn't fast.

Number two: I didn't use a diet book.

Number three: I didn't eliminate any food groups.

Number four: I didn't eat any weird food combos.

Number five: I didn't have my stomach stapled, take Chinese herbs, use weight-loss tablets, diet supplements or special drinks.

The following is what I did do—but please, check with your doctor before starting any weight reduction regimen or exercise program. *And by all means, if you've never exercised, start out slowly and build your tolerance. Always warm up before starting to exercise. Follow an exercise session with slow stretches.*

I. 48-hour Fly-Me-To-L.A. Crunch Diet: To up my motivation, I jump-started the program with this skimpy plan that—I have to admit—is nutritionally inadequate. But because it's severe, you stay on it for just two days. It can start off the process dramatically, although initially the loss is largely from water. I also used this as a red-flag regimen. If I overate or lost control for a few meals, or suddenly found that the scales "inexplicably" showed weight gain, I quickly resorted to the 48-hour plan to get myself back on track. I also drank at least eight glasses of water a day and took multivitamins. *Caution:* Don't try to do heavy aerobics while eating so lightly. On this regimen, I restricted myself to brisk walking, twenty minutes in the morning and twenty minutes at night.

II. *The Hollywood Stripper Plan:* After the 48 hours, I progressed to a more liberal plan of around 1500 calories a day (see below), but I'm not big on counting calories.

III. *Cheat Sheet:* I began to look at every recipe and every meal with an eye toward cheating. Cheating? Yes.

* How I could switch from high-calorie ingredients to low ones,
* How I could shave off calories, and
* How I could eliminate foods painlessly or at least eliminate parts of them.

I'm going to give you twenty-five of these painless changes that you can make in your diet. These are the kinds of tips that are easy to make and stick with. And over the course of a year, you'll be amazed by the number of calories that you can eliminate from your diet.

FIRST: How to get an idea of what your calorie intake should be to lose weight, or maintain ideal weight. (You should be so lucky.):

Figure out your ideal weight, taking into account your body type. A current weight chart may help if you're not clear on your goal.

Multiply ideal weight by 15 if you're moderately active, and by 20 if you are very active. The answer is the number of calories you'll need to maintain your ideal weight.

But you need to lose, right? In that case, to reach your ideal weight subtract 500 to 1000 calories from the number of maintenance calories. The result will be the number of calories you can take in every day in order to lose weight slowly and safely. Don't let the number of calories fall below 1000. You need at least this many to lose weight safely without sacrificing proper nutrition. Remember, the heavier you are, the easier it will be, at first, to lose the weight. Those who have to lose just a few pounds will lose it more slowly because they're probably consuming a calorie count closer to the amount needed to maintain ideal weight.

I. THE 48-HOUR FLY-ME-TO-L.A. CRUNCH REGIMEN

Day 1:
Breakfast:	California Dreaming Cereal
Lunch:	Hollywood Gazpacho
Midafternoon:	Fresh Fruit
Dinner:	Celebrity Stir-Fry
Beverages:	Coffee, tea, club soda, water

Day 2:
Breakfast:	Oscar-Winning Omelette
Lunch:	Pacific Palisades Punch
Midafternoon:	Fresh fruit
Dinner:	Silver Screen Casserole
Beverages:	Coffee, tea, club soda, water

RECIPES
DAY 1:

CALIFORNIA DREAMING CEREAL:
⅓ cup old-fashioned rolled oats
½ cup skim milk or vanilla soy milk
⅓ cup orange juice

¼ cup plain low-fat yogurt
½ apple, peeled and grated
2 tbs. raisins, dried cranberries or dried currants
½ banana, thinly sliced
2 tsp. toasted wheat germ

Combine the rolled oats with milk in a bowl and let stand for 20 minutes. Add orange juice, yogurt, apple, raisins, and mix well. Top with sliced banana and sprinkle with wheat germ. Serves one.

On the run? Grab ⅔ cup cold cereal—opt for the healthier ones, not Frosted Flakes or Froot Loops, with ½ cup of skim or soy milk, and half a banana.

HOLLYWOOD GAZPACHO
l cup of mixed-vegetable juice
½ small green pepper, chopped
½ small red pepper, chopped
½ small cucumber, sliced
½ stalk celery, sliced
2 tbs. chopped celery leaves
1 tbs. chopped onion
1 tbs. lime juice
1 tsp. Worcestershire sauce
Freshly ground pepper

Combine all the ingredients except ground pepper in a blender. Mix for 30 seconds. Add pepper to taste. Serves one.

On the run? Order a large salad—about 3 cups—with balsamic vinegar, and a cup of vegetable juice.

CELEBRITY STIR-FRY
4 oz. lean steak, chicken, shrimp or bean curd
1 tbs. soy sauce

1 tbs. sherry
1 tsp. water
½ tsp. garlic powder
2 tbs. olive oil
1 cup celery, sliced thinly
6 oz. package frozen pea pods
8 oz. bean sprouts
2 scallions, cut into 2-inch lengths

Marinate meat (e.g. chicken, beef, shrimp or tofu) for 15 minutes in a mixture of soy sauce, sherry, water and garlic powder. Remove meat from marinade and reserve liquid. Heat oil in a skillet or wok. Then add meat and stir until browned. Add celery, pea pods, bean sprouts and scallions, and stir the mixture rapidly for two or three minutes or until the vegetables are hot. Add marinade, stir and serve immediately. Serves two.

On the run? Get take-out Chinese: mixed steamed vegetables with white meat chicken.

DAY 2:

OSCAR-WINNING OMELETTE
2 eggs
1 tsp. butter
1 tbs. snipped chives, parsley, tarragon or dill
salt and pepper to taste

Mix eggs until whites and yolks are just blended. Melt butter over high heat in a nonstick pan; add the eggs. Stir with fork in swirling motion. After eggs begin to thicken, add the herbs. Tilt pan and run the fork under the edge of the omelette so that you can fold it in half. Serves one.

On the run? Grab two hard-boiled eggs.

PACIFIC PALISADES PUNCH
1 cup cappucino soy milk
1 small banana
¼ tsp. rum extract
¼ tsp. coconut extract
2-3 ice cubes

Pour all ingredients, except ice, into blender. Blend, then gradually add ice until smooth. Serves one.

On the run? 1 cup low-fat yogurt, such as coffee, lemon or vanilla, and a small banana.

SILVER SCREEN CASSEROLE
2 tbs. olive oil
1-½ lbs mixed zucchini and red pepper, thinly sliced
8 large mushrooms, sliced
¾ cup tomato puree
¼ cup bread crumbs
¼ cup grated Parmesan cheese
½ tsp. chopped fresh dill
½ tsp. garlic powder
pinch freshly grated pepper
pinch of oregano

Heat the oil in a skillet and sauté zucchini and red pepper for about three minutes. Push aside. Add the mushrooms and sauté for one to two minutes. Place in a shallow baking pan. Pour tomato puree over the vegetables. Mix the bread crumbs, Parmesan cheese, oregano, garlic powder, dill and pepper. Sprinkle over casserole. Bake one-half hour at 350° F. Serves two.

On the run? Buy two cups of roasted vegetables from Italian takeout. Blot off excess oil before eating.

II. THE HOLLYWOOD STRIPPER PLAN: HOW TO TAKE IT OFF.

Breakfast:
One slice of toast with 1 tsp. of butter, or ¾ cup cold cereal with one glass of skim or soy milk
1 piece of fresh fruit
Coffee or tea

Lunch:
2 hard-boiled eggs, or 3 oz. fish (tuna, salmon or shrimp) or 3 oz. white meat chicken, turkey, veal or lean roast beef (with mustard, if desired), or 1 cup low-fat cottage cheese
1 slice of bread or ½ baked potato, ½ cup cooked pasta or rice
Large tossed salad with lemon or vinegar

Afternoon Snack:
Fresh fruit and 1 cup of skim milk or soy milk, or Blender shake with 1 cup milk, fruit and ice

Dinner:
3 oz. protein (lean beef, poultry, or fish)
½ baked potato, ½ cup cooked pasta or rice with 1 tsp. olive oil or butter
1 cup of steamed vegetables
Large tossed salad

Evening Snack:
Fresh fruit and 1 cup skim or soy milk

Note: 3 cups plain, air-popped popcorn may be substituted for any one serving of bread, potato, rice or pasta.

III. CHEAT SHEET

Even if you don't diet or exercise at all, you can still lose weight just by making some small but significant changes in the way you cook and eat. You can easily come up with your own ways of cutting calories, but here are twenty-five of my favorites to get you thinking:

1. Wait until your bread cools to butter it, it will absorb less.
2. Have a whole orange instead of just the juice. It has higher satiety value and more fiber.
3. Opt for a teaspoon or two of sprinkled sugar instead of maple syrup as a sweetener for waffles, French toast and pancakes. Most of us pour with a heavy hand and end up using a quarter of a cup, a whopping 210 calories versus 16 calories for each teaspoon of sugar.
4. Think breakfast foods when it's lunchtime. A bowl of ¾ cup shredded wheat with ½ cup of skim milk makes a great low-cal, low-fat, high-fiber meal for only about 150 calories.
5. Fruit juices may be healthy, but they can add a major-league load of calories. Scale back on calories, and up your water intake by mixing equal parts of fruit juice with water or club soda.
6. Wean yourself off sugar in coffee or tea. Yes, you can do it, just give it a month. Week one, you'll hate the taste. Accept it—there are only seven measly days in a week. Week two, you'll be less unhappy. Week three, it's better, and by the fourth week you won't mind and will appreciate the taste of the coffee or tea. (And try switching to good quality coffee, not the brown powder that comes in a jar.) By

cutting your daily sugar, you'll save 16 calories per teaspoon of sugar. How many cups do you drink a day? Do the math. And no, I'm not a proponent of artificial sweeteners. (Don't hold me to this, but I recall reading a study way back that indicated that they can actually stimulate your appetite.)

7. Throw out the salt, and fill your salt shaker with this tasty *Salt Substitute:*
   ½ tsp. ground red pepper
   1 tbs. garlic powder
   1 tsp. each basil, marjoram, thyme, parsley, savory, sage, onion powder, ground black pepper, mace

8. Divide lunch into two meals. Have your first half sandwich with a drink at 11:30, and the second half at 1:30. It'll keep you feeling satisfied longer.

9. Always have a late-afternoon snack of fruit so that you don't go into the kitchen starving when it's time to make dinner.

10. While you're cooking, keep a tall glass of mineral water or V-8 around to sip.

11. Add sour pickles to the plate of safe foods—like cut-up veggies—to grab when you're starved. (People who are trying to quit smoking find pickles helpful too.)

12. Opt for blender drinks for a snack rather than just fruit and a beverage. A glass of skim milk or soy milk blended with an apple or banana, ice cubes and a teaspoon of sugar is more satisfying than just a piece of fruit and a glass of milk. The air incorporated into the drink will fool your stomach into feeling fuller than it would be from just the milk and fruit alone.

13. Next time you feel like having a frank, cut calories

in half by slicing the frank in half (give the other half of the dog to yours) and filling the half-empty roll with sauerkraut and mustard. Use the same trick with hamburger—that's where all the calories are, not in the poor maligned bun. Add two slices of tomato and lettuce.

14. Start lunch or dinner with a generous salad and a low-fat or no-fat dressing, then wait fifteen minutes before going on to the next course. Sanity will rule. Try this creamy stuff as a dressing or dip: Combine 1 cup plain low-fat yogurt with 1 tbs. dehydrated onion flakes, ¼ cup chopped fresh dill, 2 minced garlic cloves and 1 oz. crumbled blue cheese. Use 2 tbs. per large cup of salad.

15. Think of soup as the main course, not an appetizer. You can steam and then puree a pound of any fresh vegetable with four cups of low-fat chicken broth combined with one chopped onion and 1 ripe pear, which have been sautéed in 1 tbs. of butter. Makes four servings. Freeze each one separately so you can microwave for a low-cal quickie dinner.

16. Turn side dishes into main courses. Make a baked potato or a cup of brown rice the centerpiece of your meal. Top with ½ cup of cottage cheese and a cup of roasted or steamed vegetables.

17. In all recipes that call for sour cream, substitute low-fat yogurt.

18. When you buy meat or fish at the butcher shop or fish store, make sure you have it cut into 4 oz. serving pieces. If it's presized, before cooking, you'll be less likely to overeat.

19. Instead of spreading a tablespoon of mayonnaise on

your ham, chicken or turkey sandwich, try using mustard. You'll save 85 calories.

20. Avoid buying boxes of cookies or containers of ice cream. Walk to the store and buy single packaged cookies or single scoops of ice cream. Yes, it is far more expensive. Hold that thought and let it be a deterrent.

21. Keep a piggy bank and deposit all the pennies you would have spent on things like Sara Lee cakes and didn't. At the end of each month, take the money and buy yourself a nonedible treat— a Chanel lipstick, maybe? You deserve a reward for abstaining.

22. If you must buy ice cream, choose the less expensive, nonpremium brands. They're lower in calories and fat.

23. Can't resist the chocolate temptation? Instead of eating a fattening chocolate candy bar (most have over 220 calories), opt for one Oreo cookie (50 calories) or one Reese's 0.6 oz. Peanut Butter Cup at 92 calories.

24. Can't give up your favorite pies? You don't have to. Simply eat the filling, but not the crust. You'll be eating about 25 percent fewer calories.

25. When baking a cake from a store-bought mix, substitute ⅓ cup applesauce for an equal amount of cooking oil. You'll shave 612 calories, and 72 grams of fat.

ENOUGH OF MY TRICKS! You're on your own from here. Just remember, shave 3500 calories from your diet (or burn that much through activity) and you lose one pound. Get creative! Just switching from a can of Pepsi each day to a bottle of mineral water will save you 150 calories a day and net you a one-pound weight loss in just over three weeks.

EXERCISE

I'm not going to pretend that this part was easy. At least not at first. But I don't have to tell you about the dividends: A stronger heart, a thinner body, reduced risk of osteoporosis, diabetes, heart disease, even some cancers. *Start slow and get clearance from your doctor first, before beginning any exercise plan. This is vital.* And forget about no pain, no gain. The easiest way to start is with brisk walking. I graduated to the NordicTrack, slowly building to an hour a day, Monday to Friday, with weekends off. If you're out of shape, start with just your legs. When you've built up your *aerobic* capacity (and you're not huffing and puffing), add the arm movement. I also added a set of sit-ups to the aerobics every day, working my way up to forty-five crunches, and an additional thirty-five crunches to work the obliques (muscles around your waist). And remember, start every exercise slowly so that your body warms up first. Never stop abruptly, slow down little by little, over the course of a few minutes so that your heart rate slows down gradually.

I can't write a whole exercise plan in the space of this column, but it's sufficient to say that in addition to the benefits of regular aerobic exercise, your body will benefit from sit-ups and weight-lifting to tone and firm muscles. Wanna know my advice: Go to your local health club and book a session or two with a trainer to assess your condition and get you started. Once you're taught the proper exercises, you can buy some light weights and do the workout at home.

Here's a quick list of how many calories the average 150-pound person burns in one hour:

Biking (moderate exertion): 572

Jogging: 501

Weight Lifting: 107

Aerobics: 429

And, wanna laugh? You'll enjoy this. It takes

* 2 hours and 44 minutes to walk off a 9 oz. slice of apple pie
* 35 minutes to run off a 9 oz. bowl of ice cream
* 47 minutes to run off a 9 oz. slice of cheesecake
* 59 minutes to run off a 9 oz. brownie
* 4 hours and 39 minutes to walk off the brownie
* 1 hour and 55 minutes to bicycle it off

Bottom line: Keep your sense of humor. Unfortunately, I couldn't find statistics on how many calories you burn when you laugh. But whatever, it's good for your soul!